Luther

LUTHER
una storia fiabesca delle chiave

Alec McGuire

demiHorse Books

First published 2009

demiHorse Books
34 Gledhow Wood Road, Leeds,
LS8 4BZ, UK

Copyright © Alec McGuire, 2009

The right of Alec McGuire to be identified as author of this work has been asserted by him in accordance with Section 77 of the Copyright, Designs and Patents Act 1988.

All rights reserved. No part of this publication may be reproduced, stored in a retrieval system, or transmitted, in any form or by any means, electronic, mechanical, photocopying, recording, or otherwise, without the prior permission of the publisher.

This book is sold subject to the condition that it shall not, by way of trade or otherwise, be lent, re-sold, hired out, or otherwise circulated without the publisher's prior consent in any form of binding or cover other than that in which it is published and without a similar condition including this condition being imposed on the subsequent purchaser.

This is a work of fiction. Apart from the character of Luther the cat, any similarity between any character depicted herein and any actual person living and dead, or between any scenario described herein and any real event, is entirely co-incidental.

ISBN: 978-0-9561560-0-6

in memoriam JMcG, JMP, CJP & RLW

A thousand tymes have I herd men telle
That ther ys joy in hevene and peyne in helle.
And I acorde wel that it ys so;
But, natheless, yet wot I wel also
That there nis noon dwellyng in this contree,
That eyther hath in hevene or helle ybe,
Ne may of hit noon other weyes witen,
But as he hath herd seyd, or founde it writen;
For by assay ther may no man it preve.
But God forbede but men shulde leve
Wel more thing then men han seen with ye!
Men shall not wenen every thing a lye
But yf himself yt seeth, or elles dooth;
For, Got wot, thing is never the lasse sooth,
Thogh every wight ne may it nat ysee.

Geoffrey Chaucer
The Legend of Good Women, Prologue.

LUTHER

CHAPTER 1

A man's mind will very generally refuse to make itself up until it be driven and compelled by emergency.
Anthony Trollope
Ayala's Angel

In the beginning, the very first thing is for you to forget all you ever heard about dragons. Nobody ever tells the truth about them: it's too risky. You see, child, every time a little boy or girl says anywhere in the world, "I don't believe.", another dragon is born.

And then you can't just go up to a dragon and say "Good Morning"; dragons are really timid, so the dragon thinks you will hurt it, and burns you up quick before you can do anything else. No, to meet a dragon, you have to be properly introduced by someone who loves that very dragon. Then, if you are especially careful, and don't do anything sudden, the dragon will sit still and let you stroke it - though you must only do so between its armour plates, where the skin is soft. That's the one place where the dragon can feel anything at all. If you try to stroke it on its armour, it can't feel a thing, and just sees your hand moving over, and thinks you are trying to find a way in, and it gets very, very frightened. And you know what happens then. But if you do all I tell you, exactly as I tell you, and if you are very lucky indeed, and if the dragon happens to be in a good mood that morning (which is if there aren't any people about it doesn't like, such as knights or young ladies in thin white dresses), why then, it will roll over on its back, and let you rub the soft skin on its belly. It will even gambol with you through the fields, like a young unicorn. And if that happens, he will be your friend, your best friend, always. Yes. He will even save you from destruction.

Once upon a time, yesterday will do, and once upon a place, anywhere you like, provided it isn't as far away as the next street, there was a dragon. No one had ever loved it, not even its mother. But then, no dragon was ever loved by its mother. After ten years with a dragon growing inside you, you'd be pleased to get rid of it. Every time it moves, one of your organs gets cut by a piece of armour, and just every time it breathes (or practices, anyway, since you can't really breathe before you're born) you get burnt up inside. No, you wouldn't like to give birth to a dragon. What makes it worse is that there are only a few mother dragons, and they are all waiting to give birth, so they always feel bad. And so as soon as one is born, they drive it away. Yes, they all live together, so they can complain all day about what it's like, no-one knows what they have to put up with, and how for two gold pieces they'd give the whole thing up, and move to somewhere nice, with some good-looking young man called George - he's always called George, don't ask me why - who would really appreciate them, not like. No, they don't listen to each other, they're not really interested, even if they do pass on what the dragon next door but one said, did you ever; they just need someone to look as if she might be interested, and they do the same so the neighbours don't think they're odd. Anyway, they drive the young dragons away, without even a word of Goodbye, without even a word. No dragon was ever loved by its mother.

So how do dragons ever get anyone to love them? Well, that's the point of the story. Well, No, it isn't really, but perhaps we'll find out as the story goes on, so that will be all right, won't it?

No, there aren't any daddy dragons, or, at least, no one knows anything about them.

What's that? They taught you in school. You can't have a baby dragon without a mummy and a dragon. How very strange.

Right. You wouldn't really like me to tell you, but I will anyway, I warned you not to ask awkward questions. The daddy dragon and the mummy dragons - yes, there's only one daddy - don't meet very often, because the mothers haven't got time for that sort of thing.

So when they do meet, it's always where there are lots of children. Human children, of course, what did you think I meant? And they take each egg as soon as they can, and put it inside a child, and when the child says it doesn't believe, they tear the egg out of the child's belly, and the mother tries to give birth to it, and they put two back in the child's belly just to serve the little so-and-so right.

Well, I did tell you you wouldn't like it. Dry your eyes, look, here's a handkerchief. All right, have a paper tissue out of the box, then. If we get on with the story, you'll forget all that. How should I know how many dragon eggs you've got inside you? What a way to spend an afternoon!

Do you want to hear the story? Well, then. Listen. And don't ask stupid questions - this is a story after all, and it doesn't matter if everything doesn't always make sense, not straight away, not like real life. Well, don't you always make things make sense, even when they don't or won't? Even when reality just sits and kicks and kicks, because it just refuses. Right. So no wondering about what's not being said, yes? Good. You promise? You promise.

So. The story. Once upon a time. Yes, I know I've said that already. What's that, you want to skip that bit, that's how I made you cry? Mm. How do you know I won't make you cry again? You think I'm horrid. No, child, not me.

Well, there was this dragon, and no one had ever. That bit as well? All right. So one morning, he decided he had a QUESTION. No, not a quest, a QUESTION. You'll find out in a minute. So he thought, which was quite hard, since with no one to love him, not that that was unusual, he'd always been too busy just keeping himself to himself, and finding a cave to live in, and finding enough food. What do dragons eat? Now there, though I told you about questions, well, not that question, but questions, you have me. I mean, I've known several dragons, and listened to them, and played games with them, always their games, I'm not stupid, but I've never seen a dragon at meal times. I think they eat. In fact, I'm certain they eat, because they used to complain about being hungry, even if

I never did see one doing anything about getting a meal ready. Well, this one had. Though I can't tell you how. Or what.

Now, he had to think. Have you ever thought about thinking? No. Right, if you can't think, you can't sit down and think how you would think, if you knew (which you couldn't, not being able to think and all) that you needed to think. Yes, you understand. So how he began we'll miss out. If he hadn't got started, there wouldn't be a story, and I'm telling you the story, so he must have got started, which means. Riddles are later, are they?

Back to the QUESTION. The dragon already knew he must find an answer, otherwise he would live, or not, for ever. You can know some things without thinking them, you see. But he'd never been taught anything, so he certainly had no idea how you got a QUESTION answered. So having found out for himself how to think, and deciding he quite liked it. Well, because it was new, and no-one could take it away. Well, probably it's better than teddy-bears, and, before you ask, I don't know if dragons have teddy-bears. Deciding he quite liked it, he thought a bit more. Then he decided. If he didn't know, then he must ask someone else. And that made him very sad, and he began to cry. You see, if he had to ask someone, he would have to know that person really quite well. And he didn't know anyone really quite well. He didn't know anyone. And what really made him cry was not that, since he'd never cried before. No, because he'd thought, he'd realised that he didn't know anyone at all. And worse, now he realised that he didn't know how to know. And if you don't know, and you need to ask, and you don't even know how to meet someone to ask them, then you really are stuck.

You've gone too far. Its lower lip is quivering.

Carry on. It'll get over it.

So he cried for a very long time, and got so he couldn't breathe properly, because his fire kept getting water in it, which made it spit. Which hurts. And then, he stopped crying, and just sat. And sat and thought. And then, he didn't decide, because he was afraid to decide something else, in case things got worse, he just did something. And, if you can imagine it all, it was amazing he didn't stop thinking completely, but he didn't. He just did something. He left his cave and started walking.

That's cheered it up. It's almost smiling.

"That was very, very brave, and very, very beautiful. Wasn't it, Grandpapa?

"Why are you crying, Grandpapa?"

Now that I am an old man, I shall stand in the middle of a room, and hold a pure white handkerchief. And with each tear, I bring the end of the world a little nearer. It is always so with us who are very old.

We pray in the kingdom.

"Grandpapa?"

Yes, child.

"There's something I don't understand."

Yes, child.

"You said when they tore a dragon egg out of a child, its mummy tried to give birth to it, didn't you? And you said she always as soon as a boy or girl says "I don't believe" a dragon was born?"

Yes, child.

"Well, if she just tries, she mightn't. And if she always, she needn't try. Why does she try? Is she afraid?"

Yes, child, she is afraid. You know how it is when you have got toothache, and you know you've got to go to the dentist to get rid of the pain, and you go to get made better, but you're still afraid?

"Yes, Grandpapa."

Well, it's nothing like that. And you know if you'd always had the toothache, or had it for a very long time so it seemed like almost always, you might be afraid that if you lost that toothache, you might get yet a worse one later?

"Yes, Grandpapa."

Well, it's nothing like that either. If you'd had toothache so long that you couldn't ever really remember not having a toothache, you might be perhaps afraid that if the dentist took you the tooth away, the rest of you would go with it, and you wouldn't know what to do then, not at all.

"Yes, Grandpapa; but is it like that this time?"

Not at all, child. It's just being afraid. Just being afraid of having toothache, of the dentist, of not having toothache, of teeth that stand to give you pain, of having no teeth, of having the pain of having the toothache taken away from you. Just being afraid. So just trying is all you can do. Not what happens, see, but what you can do. The only way you can get away with just being afraid, but not being terrified of being afraid, is knowing you only try. You mustn't do anything, ever. And if the tooth drops out, that doesn't make things better; it takes away a painful tooth, but puts in a whole plateful of fear. That's what it's the like of, child, yes.

Shall I get on with the story? You're uncomfortable. Fidget, then, it usually helps. So. There was this dragon, then. And he left his cave and just walked. Yes, Grandpapa? Good. So he walked, and all around were things that he had never so much as a dream-thought of, not even in the wildest peaceful night's sleep. There, see, was the sky playing with the blues, and the blustery of the air, and the trees all dancing to the wind-beat, and the grass applauding, and all the flowing and flowering of the ever-so-many-things, and the surprising fact was, once he began, he didn't feel even a little afraid, he was too busy. In any case, you can't, they say, feel fear if there's nothing you hope for. Which then he hadn't, even if he ought. Not yet, anyway, a while. No, he wasn't afraid. Why not, really? I've just told you. So on he went.

If you or I had gone there, and walked along behind him unseen, you would have noticed something he didn't. Do you know what it was? Correct. There was not a single bird, or animal, or person, anywhere about, to be seen. Not one. They'd all run away, of course, as soon as they knew there was a dragon, as they say, abroad. And that helped, since, if there had been, he might have remembered that he was a dragon. Remembered, you see, though he didn't know, had never known, he was.

Only, and this is important, there was one indeed who hadn't run away. It was strange, because that one you might expect to be the first to run from trouble.

It was a cat. A perfectly black cat, rather stout. Well, he did have just a few white hairs. On his stomach, and on his chest even less. And his eyes were very large and round. Bright yellow, they were, fading to green in the middle. His ears were quite usual, you know, pointed, but one had just a little tear in it. It did make him look a mite rakish if you noticed it. But usually his face was like a kitten's. A bit sad, though, it was perhaps, or better we should say thoughtful. He looked as if everything were to him just very slightly unpredictable. He would sit and stare at you, with his head tilted to the right, trying to work out what you meant. But, when the sun shone, he was different; the beams played catch-as-catch-can in his fur, and made a cloud of gorgeous rich chocolate and cream-of-sugar threads: he became a feline god in cat's clothing.

His name? Lutherius. Originally he was called Luther. Because, child, his master said he protested a lot. No, I mustn't tease. When he was a tiny kitten, just an explosion of fur animated by a mischievous soul, he went for many days without any name at all. But his favourite toy was one of his master's Roman collars. He used to pounce on the collar, and wrestle it to death. And then it turned out to be just as impeccable a collar as before. So he pounced again. So Luther he became - it was the giving him a character, like every naming a person chooses. The Vet said, when his master took Luther to have the inoculations, that it was not the name to be giving a good catholic cat for the lumbering of him with it. Too late, as many a theologoumenon is, for it was settled by then, and, then, it was always the right-seeming name after.

It became Lutherius only much later on, when he became middle-aged and learnt Latin. He grew to write impenetrable works of philosophy under a pseudonym. Mieo, mies, miat, you know. He was at least as old as you.

Why? He learnt Latin because he had to become a famous philosopher. He had once been very ill, and might have died; only his master nursed him very carefully for a long time. He had to give him fluids by syringe just to keep him alive every two hours. After that, he was never the same; he became very docile with thought. In his youth he had never been quite tame. He caught hundreds of birds, and scratched plenty of people, and terrified lots of dogs, and once he saw off a Great Dane by swiping it across the nose. Only, now he remembered nearly all the time what had come near to be. He did, it is true, and I cannot deny it, that he had fits of absent-mindedness when he would catch himself having caught a mouse, and he couldn't bring himself to feel guilty about it.

I tell you all this because he was a very special cat indeed. He was not merely a great philosopher, but had gone on, as all philosophers should, but so few do, to become a stone as well. For his own philosophy, you understand. Remarkably gifted at solving people's insoluble problems. His master was a sort of teacher when he could, you see, and explained things that other people wouldn't, which was possibly or probably the origin of Lutherius's career. So when people came to sit at his master's feet, Lutherius would sit himself at their feet to judge the state of their souls. And would look round, and select the needful someone. Would wait until that didn't suspect. Then leap. Then, of course, it was easy. He insisted on being well stroked all over - he had the softest fur - purring very loudly, like a two-stroke engine on a Motorway. When he had done that to them, Yes, for they were the passive one, he would relax altogether completely, and go to sleep in their laps. And they would feel ever so much better. Ever so.

That's the point, child, but Yes. He was just being a cat. But completely. That was what made him remarkable. He wasn't human at all. He was a cat who specialised, you see.

The dragon? O, I haven't been forgetting him. No dragons don't have names. Not even the ones who have met someone.

So the cat hadn't run away. In fact, he had stayed curled up fast asleep, with not so much as a chink in an eye left open. Though he knew perfectly well that there was a stranger about. He was a philosopher, after all, and knew all there was about many sorts of strange beasts. What? Like the double-horned lemma, which can only catch you if it uses both horns at once. Yes, so he wouldn't be as foolish as to frighten it away. If he was going to solve its problem, and he expected it probably to have a problem, he had to let it be. Absurd petitions reduce no principalities. Therefore, that is, he waited. Like the English. No, I told you, riddles come later before.

The dragon saw the cat. Then, Guess. The cat saw the dragon.

He opened one eye. Probably the left. There before him was a beast such as he had never seen. He thought it about seventy-two paws in height. That's right, three licks equals one paw, eleven paws make a tail, and five tails are one fight. At the least. But mostly you measure size in paws. Seventy-two paws in height, and about twenty-one tails long. What? Don't you understand anything? Look. Size and height are in paws. From the verticality of them, you have. Length is in tails. Horizontality or in circle, obviously. (Cats never keep count when they're feeling pleased with themselves.) Movements in fights. Well, why not? Why shouldn't you keep your measurements separate if you use them for differences? It's the sense of it.

Think, child. Your old woman measures the length and success of a stroll in the number of gossips that come or she can make. A blessing on each, there is. Therefore three gossips make a good stroll. And but isn't it on a summer afternoon your da goes on a long six-pint amble? Yet if you asked his dog you'd learn it was so many walks make a day. Yes, that's right: Fifty points make one sherry glass. Three sherry glasses make for a quiet life. Everything makes its own measurement.

So, seventy-two paws high, a sort of coppery-red, lots of armour plates all over at all kinds of neat angles, nicely-curled dark eyebrows, a moustache and a little pointed beard. And sixty-four teeth of course. The nearest Lutherius could get to assigning the proper category, after searching his memory, was that this must be the fabled tautology.

Cats don't often meet tautologies; in fact, there never has been a cat who could be truly certain he's met a tautology. They're not much given to applied logic, aren't cats - they prefer intuition and empirical moral science. Logic, they keep pure. Lutherius needs knew about tautologies by reputation, from his studies of philosophy, and had always wanted to meet one. They sounded such simple creatures. So he always lived with a slight, mild hope that the next strange creature he met would be a tautology. Now, and I hesitate to say it of such a distinguished cat, he was far from correct. No tautology can have an unanswered QUESTION. They know everything they are able to know, and nothing else at all ever occurs to them, you see. It makes evolution a problem, poor dears, popular though they may be. Though actually they disprove evolution. Since they can't change, they can never acquire a disadvantage, or reproduce or die off. Though they can come into existence. How, no-one knows. Except Lutherius. And he isn't telling.

What? Well, what would you do? The cat thought he had better wake up completely. They can choose, you know which bits of them they have asleep. So he did the prescribed: stretch in three different directions all at the same time, scratch an ear, lick yourself over and about, sit up, and wrap your tail around your front paws. To keep them warm.

And then the cat realised.

Something terrible and hideous and awful and, not to waste words, really quite mildly frightfully interesting was here. Indeed, he thought of doing the back-arching and fur-raising routine, but decided against, on the ground that it wasn't empathic or appropriately non-aggressive. Nonetheless, his professional equilibrium was troubled. In all his days, he, Lutherius, Cat of Cats and Mog of Mogs, had never seen such a thing.

The beast before him had, O how could it be!, nowhere to sit on. No lap! No surface anywhere on which to perch. No part of him which wasn't covered in armour plates. That such a creature could live ... Philosophers don't cry, but Lutherius came close to being tempted. He couldn't make it feel happier. He couldn't give it a convincing demonstration of his skills.

And, therefore, he just sat with his head tilted slightly to one side, and contemplated the eternal verities. Doubtless, this too must be part of life's rich basket-weave. And, though many, nay, all, cats would be moved to have their teeth chatter, Lutherius was filled only with a sense of wonder: O brave world, that could bear such creatures in it.

He just sat.

And this was just about the best thing he could do. Indeed, if he had done a single other thing, he wouldn't be around now to tell the tale. No child, the dragon would not have been wicked, it would just have been a reflex action. Which is a sufficient cue for tea.

So we sit, silently at table, eating and drinking separate meals. The child wants the story to begin, really begin. Let it be a good story. Please. This old man, he wants not to say too much, not to let the child know. How to do it?, when making a story as you go along. The child must remember; the child, is it I who designs?, must forget the story but remember the telling and through it. What is by this telling made?

Now, as we were saying before tea, the cat just sat and did nothing. And the dragon, being a dragon, felt this to be curious. Dragons have most generally of their reactions built in; they expect either flight or attack. Something that doesn't either, doesn't occur to and for them. So, feeling that it was curious, and not having anything better to do, he just sat down as well. And being at least as well brought up as dragons ever can be, which is not at all, he was as polite as he knew how, and wrapped his tail round his front legs. With difficulty, because a dragon's tail isn't meant to be able to do that, though there's no obvious reason why not, but there we are, and only reaches round as far as the heel of one leg, but it was the best he could do. And having sat for a while in this uncomfortable position, he spoke.

Excuse me, he said, but are you, ahem, are you a living creature? I'm not terribly sure about these things, but if you are, and if it's not too much trouble, I wonder if you would talk to me.

Interesting, thought the cat, it does have a problem. I will answer.

I am, indeed, as you say, a living creature. And I am, as you hear, talking to you.

I have many questions. A QUESTION which must be answered. But I do not know who can answer my QUESTION. Do you know?

I know many things. I can solve many problems. I can make you be ever so much better. I can relax you so that no problem is a problem. But, I answer no questions. It is not permitted.

Who knows, child, what language they used? Not Latin, certainly, and not English, probably. Lutherius, indeed, knew Greek just as well as Latin. Indeed yes, child, truthfully. Mio, miois, mioi. And Sanskrit, too. Mayeyam, mayeh, mayet. But perhaps they made up their language as they went along, or perhaps the one taught the other a power of some speaking tongue. The dragon, remember, is little learnèd, like one called to be just born out of due time. I do not know the what of what he could say, let alone the of what. Well and indeed, the truth is I know what he did say, in substaunce, but not the manner of it. So whether and how the cat taught him, or he the cat, I cannot be saying.

So there they are then, and with me telling you the story of it when I can remember, the dragon and the cat talking about a question. The dragon seeking peace, and the cat the absence of trouble. Or perhaps it was the other way round. And don't be telling me I tease: I don't.

How long did they just sit there now talking? For as long as forty long dozens of dozes. And yet, they did not gain one day of age in all that time.

And you, child, will well be having guessed that our two friends, they decided to go on to the journey - the obligatory one, is it not?, for all questions and QUESTIONS, you see. The day-spring of the most high might himself have dawned upon that journey. And so on the very next bright, sunny spring morning - pouring it was, with rain that a fish might fly in, enough to make a man grow a macintosh-and-galoshes skin - they went off on the way of all flesh, Luther (he wasn't feeling philosophical that morning) carrying a yellow, green and crimson-all-over golf umbrella and a bag of pilchard sandwiches, and the dragon with a broad smile draped in a tarpaulin and a sack of, yes, coal or whatever it was would be a snack at lunchtime. Follow, shall we, this sweet sight's progress?

It is, ahem, really quite kind of you to do this, you know, we can hear the dragon saying in a mellifluous kind of roaring whisper, you didn't have to. Not at all, says the cat, thinking of being curled up on his master's lap and covered with newspaper he'd be reading the while. For to tell the truth, Luther was not a little worried about being homesick and getting his feet wet. To tell the truth truly, he was feeling ashamed of having left his master behind him, to pine and fret alone.

Not at all, it is, I am sure, a pleasure. It will be very interesting to accompany you on your journey; anyway, I promised to take you to someone who would know how to find the answer. So, that I will do.

Where are we going? You didn't tell me, ahem, who this person is, or why they can help.

No, I didn't, did I? All you need to know is that there is only one authority with whom I am acquainted who can be consulted in matters like this. And there are no other authorities in this particular field.

For a little while they walked onwards. The dragon was feeling confused. This nice cat had promised to help, and had been kind enough to give up his valuable time, which he could have been using to read Spinoza, as he said, to go on this fool's errand. The cat had been gracious, and had even offered him a plate of left-over rabbit stew that his master had made and then not eaten, but now everything was tense and tight. I wonder what the rabbit would have tasted like.

A shiver passed from the tip of the dragon's tail all the way along to his neck, and he sneezed. Twice. It would be terrible if he had a bad attack of tepid. Thoughts of quietly erupting volcanoes, and swirling hot mud pools bubbling with methane, kept offering themselves to his mind, but the dragon didn't quite know what to do with either. He sneezed again, and had a richly satisfying vision of hell-freeze. Curiously, it was full of mewling cats. Had he been able to put a name to his emotion, he would have discovered what people who go to the wrong kind of therapist call guilt. The others would call it a shame. Therapist?, - a therapist is a person who gets paid for letting other people talk to them for longer than anyone sensible would ever put up with.

Another shiver and a sneeze. The cat snorted and leapt in a single bound on to the dragon's tarpaulin, where he proceeded furiously to clean and sharpen his claws. The golf umbrella rolled on the ground, getting muddy. The dragon felt pawsteps go along the tarpaulin as far as his neck, and then sharp little teeth grasped an armour plate and shook from side to side. The armour plate remained unmoved.

Indeed, child, Luther has forgotten his Aristotle. A thing is what it is and not another thing. No dragons are kittens.

Excuse me, but what are you trying to, um, do? I hope it makes you feel better, whatever it is. -- Thus, the dragon.

Luther rolled his eyes, and, rather gingerly, came down from the tarpaulin. He looked at the golf umbrella, fixedly, for a few moments, as if everything was its fault, picked it up, shook it vigorously, and then rolled the cloth up into neat folds. He stood quite still, with not even so much as a whisker's twitch to spoil the effect.

What is it, he said suddenly sitting down, that knows nothing at midnight, everything in the morning, less than nothing at noon, and precisely nothing at evening? And, just to add the necessary emphasis, he prodded the dragon quite firmly under the chin with the golf umbrella.

There came, before either one might do another thing, the sound, the one that you and every other soul hears at the last moment before you awake, but which you can never remember.

Luther fell to the ground, and covered his face with his paws, like a cutely trained dog, and, with the same terror, gave a single cry. The dragon, not having learnt how to fear, stayed as he was, and he looked and saw. His eyes turned the colour of opals set in silver, and as opaque. For child, I tell you, only the pure spirit of a sinless animal can see those hinder parts and live. And, sightless, his mind filled with white, until there remained not one imagined drop of hope or prayer. That plated head dipped slowly to touch his breast, and bone-locked rigid.

I am an ancient, a man whose lips slobber with truth and drool with wisdom.

Cat?, said the dragon, who didn't know what names are, Cat?, Where have you gone? Just now, there was the wet, and the path, and the sound of you talking. And there's only light. Please, I don't like this light. Where have you gone? The dragon's head and the rigid neck like a glass swan, child, you could have snapped.

There was no answer at all, not from the cat. No, my little one, my dearling, we dare not call him Lutherius, by any name. Because he could not speak, or hear, or move, or remember. His head was being filled as for ever with a wild song, like it was the angels screaming and crying to another in their agony of Holy. Before that throne there is no sanity.

I am old, child, I have been born thirty-and-one thousand days. Do you think I do not know? What mercy will there be in a last eternity? It is your eyes that are sightless.

But I must tell you the story a little longer. Do not look at me, my melancholy will burn you. Listen, my sweet, and come again tomorrow, and I will invent you a little more to charm you.

CHAPTER 2

> I that in heill was and gladnes
> Am trublit now with gret seiknes
> And feblit with infirmitie
> *Timor mortis conturbat me.*
> **William Dunbar**
> **Lament for the Makaris**

And there you are! Sit yourself into that chair there, and listen comfortably, and I will continue. What? Don't squeak at me, child; has your mother not oiled your jaw recently? You sound as if your tongue is rusting.

Now, I was weaving you this story of the dragon and the philosopher. Gently spelling it out to you with silk, while you are not quite succeeding in playing my Glaucus. But, that may still improve.

So, the dragon cannot see, and the cat cannot hear. And both are struck down with the black dying of plagueful terror. By all the rules, what ought to happen out is that the dragon, somehow, very O so carefully, places the cat upon its back so the cat has the eyes, and the dragon the ears, and together so they continue upon their journey. Is that not so? Precisely.

But it is not so with us. I cannot be doing with such nice little sentiments. Do not interrupt me. I have decided what shall be, and you shall not go play in the garden instead. You made me begin this story, and I will make you a finishing of it. That is justice.

What happened next frightened them the both to their very souls.

Souls? We have many souls, child. We wear them like clothes, and just as cloth do they wear away. From our very first day we are set to work, knitting and sewing our next soul, and when we can't stand the look of the old one, so shabby it is, we put on the new one, and twirl it about - to have it admired, by our own soul not least, of course - and to see what it looks like in the mirror stage - but mostly we twist it round to make the creases drop out. For, shameful, we can't take these robes even one off, and every soul must serve to cover all the rotting tatters, and you can never get the hang of it right. It's that gives the impetus, to make us start knitting and sewing with all the gusto we can have for the next.

But the very first one is the soul of our naked skin-cover, and isn't that the one which is cut to shape for you? Not that you can lose any of it, slice away as they will. Perhaps mother, a mother, carves away in your liver, neatly as she liked, to make a pattern in dark. So you are left with for eating: you have a soul without anger as the you you can taste. Your fleshly soul. You have eaten and were sated. But the other soul is all bile. And you remember it. You remember (sans tongue) you once had something. You cannot say: you are never told. But you remember it, like the man remembers there was more than a stump. And like the leg remembers, even as it is incinerated, that there was once a reason. That anger misses you. Like a sleeve in a pocket.

Or you had a father who cut away a hand that's grasping some life for life. Then the flesh, soul, has nothing but a reminiscent that won't hold, while a loose hand grips hard to no good for nobody.

Or your carved away is lust, love, fear. Each existing and not, at the same right hour.

I know a man on whom was made a delicate work of dissection, to the seventh order, with no gross butchery, in that no part was severed lost, but was left with, as it may be, a nerve and a little blood to connect it. He resulting had no form, but only substance of cutting, until he held together only by wearing the darkest suits. Into them he had to be sewn with strongest silk four-cord, if he was ever to keep to a shape for more than a moment's glance. It was never, to please you, a design, a line-crossing to make a man, but it moved according to a tracing of lungs as long as he smoked opium to the notes of each breath's rustle.

And another man was left to a mid-day's sun, until the touch of any cloth screamed him.

And another?

That's a soul worth painting with shellac, to be frightened to. To the which our lutherous cat and dragon are brought.

And I make it was over them stood a form informed, to release to us our next action. Who gave them sight, and now forgets them a little to continue.

It was a dog. I shall not, child, sully you with such a thing as the description of a dog. You may use whatever portion of your imagination is dedicated to anatomical mistakes and nightmares (and the like) to provide any details you feel necessary.

Luther sat and calculated. It had been a long time. Had he still the speed, the skill? To do the Chessman's Taunt, you begin by leaping into the air. Yes, it is the Chessman's Taunt, not the Chesscat's. Well, cats call themselves men as well as having all the feline terms. They don't call humans anything really, just "those". Leaping into the air, at an angle ever so slightly, but not quite nearly, more than you would think, *with your paws crossed.* Just as you descend onto the dog his nose, you uncross, recross and unrecross (or reuncross, according to taste) with the claws at full extension, faster than the blade of a lightning shaft skating down the air. If you have practised lots (and it was for this that Luther was hesitant), it is possible to have the inner claw on the recross at just exactly the position of the outer claw in the original sweep. If you do that correctly (and it is really very difficult to avoid the appearance of a double line when the match isn't exact), and if the paws were crossed precisely at right angles, then ... the scars provide a perfect chessboard (coloured crimson, black and blue).

It has long been understood by all right-thinking felines (which is all of them) (without exception) (honestly) that their innate and effortless superiority is shewn in four proofs.

§ Item, that dogs do not play chess.

§ Item, that dogs do not appear to appreciate the great honour of being allowed to serve as chessboards.

§ Item, that if one should try to explain chess and chessboards to dogs, they will not listen.

§ Item, that they try, albeit that this is not allowed, to get their own back by playing fetch with the chesspieces, and then losing them when you whistle.

Charges drawn up on these lines against the very concept of the canine resulted in outright convictions, carried by a majority of $9.999\ldots \times 10^{1,000,000,000,000,000}$ to 1 in the Supreme Court of the Catoline Hill about three millennia ago. The 1 was a chihuahua who got in by mistake. The Supreme Justice thought it was a new breed (he was very short-sighted) and no-one ever contradicts the Supreme Justice.

It was, indeed, chiefly because of the difficulty of finding suitable chessboards (together with an entirely natural distaste at using stuffed mice to represent feline armies) that cats long ago gave up playing the game other than in their heads, corresponding with their partners by post or telepathy. Sending your opponent your gambit delicately engraved on a sheet of smoked salmon is thought to show style; sending a pre-paid slice for the response, however, is just a trifle over the top. Mind you, it is only cats who realise that serving smoked salmon with trifle over the top is absolutely delicious.

The longest chess game in the history of any species is still being played by Miss Ann Mimosafield's late Tolstoy - a cat so venerable as universally to be honoured as a Statespuss - and Mrs Annabelle Trahison-O'Clerck's Whimsy - whose daring moves and unpredictable gambits, often involving breaking china pots to distract observers while mentally rearranging the board, are unequalled even by the legendary Pussowitz. The game is now into its fourth century (both cats having gone through numerous reincarnations rather than resign) with Whimsy having two paws lead over against Tolstoy's extra bowl of cream.

Oh, for goodness' snake, Yes, child! Don't you understand anything at all? Look, cats have no religion, so bishops were out from the start. Even Anglican ones. And "Rook" is a four-letter word, so you couldn't have them. Therefore the pieces are renamed all and some and singular: the object is to capture the Tom, with the Queen being the most important piece on the board - be the board real or not, it doesn't matter. Then you have two bowls of cream to give comfort, spiritual and temporal; two salmon to inspire the fight; and two cardboard boxes to hide in. The front row consists of eight paws, of course. Don't groan, child, it doesn't become you.

Such stupidity you have. Feline chess has decided the fate of nations. When I was your age, or a little less, I was allowed to see one of the truly great animalick circuses. Your Olympic Games are no more interesting than bagatelle in comparison. Mm, I must beg to differ; Vicarage tea-parties are, in my experience, extremely vicious war-games, usually between the Enrolling Member of The Mothers' Union (Yes, I know - they've organised) and the Choirmaster's wife about whose turn it is to run off with the Churchwarden, with the loser getting regular "pastoral" visits from the Curate as a consolation. Truly. But as I was saying. The cats have Wrestling, and High Jumps, and Hammerbill-Throwing, and Shutting the Draw, and Tangling the Laundry - that gets the audience going -, and then there are the Horses. Yes, it's run under the auspices of the League of Species, which was, as you remember, set up to defend evolutionary liberty.

The Horses are the high-point. When they've learned to balance properly by practising with people on their backs - chiefly so they can overcome temptation, and get used to the itchy feeling of having their hair brushed the wrong way by someone who isn't their mummikins. When they've learned, as I was saying, to balance, then they can graduate to books on their nose, ready for the supreme: the art of dressage. The Horse (Lipizzaners are best at this) stands with its nose at the centre of the Circle, with the Cat-Fancy Yearbook poised with perfect symmetry on the very tip. Then the Horse side-steps until it has gone round 360° exactly (or *Au Point*), twitching its nose meanwhile so the book always points the same way. Presumably so the judges can read it - how should I know? You lose points if the circle isn't perfect and if your nose isn't exactly at the centre throughout. But the greatness of the art is this: the whole must be done so slowly and steadily that no-one can see the movement. Not a ripple, not a flicker of a hair must be visible. It takes years to learn, of course, and then the performance takes so long that no horse ever lives long enough to do it twice. Or once. You're disqualified if you drop dead in the middle of it. They use tortoises as the judges, and it's always held in the Galapagos. If you can spend an entire century stretching yourself first thing in the morning, then you've got what it takes to judge dressage. But purists know the real thing. They don't need action. And certainly not change. Stasis, that's the thing. Possibly.

Cows? Ah, now there you have real skill. They build this wall round a city, you see, and the cow walks round seven times, mooing, until. Now would I tell fibs? Well, there's tennis. Yes, with their tales, knocking flies over the net. They use calves that have escaped from veal factories to catch any flies that go out of court. It's much more fun if you use live flies: then you have to judge exactly how hard to swish your tale: stun them too much and they die, but too little and they escape.

Now, let me tell you a secret. A lot of trouble is caused by people not understanding this. The umpire uses red rags to signal the score. The umpire stands by the side of the net, on top of a topiary bush, waving the rags about: in the left hand to indicate a hooffault, and in the right to award points; for a match point the umpire has to balance on one foot, and wave three red rags, one in each foot. Hands, feet, it's all the same, child. Bumpsadaisy to you too. So of course, when the cow's partner sees the red rags being waved, he rushes on to court to congratulate her. Terrible misunderstood little gesture.

Remind me, and I may take you to the next Circus Games. There's only 392 years to wait. The cats won the last lot. They always win.

So. It was in the great games of. What? I was about to tell you a story of how the cats decided the fate of the free world. No? I always said you were a Philistine.

Right then. There was this dog, see. And Luther was sitting there, calculating and computing and working out the logistics and the ordnance. You can think through the voices, you see; you just can't switch them off. Heaven goes on for ever.

There was this dog, see. Of course, there needn't absolutely have been. This is history, after all. I could make a thousand million trillion thunderbolts come out of the sky in the next thing I say. And nothing in the world, the world you know, would be different. But I don't, because there'd be no point. There wasn't even one thunderbolt, so I don't put even one in. But in another life, someone can be driving down the road, listening to the radio, and hear suddenly that an earthquake has killed five hundred people. And that can't make sense. So you look round for a meaning, a reason. Five hundred people can't just die. So they must be evil. Or God was angry because they all slept, possibly with each other.

Or maybe you're differently rational, so it must have been the Government's fault. The Government should have employed more scientists, better scientists, so they'd know when there was going to be an earthquake, and move the people out of the way to somewhere they wouldn't get killed. Or else they told the people, and the people wouldn't move. Or something like that. So, what we find, as a universal law, is that in history, where nothing needs to make sense, everything has to, whereas in this our life, where everything needs to, and where there's God or the Government in charge of everything, nothing means anything. Which is only logic after all. So I'm telling you beyond any possibility of contradiction that there was a dog, though without bejewelled head.

31

With the words I lay out, so it becomes, and the so is not as you have been prepared, but as I will. The so is not what you can tell, but as I raise it to be, as some bare-grained truth perhaps, or some other body. Is it not written so? Do not trouble me, child, for I bear in my soul the marks I shall make.

CHAPTER 3

Students of the heavens are separable into astronomers and astrologers as readily as are the minor domestic ruminants into sheep and goats, but the separation of philosophers into sages and cranks seems to be more sensitive to frames of reference.
W V O Quine
Theories and Things

Ah! You have returned. I knew it would be so. It is raining, and here there is a fire.

And there; there there is a dog. Well, Luther calculated no more, for the dog began to speak.

The dog, what did it look like? Luther had, despite and beside himself, been wonderfully amazed. The dog had four heads. Only one at a time you understand. As one rose up from out of the neck to be a face, so the previous one faded like a phantom and slowly passed back down in through the new. Well, it had four heads because there were four faces. For if the faces were the same, then the heads must be the same. Else there is no identity in anything. Right? Now, the first head was an alsatian, but its ears had grown and grown, and the mouth was most exquisitely formed, and the eyes had shrunk to almost nothing. And the second was a pointer, but its nose was so very long it seemed that the jaw and the head all together was just a scaffold to it. The third, ah, that was a mongrel only, but its eyes and ears and nose and face were so perfect you could cry to see it, and out of it came such lifely health that it was like shimmering in the air all round, drawing your eyes to it with awe, with awful rapture. But then you saw that the top of its head had been hollowed out and was filled with something that was neither water nor wine nor honey nor nectar but was nothing but them and was so delicately scented that you would smell it for ever if you could, even as you knew the scent would make you feel sick and take away everything good about you. Then came the fourth head, and you couldn't quite tell what it was - did it have eyes? You could not be certain. Ears? You did not know. Not one feature was clear but a small and rather sarcastic mouth. And when it went, you could not remember anything about it. But when it returned, whenever it returned, to the last day of your life, you knew you would recognise it instantly. And the heads all always appeared in sequence.

I was going to tell you much more. I was going to tell you that the four heads, they each had their own voice and their own character and their own thoughts and memory and imagination and their own peculiar and particular words. I was going to tell you what each one said, so carefully gentle that you would feel the vibrating of the air with your ears and could tell by the slide of the air over your forehead what each particle of each separate sound brought you to think. You would feel how the air did the bidding of those voices. I was going to tell you how that dog thought, how that dog spoke to themselves. I was going to tell you lightly the tale of what they did to the cat and the dragon, so brightly that your eyes would see it more real than the sky. I was going, but I cannot. There is some blue screen, an Unprintable Error. I have succeeded, you know, to forget it so I can remember only the effects, all of them for ever, and yet not one of the acts. The acts never happened for me now. There is so much I cannot remember.

But what I know, I know. And therefore I will construct you a hypothesis for a creed. I believe that the dog rose up on its hind legs, and as it did, so the other heads also appeared. And one faced to the rear, looking (so it seemed to the cat) forward down the path, while the other three looked the other way. One to the side, and one to the above, and one, and you know this one, looked nowhere but saw, well, you know what it saw.

And I believe that the front legs picked the cat up, as gently as a helicopter dandling a stretcher out of the sea, and laid him down on the dragon's neck. And Luther felt himself sinking, falling, for thousands of miles, until his nerves spoke him only no word but stillness and gravity. And, when he came to rest, behold. No. This I know.

What I have known, I have known. So I tell you this, that when they had done to him, had done what it did to them, Luther was on the dragonis neck, sinking O slowly into that dragon until only his head was neck, and his nerves cursed with the sensations of the dragon's body as they led to his brain. But not the; any other way.

But Luther could hear. He heard true still the voices of the angels. And yet he heard all that was about and around him. Perfectly.

You would think, would you not?, that all this was enough to be getting on with. If that was what your afternoon brought, then by tea-time you would give up, and have a crumpet or two, and put up your feet by the fireside, in your nicest red-leather fur-lined slippers, and reflect on what an interesting time you'd had, and read the complete works of Anthony Trollope. I had an uncle who was always going to bed with a Trollope. Or something like that. You'd give up, anyway. But not Luther. He was a philosopher.

Philosophers are very strange things. They are concerned, so they say, and no-one else is qualified to argue with them, since if you argue with a philosopher you are instantly transformed into one, which is not a pleasant thought, and so, few people do, with what necessarily must be the case. With what is logically necessary. With truth. With the ultimate nature of things. With metaphysics. With virtue.

But not with what actually is.

Because what actually is the case might perhaps have been different, and if it might have been different, then it is not necessarily the case. And philosophers can't be bothered with anything that is that unstable. After all, you might go away and then return, and find that nothing had changed at all, but be concerned that it might have been different while you were absent. How do you know that the tree in the garden out there, where we had tea the last time there was any sunshine, and you ate far more blackberry jam than there could possibly have been in the jar when you started, and where you got stung by a wasp last summer, and where we are going to put a swing next week if you're very good and the sun is still shining; how do you know that that very tree doesn't disappear as soon as you're out of sight?

Well, I might be telling fibs. And your friends might be telling fibs. You see, you don't know do you? Well, yes, you do, of course, but you don't really, not really really, do you? Indeed. Philosophers are very strange things. Which is what we started out with, which is *petitio principii* or begging the question, which means that this doesn't prove anything, and so philosophers might not be strange things, which means it can't be *necessarily* true that philosophers are strange things, which means a philosopher can't be bothered with such a proposition, which means that no philosopher ever thinks that philosophers are strange things. Which proves that they're *very* strange things indeed. **QED!** This is called an argument *a fortiori*, because you have to have a very strong head to get away with banging it against brick walls for a living.

Philosophers, being very strange things, and thinking accordingly, go in for conducting thought experiments.

This isn't like conducting an experiment in any meaningful sense *whatsoever*. What you do is imagine an impossible situation. Well, it has to be impossible, because if it wasn't you could do the experiment for real, and find out the answer, but that would be something that actually is the case, which we've already disposed of. Of course, were it completely, logically, impossible, you couldn't imagine it, so it must be something with the right sort of impossibility. Not *necessarily* impossible, and not *contingently* impossible, but a kind of impossibility that slips between them. Yes, exactly, it does remind me of when you spilt treacle on the piano keys and didn't tell us until it had mostly dripped through.

Anyway, when you've got something that is impossible in the right way, you imagine it, and you work out, using the strictest logic - well, it has to be strict to keep everything in order, otherwise one of your concepts might decide it's had enough and wander off to look for another mind to live in -, you work out what would happen to the thing that you're imagining under certain circumstances. No, you're not allowed to make anything up at all. It has to be what must be necessarily imagined once you - or anyone else, for that matter, not that there's any matter around - actually starts from the properly impossible beginning, you see. And then if you discover that the conclusion you have to imagine in the end is self-contradictory so that you can't imagine it after all, then you know that what you started with was truly impossibly impossible. And, if you don't, it wasn't. This one is called an argument *a posteriori*, which I shan't explain. Well, I'll whisper it if you like, but only if you keep your eyes firmly shut.

Anyway. Lutherius is a philosopher, so he performed a thought experiment. Suppose there were two minds, and a single body for both of them. Under what circumstances would one of the minds know that the other one existed?

Now consider as he considered. Suppose you had a pain, yes, you that it is, not me, you had a pain in your left front paw, and suppose that I could feel it too. What I would feel would be my pain. I would be having a pain in your left front paw. And it could, in fact, well be, that at least sometimes when I have a pain in your left front paw, you do not have a pain. You could be thinking that your left front paw felt the nicest it had for ages, while I could be in some wonderful agonizing from it. So even if I could feel a pain in your body, I wouldn't be feeling your pain. And even if I could see out of your eyes, I would not be seeing what you are seeing, for you might be daydreaming and having some wondrous vision, while I am staring at the blank wall in front of your eyes. No, if I sensed a sensation from every particle of being in your body, it would all be my sensation, not yours.

What then stops your body being mine as well as my own is?

Philosophy?, you ask. What is philosophy? Luther had once seen a sign on the side of a van that said in big gold-on-blue letters "J J SMITH & SON GIVE OMPT ELIABLE ICE", and he'd heard about Icemen, so he thought that Mr Smith and or his son must take pride in providing ice that was eliable and ompt. Clearly, you wouldn't advertise second-rate ice - supply the "as" if you want -, so eliable ice must be a particularly good sort of ice, and ompt ice must be very good too. He had wondered, as one would, don't you think?, whether ompt was an adverb, so that it was ice that omptly was eliable that Mr Smith sold, but decided that ompt must be another adjective since Mr Smith seemed to be a man of fairly few faintly words and he surely wouldn't, being such a man, want to use adverbs which are not, after all, as necessary as adjectives. Of course, adjectives aren't really necessary either, since Mr Smith could just have put the word ICE in big gold-on-blue letters on his van, but then anyone could do that and if ELIABLE ICE was better than ICE then probably eliable, though it was an adjective, was a sort of defining and pointing-out, kind of, word and therefore it must be an honorary noun as well as being an adjective.

Anyway. Revenons à nos mots tôns. But what did eliable mean? Well, what do you use ice for?, and, what makes one lot better than another? Because it's cold, yes. So, if you've got very, very cold ice that must be better than just medium to quite sort-of-it's-not-really-all-that-cold-at-all,-I-suppose,-if-you-think-about-it-though,-so-I-guess-it-will-just-have-to-do,-I-mean-to-say-what-do-they-expect-I'm-only-human cold. So very, very cold ice must be eliable, so eliable must mean that the thing is extra-good at doing the thing you're using it because of, because it has that quality. You see? Good.

And OMPT ICE must then be ice which is easier to use because, Oh, it doesn't melt. And so ompt means that the thing doesn't have unwanted drawbacks. No, some drawbacks *are* wanted. To make it surely so you can always be surly sore that you've got something to complain about. Which is very comforting, don't you agree? Because whatever happens it can't ever be totally your fault. And that means you don't ever deserve anything that happens to you, no matter what you are or did. And so too whatever happens, no matter how nice it is, you always always and just always have the complete and utter and irreducible and unavoidable and absolute right to be angry. At anything at all. And that's a right that is worth a great deal in drawbacks.

Of course, even Luther could be wrong occasionally. No, not bad or naughty, just wrong. And he was wrong here. Because if he'd seen the other side, then he would have read J J IT SO ROMP ABLER VICE. Which would have lead to different conclusions about the whole nature of things. So you see what a slender web spun out of the purest artifice philosophy is.

And then, too, there's the question of what message he would have got if we didn't have vowels. There are languages that don't.

Well, vowels sort of lubricate words, to make them pass down into the ear more gently. If you had to read JJ SMTH ND SN GV MPT LBL C or JJ TH N RMP BLR VC or even JJSMTHNDSNSGVPRMPTRLBLSRVC then don't you think the whole way you hear the thoughts of your mind and the thoughts that hang in the air all around you waiting to be heard or read or seen or just noticed or, as they hope, acknowledged and responded to too would be wholly and wonderfully and totally, well, different? No? No. Oh dear, my dear poor little dear. You can't convince everybody, quite clearly. No, dear, not me, you.

Another time, Luther saw a van that said "LOTHING MANUFACTURER". He felt that this aided his understanding of those quite considerably. Apart from the fact that they can't spell - everyone knows that cat should be spelt qkqatt, of course -, humans clearly need to have large supplies of nasty emotions manufactured for them at regular intervals, otherwise they might come to their senses and realise that they could be having a nice time, instead of whatever kind of time it is they do have.

It seemed to Luther that humans had had a terribly raw deal from evolution. Humans haven't survived that long, and the world got along just fine without them until a few long thousand years ago, but now they're here, they seem to be rather *too* successful. It's like a new virus that breeds and breeds and breeds and, since viruses have no brains, can't do anything about the fact that when the host dies the virus dies too.

Altruism? As for altruism, are we not talking about the species *homo sapiens sapiens*? The doubly unwise. So I'm not being ecological, child; I'm never on the losing side.

So, humans and emotions, then? Well, yes, they could produce their own emotions, but you get more for less if you put it out to tender. Of course, in a free-market emotional economy, there's a lot of haggling - I can do you a nice line in ire, this week, special, really fresh, and I'll throw in a righteous indignation, just because it's you -, and there's the law of supply and demand, so that when just everyone's wearing mercy this spring, the price of it tends to go up or its quality gets slightly strained, and there's special pages in the newspapers telling you where to go for the best deal. You can get a real sense of satisfaction out of doing the other person out of the last bit of free-floating anxiety. Sorry, luv, no anxiety left. I've got some hesitance, if that'll do, all the anxiety went early, rush on it there was. And you can get free gifts, too. Just buy five panic attacks, and you will receive, absolutely free, our special brand of cowardice. This week only, we are giving away 25% extra with every can of melancholy. Interesting stuff, melancholy; has quite a long use-by date.

Luther's master belonged to the Disease-Of-The-Month Institute. Every month you were sent a brochure with the Doctor's Choice. Sometimes you got quite a nice line in bacteria, or a fungus, or something, and all you had to do was agree to have three diseases a year for the first ten years as your only commitment. And every disease was guaranteed to be at least 25% more virulent than you could catch in the shops. After the first two years, every disease counted towards your next FREE bonus disease.

If you wanted you could join a special division run by psychiatrists, where instead of a physical disease, you got to go crazy in a different way each time. When you joined up and promised to acquire a mental illness or a neurosis out of each of a minimum of six manuals which would be sent to you at intervallic inconveniences, you were allowed to have four free introductory Conversion Hysterias for only £9.95 plus postage and packing extra.

Sorry, I got carried away. Yes, you're right, we were talking about why your body can't be my body, even if I have all your sensations. It could only be that I had no control over your body. That I will something to happen to that your left leg of mine, and nothing happens. Your left leg is itching me something terrible, and I try to scratch it with your hand, and you carry on reading the newspaper unabashed.

By itself, that wouldn't be enough. Because? Because I could simply conclude that that body of mine over there was paralysed, or was having some kind of strange epilepsy causing it to move without any control from me.

No, what I would need would be to conclude that there were some rationality about that body's movements, some purposing, some willing, that was not mine, not mine at all. And I would conclude that there was some other mind there, controlling this part of me that I sense but cannot move.

And speech. To hear from that this my mouth, this that which I can see opposite me and feel myself within, words of language that do not proceed from my consciousness. To hear that this, you, my body address me as an other. That might make me conclude I was not alone in your body.

So. Consider as he considered. It might be that all this, this that is true of my experience of my body and yours and your mind and mine, you too were aware of, as in a mirror. Though I can never know that. That that that that sentence speaks of, that that is a that that I cannot know.

But for this our experiment, what use have we made of our own body? Our as in mine, yes.

None. It has been there simply to provide us with a difference, a source separate, from which our construction, as of Dis, can emerge.

So in one body, we could do all this. I could sense it all, and control only part. And hear coming from my mouth words that are not mine, nor to be found in my deepest unconscious, yet making some truth. Some truth that is a person's truth, but not mine. Someone else in here. And I would not be we. I would still be I, and it be it.

It could even be that the other one, this stranger inhabiting me, didn't need to use me as a hypothesis even for a moment. That it willed all the things that I fancy that I have done. Willed them for some other reason, that makes perfect sense to it. So its being is as at unity in itself. Like Jerusalem is builded. But I, I still exercise my will fully. And the stranger is not one second of unease aware of anything but the sense of what it does.

Consider as he considered. Luther felt the body of a cat and the body of a dragon. And he could move neither. Only his ears and eyes and whiskers and mouth remained to him. Everything else was dragon-willed or self-inscaped.

Now, in fact, the dragon was also a philosopher. A philosopher essentially greater than Luther; one with knowledges which it is impossible to know that you know. And one whose grasp of logic was superb. He had grasped logic firmly by the throat, and singed it with fire, and strangled it by tying his tail round it, and it still worked. So he had never let it go. Because if you are in a cave where you don't know what is and what is not, and if every other cretin is a liar, then logic is all you've got to keep you true. No, you don't need to think to understand logic; logic has its conclusions carefully included in the beginning, and they come out the other end inevitably and unchangedly. (At least, that's what basic logic is like, and while the dragon actually knew thousands of logics, he was only conscious of the basics.)

Another time, Luther had seen a van with the word AULAGE written on its side, and he thought that this was a perfect idea. A wonderful firm that would come and create round you exactly the right space for you to be in, moulded to every last little bit of your psychoanatomy, with utter comfort and added space for those sort of niggly places that we all have. Though, of course, if it were absolutely right, then it ought to feel wrong, because it would be moulded to your unconscious as well as your conscious. But perhaps you would be unconscious of the way it moulded to your unconscious, so it would actually fit perfectly, and it would feel as if it fitted perfectly, and you wouldn't know the difference. Which would be perfectly imperfect instead of being imperfectly perfect if it were to be the first way.

Of course, if you showed it to your friends, then there would arise the question of whether it was then to be imperfectly imperfectly perfect or imperfectly perfectly imperfect or perfectly imperfectly perfect or perfectly perfectly imperfect. Because it might be that your friends could see the mismatch and you could, or that they could and you couldn't, or that they couldn't and you could, or that they couldn't and you couldn't (which is actually rare, but it's what we all pretend in polite society all the time, so it must be true at some level don't you think?). So you see that you must so perfectly arrange things that they are fundamentally imperfect but perfectly so. And that applies to your arranging too.

Now when Luther Dragon went to heaven, he discovered that there are seven orders of heaven, with an eighth that we'll come to later. Which is exactly as it should be according to St Paul.

In the first order of heaven, it's always morning. Everyone is just waking up, and blinking in the extraordinary light. The light is completely white. There's not a trace of any colour visible. And that's because one colour can't be more important than any other colour; they have to be exactly equal. And when all colours are mixed, then there is whiteness. An utter whiteness that pierces your eyelids and scorches your retinas until you are blind from a million million suns' lookings into you. But since, in this heaven, nothing ever dies, nothing ever ends, it has to be a beginning always; and so you are always just waking up and always being blinded by the first shaft of light you've ever seen. You're not even at the point of screaming.

Most people just stay here, in this heaven, their being too scared to go any further stopping them working out how to see with all the light. Every sort of heaven asks a question which you have to answer to get any further, and this is the question of the first order of the heavens. And usually the answer is to realise what question it is that you need to answer. And here the question isn't, How do I see with all this light?, it's, What is it that makes the light?. Because if you know that, you can control how the light shines. And you can find the right sort of darkness to walk in. But most of them, most of the time, just are dazzled at being dazzled. Which isn't any enlightened good.

And so not many go further. Not many go to the second order of the arch-heaven. In this, the Totally, Utterly, Real, Perfect World, everything is as perfect as it ought to be or should have been or could have been, and everything is utterly itself, and everything is as real as reality can get. So, of course, Socrates isn't there; No, there are three Socrateses. There's Socrates, as he was, but perfectly so; and then there's Socrates as Plato described him, because he ought to have existed and therefore so he does; and then there's Socrates as Xenophon described him, as well, because Xenophon was a nice chap, and so his view of things is quite valid too, well, sort of, but anyway a nice chap, so he shouldn't be disappointed of his hope, and so there ought to be a Socrates as he described him, and therefore there is.

Yes, that's right, everything you ever wished for is there, provided it's a wish you ought to have wished, and it is there exactly as you ought to have wished it, so sometimes people don't recognise it as what they wished for, and wish for it again. But that doesn't do any good, because it's the same wish, and therefore it oughtn't to come true again, because it already has, and if you can't see that it has, it's because you can't recognise it. But of course, that can't really happen, since you're perfect too, unless the perfect you can't recognise what it wished for, in which case you'll never get it because if you did then you would be less than perfect, which you can't be, since you're perfect, of course. So what you get then is a tragedy, and there are lots of utterly perfectly real, perfectly tragic, perfect people too constrained by perfection.

Now, of course, if the perfect you conflicts with someone else's perfection then that might be difficult. You see, it might be that for your life to be perfect someone else had to be a particular way or do a particular thing or so on. And it might be that there were two or three people like that for you, or there might be lots, or, if you were very, very famous or something like that, there might be millions of people who had to respond to you in some way, or believe in your message, or die for you, or be liquidated because they couldn't ever have believed, or things like that. Which is all very well for you, but maybe it's not too nice for them. Maybe for the other person or people to be perfectly them they had really to be utterly different from how they had to be for you. Now that's not at all perfect.

And so to make it just right, there's another them, completely real, of course, and utterly perfectly how you need them to be. But there's then yet another them, who's the them for them, as it were, and who's exactly perfectly just as they ought to be, right down from the very first flake of dandruff all the way to the steel cap of their boots. Only, and this is what makes it so, what's the word?, beautiful?, no, apt?, mm, not quite, just?, never so surely, proportionate!, that's the word, proportionate. Mathematically, severely, meet, right and bounden in a bond. Yes, what makes it proportionate, is that you will never recognise them, never even see them, because you can't, because you're perfect and real, and they're perfect and real, and you don't match, so you can't exist together even for a second, otherwise you'd both destruct, like matter and anti-matter, and so you never encounter them and they never encounter you.

But, of course, if it were just like that, then, though you'd never really be lonely, since the perfect world would be perfectly peopled just for you, and though you'd never be busy, since if you changed things it couldn't be more perfect, so it would be less perfect, which isn't allowed, and though you'd never be bored, since you'd be surrounded by all the things that you would be perfectly delighted by, there'd be no integration, no fitting of the millions of perfect, utterly real wholes into any kind of what shall we call it?, an über-whole, or superomnes, if you like, even though each whole occupied exactly the same piece of utterly perfectly thus eternity. So two utterly perfectly people can't ever really come into contact with each other. So you have no-one to talk with, even though you're not a dragon. So there are ideas. And these are the realest utterlymost perfectest things of all, so far.

Which means that there is a next order of heaven.

And Luther is still there where we left him in the dragon. Consider as he considered.

What did he feel? What he felt was shame. Shame is made of relatedness, the connectedness you can't escape. When you are ashamed you know that even to cast yourself off the top of a mountain would be of no help, because you would be universally and for ever known just and justly as the one who had cast themself off the mountain. Your name would be made ineradicable and irredeemable and irretrievable. And if you dreamed that the earth opened up beneath your feet and swallowed you up, because that is what the earth ought to do if it knew that you were standing on it, then you'd know in the next second that the earth wouldn't be that merciful, that it would vomit you out and that the earth would make you stand there and would turn to mud to slow your footsteps so you cannot run, and make itself slippery so your feet will make you trip up and slip and slide and fall, and you'll be laughed at because you can't even run away properly. And if you cried to the mountains, "Fall on me." then your voice would echo for ever until the smallest child in the furthest places unimaginable would laugh at such a silly sound, whoever heard such a thing?. And you don't have even to walk down the street to be condemned. It is known that you are where you are, so even your cell is no sanctuary.

For you must understand, *you are not being punished.* Your punishment would start the moment you might begin to expiate your sin. But now, anything you do, anything at all, even nothing itself, will just add to the wasted weight of your unspeakableness-itself crimes. You add shame to shame with every second you dare to let pass. And they have all received of your shame, and shame for shame, shame upon shame.

And if you walk down the street, if you dare to show yourself, and you will hold your head up high or fold it on your breast, it doesn't matter which, because it will be fixed in place by bands of the will, stronger than the purity of steely silk, if you will do this thing, then someone will look at you with their eyes, and you will see what they know. Or another, they will not look at you, and you will know that they, too, know. It doesn't need to be said in your presence, what your condemnation is: that would be to give you more notice than you are worth. You are impaled, so that every consciousness knows of your being and despises you, for merely being, and dismisses you, as being worth nothing. But you know that they talk about you. You have heard them laugh. You know what about. You would laugh too if you were them. It isn't funny, of course; it is just laughable. And if you were to speak about it, if you were to protest your innocence, or if you were to admit that your sin is ever before you - which is the same thing inside your soul -, then they would not know what you were talking about. They would ask you what you were afraid of. They wouldn't pat you on the head, not with their hands, not at all, would they?.

And you, you are not worthy even to hate them.

And hope not for your death; death would not help you. They would know why you were dead. And your being dead would prove that their knowledge was just.

So the only thing that comforts is that which is inhuman. A fly that buzzes round your head, because it doesn't know any better. Or best, a stone or water or the still, still-black sky. They are your friends. The stone will let you touch its solidness and will not flinch.

The water will run through your fingers and wet you. The sky will not accuse you. The fire will not deny to burn you. The knife will offer you its sharpness, and let you bleed your blood onto it. And the bullet will pierce your own heart also. All hearts. All flesh.

That's why you have to kill. It doesn't matter who you kill, since they all know. You're helping them, you see. They have to become inanimate in order to make the world a better place.

But you mustn't be caught, and you mustn't be known. That's the biggest mistake. To keep your power, to be able to help them, to be able to heal the world of its knowledge, to cure their omniscience, you must be silent. If you speak, all your power goes, and they will say you are mad. But while you are silent, then you can see the fear on their faces and read about their guilt. And you know that they can only wait for you to purify them from your shame. Even God waits for you, for only you only keep him to be last of all. God will tremble as you reduce him to nothing, as you turn him back to the dust from which he raised you.

I think it's supper-time.

CHAPTER 4

I will not accept if nominated, and will not serve if elected.
General William Sherman

Why do cats sit on sheets of paper? Well, they're not allowed to read, because it's bad manners to appear to be working.

So instead they found a way long ago of absorbing information by osmosis. Luther ingested the whole of Kant once in an hour by dozing on top of a bookcase. He got a categorical headache. And sitting on a television is far more efficient than watching, since you can soak up all the channels at once while watching what's going on in the house opposite. In fact, they take the principle further still: you see, when a cat sits on top of a car looking at nothing very much in particular, it is in fact carrying out extremely subtle investigations into the working of the Second Law of Thermodynamics, or else, and sometimes more likely, it's speaking to its great aunt in Australia using a type of waveform that travels the surface of the earth never exceeding six feet above ground level. It was Wittgenstabby who first pointed out that if you tied a length of wool all the way round the world and then added an extra metre, then the resulting circle would be precisely 159.15494 mm (or about six inches) above sea level all the way round the world. From which it follows that a wave-form of the right wavelength can be kept in orbit at any really convenient height. Yes, but that's part of it; they need the warmth to be able to do these things. Young cats get a good grounding in string theory, of course.

Now then. What took Luther out of his thought experiments and out of his discoveries, and got him to go further still, was another apparition before him.

It was a butterfly of purest gold, with just a little lapis lazuli inset here and there to stop it from being simply *too* vulgar, don't you think?. And it took over Luther's head for a moment, and told him to pull himself together, and go and confront the Bird Who Must Not Be Caught and the Mouse Who Must Not Be Chased. Then

Luther could be pulled apart again, and so get back to normal. And then, all this confounded nuisance of a business about the dragon could be sorted out, and with a bit of luck Luther could be back curled up in front of the fire by, Oh, probably Thursday week, how does that suit you, Squire? At which the Butterfly gave a deep sigh and flew off, only to be promptly blown back by the wind. At which he sighed even deeper.

Well, he was a King Butterfly, and they have special powers. Well, to be more accurate, he thought he was a King Butterfly, and he thought it so strongly that he had the powers anyway. Which is called faith.

A butterfly is the true counter-pole to God. The devil is only God in a sulk, or God feeling forgotten about. But perfectly, perfectly explicable in its own purity of logic. What destroys God is randomness, the glory of chance, the magnificence of accident, an eminence of happenstance. And if a butterflying pair of wings can precipitate disaster at the other edge of the world, are those not the real angels to oppose God? Aren't they the ones who can never be allowed into heaven? And isn't that why they have beauty that nothing shares, totally quidditative?

So the butterfly had a mere motion, and decided that it was off-with-its-head-time, and summoned from all the corners and apices of the three axes every last one of the plagues of butterflies that move over the face of the earth. And they arrived, and blotted out the sky and the sun, and their wings blew a grave space about Luther and lifted the dragon from the earth, and held him suspended in a ball of fluttering high above the world. And the King Butterfly said, "You must tell me a story, and if it pleases me you shall indeed live, and if it displeases me, I shall sever your head from his body and you shall die and he will be healed." And he gave Luther a voice to speak.

All right then, I'll tell you another story, if this one's too scary for just now, but only a little one, and then we'll have to come back to the main one. Yes, all right, teddy can listen too.

Once upon a time, there lived a King. He had a castle, as all Kings do, but, unlike some Kings however, he never let anyone inside. Though, children, he did have several Visitors' Books.

Having heard about Wenceslas, and all that, he went out of his way quite often, taking care to ensure that his footsteps could be marked well. Pages, please note. Out of his way wasn't very far, since there were plenty of peasants, not to mention villeins, round about the castle, as far as his eye could see.

Every now and then the King noticed a peasant in some difficulty. When this happened, his eyes filled with light (a sort of gleam, really), his ears pricked up (did you know that cauliflowers can be pointed?), and he went rushing off following the sent. He would rush up to the peasant, and say "I know exactly what you must let me do.", and would do it. The peasant was grateful - peasants aren't stupid - and waited till the King had gone before tidying up all the extra mess. And all they had to do in return was worship the King for evermore, and give him extra tithes to fill his barns (etc), in utterly spontaneous recompense for their King's unwonted largesse.

Sometimes it happened that the peasant was really in trouble, but the King couldn't help with that, of course. If it can't be solved at once, then you must wallow in it, unspeakable wretch that you are.

Occasionally, too, it happened that the King found a peasant who had worked out how to go on having just the right amount of trouble, and that made him busy for weeks on end. Never mind that the estates all round were overgrown, and that there was a run on the groat. This was much more fun. Ever so. (Even more fun was the discipline - but there are some things, children, that it's not polite to talk about.)

But a day sometimes came, O woe, when a peasant said "Go away." They were very polite peasants. That made the King very angry, and he would tell the peasant that he was very wicked - that is, the peasant -, because he had not understood that the King must always have everything he wanted, and have it immediately, or else something terrible would happen. And do you know, children, that something terrible usually did? Such powers of prophecy the King had.

Even worse, sometimes one of his super-peasants - the ones who knew how to have just the right difficulties for a long time, that is - would do something that hurt him. And then the King would be very sad, and depressed, and melancholic, and blue, and down, and low, and dejected, and sorrowful, and unhappy, and cheerless, and lamentable, and pitiful, and touching, and pathetic and very sad. And he would eventually complain that he was so terribly misunderstood, and how awful it was that everyone always kicked him in his Privy Purse. But he tried to hide this mood when he was at important state occasions, like meetings of the Security Council, for instance, and would just remind people that he was the King, and if they didn't do just as he said, well, they would find out just what that meant (if he could find time to tell them) or else he'd go away and leave them to be gobbled up by the big bad wolves.

Now, it is very interesting that wolves were an endangered species, because, first, the King had domesticated them, and told them how much he liked them and valued their opinion, and gave them special jobs to do, and then he waited a bit while they got on with the jobs, and then he'd accused them one by one of plotting against him, because they were involved in state matters, and had them tortured until they admitted it, which proved he was right (and they'd been found in possession of state papers, that he'd given them, which was evidence, but he thought their confession was better for his soul), and so he had them cooked and served for his supper.

Now, children, Oh, sorry, child, I was talking to teddy as well, I hope you're not squeamish, because there is something terrible. You see, in his castle he had lots of photographs on the wall, one of every peasant he had ever helped since the beginning of his reign. But the castle was made entirely of glass - the one-way sort, so you can't tell that it's glass. And one day some of the peasants got a very sharp knife and very quietly cut a tiny hole in the wall, which was very daring and totally against the rules. And they looked inside. And what they saw was that every photograph was exactly like every other photograph. And they were framed in glass. And you couldn't see where the photograph ended and the frame began, nor where the frame ended and the wall began. And this was all quite understandable, because the King, who displayed only photographs he'd developed himself, had made sure that each and every photograph he ever looked at in his entire reign was a beautiful, perfect and completely exact likeness of himself (taken from his good side), only ever-so-slightly out of focus.

And then they realised that the King would never die, because he only existed because of the glass walls. When he went into the castle, he disappeared into the walls, and got energy from them until there was enough of him to appear again, and then he went out and did some more reigning. And they saw that he had never been born. It was always going to be like that. Orient wheat.

So they started investigating the properties of the best and of the most up-to-date sorts of paint, and wrote graffiti all over the castle, until every bit of the castle wall was covered in DOWN WITH THE KING., and BESANT's RITES KNOW., and such-like. And then they used a silver groat to open the lock on the Portcullis and stormed the castle, and painted all the walls inside and out with really thick black paint, the sort that stops you washing the graffiti off, and wrote even more graffiti than they had told themselves they were going to. That way the King would be stuck inside the walls, and all the photographs were destroyed. And they went on their way rejoicing.

And the next day the King came out of the castle exactly as usual. And, you know, he didn't take any sort of revenge, because that would have been completely superfluous.

CHAPTER 5

Almost everybody in the neighbourhood had 'troubles', frankly localised and specified; but only the chosen had 'complications'.
Edith Wharton
Ethan Frome

There it was, flittering and fluttering about in the air. Flittering and fluttering, a funny-looking little-looking birding of a butterfly, looking little at Luther. Flittering and fluttering, though certainly not flattering. To anybody, of course. Not flattering, is flutting and flitting. What? I don't know, not about fletiferous and flottering. If anyone had a right to be flotten, it was Luther, you see. Completely flottering from his flettering. Only, he couldn't flet, not in front of anyone else. When his master watched the box of flat people, his master sometimes flet at something that was magnificent, or noble, or kind, or humane, or loving, but never, never at anything was sad or horrorible. But Luther flet only by himself, for himself, because of himself, for cats have an adult honour. And he would not flet at not being flattered by a strutting, flutting, feathered unfriend. But though it flittered and fluttered, it did not move, and indeed existed outside space itself, because, as we all know, fluttery won't get you anywhere.

You know, cats' whiskers aren't so the cat can judge if it can squeeze through a gap. No, rather, whiskers are essential for good form. Etiquette. C and non-C. It simply isn't on to have feathers coming out only of one side of one's one mouth. There must be several feathers coming out of each side of the mouth, with the front of the lips gently dusted with down. It adds a certain piquancy, a certain je-sais-vraiment-quoi, to the taste of blood. It's why cats never use salt: all their food - all proper food, that is - comes ready salted.

Of course, cats can't understand why anyone should invent packaging, since all edible things come ready packaged. A nice layer of feathers or fur keeping the fodder fresh. And, of course, as you get older your lips aren't as nimble as they once were, and it's more difficult to open the carefully-kept-warm-until-you're-ready-to-eat-it dish of the day. "Young lips", you hear one old queen say to another, "O for young lips." Or something like that. Old queen? An old queen is an ageing cat whose claws are too long for its tongue. Or something like that.

Oh yes, the whiskers. Well, you see, they're there as their way of telling how far out the feathers are, and to stop them flying away. Or perhaps one should say flittering away, shouldn't one?

It's one of the things that shows that humans are incapable of being kind to cats -genuinely, honestly, kind - is that humans always have their own food warmed up, and always serve cats **COLD!** cat-food, when every sensible creature knows that proper food has been kept exactly at the right temperature - blood hot - from the moment it came into existence until the moment you are hungry for it. When did you last see a cat pounce on a tin of cat food? And then, human table manners! Every kitten is lovingly taught how to play with its food, how to pick it up, throw it in the air, shake it about, turn it over and over, and only then to take the first bite. How to scatter the feathers. Which bones to crunch and which not. And exactly how much to leave. Humans just don't realise how grossly, insultingly rude not doing that is. It's almost as bad as serving a guest meat that's dead. Or making you eat up your vegetables.

Let it be recorded, mice sandwiches never repeat on one like cucumber. He occasionally took afternoon tea at the Ratz; it was the only place one could go to in London that didn't admit Manxes, and others improperly dressed.

So Luther told a story, and guess, it was the other story I've just told you. And the butterfly said, "You must tell me a story, and if it pleases me you shall indeed live, and if it displeases me, I shall sever your head from his body and you shall die and his soul shall be healed."

And here is another story for me to tell you.

There was once a wise man, a great theologian, who sensing that he was too old, decided that he must overcome death. He took careful thought, and believed that he must rejuvenate himself. If he became young again, he would have put death in its place: it would not be a problem.

So he prayed, and meditated, and fasted. After forty days and forty nights, he arose and walked through a desert towards the holy mountain. With every step, he sensed that time was running out. Yet he knew he must not hurry. That would spoil everything.

He just managed to reach the peak of the mountain, and with a great cry, he fell down on his face, having accomplished his goal. Now he would awake and live for ever.

And in that very moment, he split apart, and where he had fallen were two utter apsqualling infants. A new-born baby boy and girl. But he was still dead. For, as infants, they knew nothing.

What am I in this telling making? There is so much I do not know.

Remember? There is so much I do not remember. One memory must serve for another until the trail ends. Like the address means the house, but nothing is there. Never constructed, never demolished. So I make a story and leave the trail behind. Altogether.

So Luther then told it a second story, and guess, it was the other story I've just told you.

And the butterfly said, "You must tell me a story, and if it pleases me you shall indeed live, and if it displeases me, I shall sever your head from his body and you shall die and his soul shall be healed."

Now, once upon a when, there was a man who could not dance, and decided, for it was that there was never another choice, to live in a wilderness. And in the wilderness he marched, and he loped, and he strolled, and he remembered that he used to be able to run. And now and just then he would think that perhaps he had not utterly forgotten a day when he was, O perhaps seven stones ago, lighter on his feet than any other child.

It wasn't really that he couldn't dance, for he knew that there was music within him, and when he listened to Mr Bach his fugues or Mr Beethoven his sinfonies, he was wild inside with leaping. Then too he had grace; he could walk as it were he were a wheel, and he could progress his hand so it would touch and not touch in the same moment any contour or range of mountains. But, he could not dance for all that he loved to dance.

He had lived more than half a life-time in a reverie of seriousness, making a palimpsest of an existence out of text-books of everything, until he was a wraith, a shadow on which the sun might never shine, lest the source be obliterated. So clouds surrounded him, and they were clouds of wisdom, for many people came and showed him the utmost respect, and talked to him and he would listen and say a littlest word, and they would marvel at what he did.

Yet, one morning there came to him a whisper that there might really truly be a spirit, some angel perhaps, a messenger from the very flesh of life. But he did not believe it, except only a little, in case he might be deluded and go mad and be driven from his wilderness to share the misery of *hoi polloi* people.

But the messenger came, whether he would or no, and dragged him to his feet, and said, Dance with me, because I would dance with you. And he was forced into a dancing pattern. He did not know whether he was dancing or not. It seemed, yes, indeed, O my gosh, like he was dancing, but it did not feel like dancing. It felt like he knew he was being bewitched and caught up, and that the messenger would suck his bowels from him, and graze his tongue with emery-board, and convulse him with longing and terror, and laugh at him through still eyes. But the messenger said, I can see your brain and swim through your veins, and I know your fear and how your skin has slept so many days, and I will dance with you, for I would dance with you.

And the man tried to believe this messenger, and quieted himself, and went limp as rag-dolls' souls. And he went on moving in this pattern. And he knew that he was dancing, and that the messenger true would dance with him.

So he was delirious within himself and thought that he might dance for ever in the arms of this strange messenger. So the messenger, knowing that the man was but a poor sad fool without even the wits of foolishness, drank deeply out of the vessel of sleep, and said to the man, Today it is tomorrow I shall dance with you, but today I must rest. And tomorrow the messenger said, Today it is perhaps tomorrow I shall be dancing with you, but today I must be recovering myself from your dancing. And tomorrow the messenger said, Today and tomorrow it is soon I would dance with you.

Then the man knew to himself what the messenger had said, and he thought and thought within that the messenger was no messenger, but a hungry siren who would cast his husk aside and smile, and say, But I did dance with you a little, and now I will not dance.

And it was that the man knew that he had always known what this messenger was, and he wanted to be sad, and to weep, and to take poison. But he said to himself, I am worth enough to be a fool to myself if I choose and to be wise to myself if I am wanting and to stand still for many days if I must. And he knew he was more deadly than any siren and more urgent than any messenger.

But he was wrong, and the messenger came again to dance with him. And he danced until the messenger gasped for air and sense and discipline. And the man knew that he cared not to an end whether the messenger was there or no.

Yet, there was this curious, that the man, he could not feel his feet at his dancing. For they moved beauteously in a frettedness of steps, and he watched his feet unbelieving as they moved. But feel them he could not. And he thought that he had forgotten when his feet had become numb, and how no messenger could make his feet to sense but only him alone.

So after much dancing, he let his feet remember, and they remembered the glorious touch of the earth on the sole. And suddenly, while the feet were still remembering, the stranger disappeared into thin green air. And the man decided that his feet could keep their memories and awaken to be true feet obedient to all rhythms to which they truly ought to be obedient.

And long after, though the man never forgot that stranger, and knew this messenger to be quite near to, the one approached him once last time begging some favour. And the man would not let the stranger go until there was an accounting for all these doings. And when the stranger had finished speaking, the man knew that for all the dancing the stranger had never once danced by a choosing, had never been free to be dancing, was the lowest slave of the dancing. And with this knowledge, and with all this discovery, the man was content. For as if in a mirror, he had recalled and recovered the surging of dancing.

So this, child, was the third story that Luther told the butterfly.

And the butterfly said, "You must tell me a story, and if it pleases me you shall indeed live, and if it displeases me, I shall sever your head from his body and you shall die and his soul shall not be healed but what will be shall be."

So Luther said, There was once an Old Man and a Child. And one day a voice as of the Old Man came out of the heavens and said, We must go and sacrifice. And the Child said, With what shall we make a sacrifice?, for we have nothing. So the Old Man answered that he would himself provide a sacrifice for any God.

They walked for many days, and rode, and walked, in heat and dust and tempest and holy drunkenness, until they reached a place in which there was a flat stone. Here we must sacrifice, said the Old

Man. With what shall we sacrifice to any God?, answered the Child him. Do as I shall tell you.

And so obediently the Child took rope that had been concealed and glue and sealing wax, and affixed the Old Man to that flat stone. Now, now said the Child - show me what we shall sacrifice. And the Man said, in my clothes in my chest pocket there is a knife: take it. So it was taken.

A voice came from heaven and said, Look about. For there were many rams whose horns were caught fast in thickets of briars. But this Child, Oh a wise Child, knew that no sinless pure animal is a sacrifice for any true God, and carefully gently released every one of the rams and drove them away to live.

Careful now. Don't falter. Face like a mask. You know you know how.

And a voice came out of heaven a second time, and said to be lifting up the knife and with it piercing the Old Man's heart.

The Child looked at the Old Man laying helpless on the slab and saw how piteous a thing he was and how foolish. Senseless as the beauty of pure sound to signify nothing silent.

And quick, quick the Child flung that knife far into the swiftermost sweeps of the wind, and went hippity-skippity away, that the rains the winds and the dust might come and wash the stone each grain down, 'til the Old Man should keep himself there by his own gravity of thinking only, from his fixity.

So Luther told too this story.

And the butterfly said, "You must tell me still a story, and if it pleases me you shall indeed live, and if it displeases me, I shall sever your head from his body and you shall die and what shall be shall be."

Once there was a greatest of scientists, who was tormented by this deepest of problems: was he alone in the universe? Or was there out there some form of intelligent life, on some far-off planet round an unknown star circling?

And being a greatest of scientists, he could get researching grants from the government of certain countries if he counterfeited that it would protect them from their enemies. For they feared enemies greatly, and lived in terror of being attacked, even though they had overcome the world. So they gave him the lakhs of billions of green pieces of paper, and he set up his grand experiment to find the answer. He assembled a team of specialists and technologists, and all that he needed to spend so much money. They laboured for the longest of time that they could get away with without the auditors getting uppity, and began to send out especial simple messages and symbols into the aether. Not that the aether exists, of course, but you can't just go sending messages into a vacuum can you? And they waited for a reply, that would, O you know, come just wanting to pass the time of day from some civilisation that is so alien from us that we couldn't understand the slightest of their thoughts, so advanced were they. Day after day they waited, glued to their instruments. Quite right:- being glued to your instruments is painful and uncomfortable. But these were dedicated people, who were paid a lot of money as well.

And every day there was a response that the line was engaged. So after many years, they concluded that they had their answer, and the greatest of scientists called a press conference. It's where ideas get press-ganged. And the scientist solemnly announced that there is no intelligent life to be found in the universe, anywhere. At which all the listeners nodded sagely and agreed that this was indeed a greatest of scientists.

So Luther told this story too.

And the butterfly said to him, "You must tell me still more of a story, and if it pleases me you shall indeed live, and if it displeases me, I shall sever your head from this body and you shall die and what shall be shall truly be."

So one day this chap wakes up and realises he's got the wrong life. There's nothing wrong with his life, you understand. He's got the good job, nice wife, pleasant home, 2.4 children exactly well-behaved, car that impresses, loyal friends, all the rest, and he's fit enough to play squash three times a week. There's nothing wrong.

Except he's got the wrong life. It's just not his life. So he talks it over with his best friend, who isn't exactly sympathetic. "What do you mean, the wrong life? You've got (*please insert long list according to taste*); you've got it made; nothing to worry about. I envy you."

So he goes to see his priest, which in his case was also a counsellor. She'd done lots of courses.

"Aha, I see. So you have this deep sense that you're living the wrong life. I suppose I'm wondering what you find wrong about it."
"There's nothing wrong about it, except that it's wrong. That's the point."
"I see, uh-uh", said she who actually didn't, "so it's just wrong for you?"
"Exactly," said the client, "it's so good to be understood. No-one else understands me."
"Mm. So what might the right life be like? Here, imagine I'm giving you this magic wand; not a real one, obviously, but real between us. So how are you going to use your magic wand to make your life the right one?"
"I don't know. That's what I wanted you to tell me."
"My task, really, is to facilitate your discovery of your own answers. So let's concentrate on the magic wand again, and this time I want you to fully engage with your unconscious and let the answers find their way through."
"I suppose I want it to be the right life for me."
"Excellent", she cooed, for she knew how powerful her technique of non-judgemental empathy was, "the right life for you."
"Exactly."

"So let's go deeper still. What comes to mind when you think about the right life?"
"Well, that it feels right. That it doesn't feel wrong."
"We have made real progress today. Same time next week?"
"O, yes please. Thank you ever so much."

So after two years, he realises that counselling is wonderful, but that he's just not cut out for it.   So he decides to visit a monk. A proper monk it was too, one who lives in a cave on a holy mountain in the middle of a desert, and eats only dried vegetables and inedible roots and drinks only vinegar.

The monk looks at him, and says, "Sell all you have, and go and minister to the lepers." "Are you crazy?," says the lost soul, "I couldn't possibly do that. I've got..." (and he reels off his list).

"Then you will be unhappy for the rest of your life."

Now this was a real revelation. For he sees the truth: that he should be unhappy for the rest of his life. It would still be the wrong life, and he'd die unhappy. But it would be his wrong life. And so he devoted the rest of his life to unhappiness, and felt that he'd found the answer. You're not meant to be happy. You just have to get on in this world and be unhappy. And that's how he brought up his children, who learned their lesson well.

Well now, he's going on with this, and one day he's looking in the phone book for the number of someone to come and service his burglar alarm, and he sees this highlighted entry. "Complete Heaven and Hell Everlasting Security Service", it says. And he rings it.

"Welcome to the Complete Heaven and Hell Everlasting Security Service Total Customer Service Helpline;" says this nice helpful lady, "this is our 24-hour seven-day a week dedicated call centre for all your eternal security problems."

"Promising", he thinks, until there's a undertone of a beep and she carries on.   "We're sorry, but, this being a holy feast day of obligation, the call centre is closed. Please try again Monday to Friday during normal office hours, when we shall be pleased to offer crucial succour to our customers. Remember, we offer our customers complete and total security for their eternal comfort. Thank you for calling. Have a nice life."

"That's it", he fumes. "I'm nothing but a complete and total customer. That's all I am. And if anyone crosses me today, they'll find out just what complete and total customers they are too!"

Being a curious sort of chappie, he looks up his diary, and there's no Saint's Day listed. So he goes and looks up reference books for every one of the world's religions, and none of them have a festival on this day. This does not bode well for his attitude towards the call centre. They're having him on. And he does not like being had. On or off.

But for some reason the following day, he rings again.

"Welcome to the Complete Heaven and Hell Everlasting Security Service Total Customer Service Helpline;" says the lady, now seeming slightly less nice and not at all helpful, "this is our 24-hour seven-day a week dedicated call centre for all your eternal security problems. For faster service, please press the hash key now."

So he does. "Thank you. Now, please enter your twenty-three-digit Eternal Security Number, using the keypad on your phone. If you have not received your Eternal Security Number, you may wish to contact your local Eternity Assistant. Otherwise, please hold, and you will be connected to our next available representative. Remember, your soul is important to us."

The line starts playing, Purcell's Suite in C for Trumpet - without restarting every twenty seconds -, and he's got through four movements and is humming along to the Irish Tune, when it stops and a reassuring baritone voice answers.

"Hello, you're through to Securiel. Do you have your Eternal Security Number available, by any chance?" George, that was his name, decides not to be sarcastic, but simply says that he's never had one.

"Everyone has one, but, between you and me, guv," says Securiel, becoming unexpectedly chummy, "the way things are nowadays, what with the state of the Churches, not too many people are getting to know theirs. Never mind, you're in safe hands now. So, would you like to know yours? It gives you full access to all truly essential services for the rest of time and beyond."

You can't really refuse an offer like that, so George says Yes, please, he'd like his.

"Sensible man," says Securiel, "makes sense really. I just need to ask a few questions to confirm your identity. Full name?"

There's a pause, since George has always been a bit embarrassed by this; but he plucks up courage.

"George St George If-Christ-had-not-redeemed-the-world-thou-shouldst-be-damned Alleluia-for-all-God's-Mercies St John Blessed Mary Saint-Smith."

"How are you spelling 'shouldst', Mr Saint?", asks Securiel, as if such names occur every day – but then, in his business, they do.

That settled, the next question turns out to be, "Date, time and place of implantation in womb, please."

"Pardon," says George, "how am I supposed to now that?"

"Essential, that is. Absolutely essential. I mean, this isn't just one of your pro-life organisations; this is the total-life service. And we need to know when your life started. That's fixed, see. I mean, if your ma is a bit late, or the doctor decides to induce her, you come out on a different day. You can't rely on birth being accurate or anything.

We do need to find when you actually began. Mind you, there's a fair number of people like you, so if we get more information, I'll try and find your trace in our ledgers. We'll certainly have a book on you; it's just finding it that gets awkward."

After recounting most of his life story, George gets his answer.

"OK, I've found you, and brought your records up on the screen. Sorry it's taken so long; the computer system's slow today, must be a lot of demand. Usually the Americans that cause the trouble. Have you got a pen handy? Fine. Your soul number, your Eternal Security Number I mean, is 2-718281828-^-i-*-3-141592654. Got that OK? Good. Please keep it safe. Anyway, now we've sorted that, how can I help?"

And George explains.

"Ah well," says Securiel, "not too much I can do about that. It's your number, see. You've just got a bad number. Happens sometimes."

There's a bit of a pause, and then Securiel says, "I shouldn't do this, George. Against the rules, it is. But you sound like an OK sort of guy, and like you could do with a break. So I'll tell you, but don't let on I've said anything, OK? It won't make any difference in the long run, yeah? It'll all work out just the same."

And George, feeling that at last his problem has been settled, offers profuse thanks to Securiel, saying he's the best friend anyone could want.

"That's what we're here for, George. Anytime, mate."

"Oh, before I go," says George, "what was the feast day yesterday? Couldn't find it in any of the prayer books."

"You are out of touch," says Securiel. "First day of the Worlds' Cup. People's Republic of Ousia playing United Upostases. Everyone was watching. Great match. Ousia won 1-0. OK?"

With which, Securiel ends the call, sighs and shakes his head slowly. For he knows how George's problem already has been settled.

Luther was telling this story also.

And the butterfly said to him, "You must tell me yet again a story, and if it pleases me you shall indeed live, and if it displeases me, I shall sever your head from this body and you shall die and what will be shall be."

There was a certain man who had waited long years for a visitor with a particular message for him. He knew what the message was to be, and he had spent much thinking of how he should respond to the salutation, that it might be not according to his immediate word, but to his deepest intent. Many times he had been tempted to suppose that he had been refused: that the one who had promised would change their attitude towards him, and award this message to some other, less deserving than him. Yet, he ever knew that this was only temptation, and that the message would doubtless come.

So, of course, this must be the story of how the visitor did indeed arrive. Pity, you must, the poor angel who had been deputed to this task. This angel, see, had spent his last thousand years on guardian duty, delegated to looking after moderately old folk. No, our guardian angels don't stay attached to us throughout our lives. No, really, they get replaced every few years so that they can each specialise in a particular developmental stage. If they didn't, then they'd really get to know us, and get properly attached to us, and they might be tempted to intervene and guide us through life, and then we might successfully negotiate the challenges that life has to require of us, and then we wouldn't have all the things go wrong which usually do, and so we'd probably be happy and fulfilled, which would mean we were in need of far less grace just to stand still, which would mean that the angels wouldn't have to use quite as much skill in order to get a far less satisfactory result for us. So you understand how it makes a lot more sense not to have continuity of divine service.

Anyway, this angel had specialised in people who were past middle age, but not yet in any kind of mortal danger, and whose job was really only to accept that they were getting old. And since angels can't intervene with the exercise of your ever-sovereign free-will, and because adjusting to age is entirely a matter of will (well, all of life is really, you're quite right, but let's not do divine intervention out of any role in the economy of things), the angel has had, not to put too fine a point on it, rather a cushite time of it. So one millennium, his superintendent Power comes up to him, and says that it's time enough for a change, and he's been reallocated to a new and exciting work opportunity, at which the angel's wings droop, because he knows what New Heaven is like nowadays, and realises that whatever it is it won't be anything like as nice. So the superintendent Power says that he's been transferred to the angelic messenger corps. And with barely a century of on-the-job retraining, here he is taking out numinous expressions of the divine will. Mind you, he did try to look on the bright side, being an angel and all, but he was still looking and hadn't found it yet.

And this was a messy job. Visions and dreams are nice and straightforward, since you just have to deliver the messages through the person's psychic letter-box. Omens and portents, they're not so bad either, since you can go over the top with the lighting effects, and the boys and not-girls over in the sound-mixing department are usually quite amenable to lend a hand or several, and, between you, you can usually come up with something just amazing. Forget House and Garage; this is Cathedral. He hadn't had anybody decide to found a religious order, or build a shrine yet, but he knew it was only a matter of time.

No, this was a direct angelic visitation. You know, the full wings-akimbo job, flying in through the window with a little too much dry-ice on the side, and crying out "Hail!", and all that. For someone who's on the shy side, it's all a bit much. And he had a bad feeling about this one.

So in he goes, and he's got no further than saying he's come with a special greeting from on high, and that you've been specially selected to take part in an offer being made to a very carefully targeted group, i.e. you, when this guy, who's supposed to be overawed and shocked and not quite sure how to react, but overwhelmed and thankful, turns round to him and says he's a bit late, but now he's here let's get on with it. I mean, the effrontery of it, mortals thinking they can demand customer satisfaction out of angels.

"How many?", says the target.

"How many?", repeats the angel, thinking roles have got a bit reversed here.

"Yes, you heard, how many? You've come to give me some wishes, haven't you? I know it, you know it, we needn't get carried away with all the mystery and stuff. This is a perfectly straightforward deal. So how many wishes do I get?"

There's a look on the target's face which says not to mess with him, you know, like he's a *real* protestant or something. So the angel thinks he'd better just go with the flow. Because he doesn't want to have to roll with the punches or get nailed to a Church door.

"Well, three actually,", says the angel, "it's what it says here on the scroll."

"I only need one.", says the target. "Omnipotence. That's all."

"I'm not sure that's allowed," says the angel.

"Of course it's allowed. Once you've made the offer, you've got to keep your part of the bargain. Heaven can't go back on its word."

The angel decides he needs to take advice, and it gets discussed in the highest circles – it would do – but eventually it's agreed, after particularly heavy thunderstorms throughout the universe, that the target will have to be allowed omnipotence, but limited to the solar system. And the angel gets sent back with a new, revised scroll.

"Won't do," says the target, after reading the scroll through very carefully, as one is always supposed to do, but so few people ever bother with. "There's no guarantee, and no returns policy."

"We don't do guarantees."

"Don't do guarantees! Guarantees is your business. Without guarantees, you folk is nothing. And you know it. Don't give me 'we don't do no guarantees'."

So there are a lot more thunderstorms, and he gets offered a three-millennium return policy, and a guarantee against inherent manufacturer's defects (the lawyers worked out how he could never successfully claim on it).

And omnipotent the target was.

So the first day, he decided he wasn't going to do anything much with the world. No, this was his day, and he was going to enjoy it. He started with the perfectly beautiful body he'd always wanted, you know, so handsome and fit that everyone in the world, of whatever predilection or outlook, wanted to have his babies. Then fabulous wealth, so that multi-billionaires was paupers to him, and the home of all homes, of course. And the rest of the usual stuff, and since he'd had plenty of time to prepare, this took all of thirty seconds to arrange, and he took the rest of the day off.

Now, on the second day he'd got things to do. His world was going to be worth living in. None of this unhappiness and sickness and war stuff. No, everyone was going to have a properly blissful time. And the first thing he's decided on, was getting rid of race and colour, since that seemed to be behind quite a lot of the difficulties of the fallenness he'd got to sort out.

So, what colour should everyone be? White, black, brown were all out – that would be favouritism, and he wasn't having any of that. Green was a bit too obviously sci-fi, so he'd settled on blue. The exact shade took a little trouble: cerulean was too pale, and the blood vessels might show through; while ultramarine was too dark. Cobalt would do, but it's a bit variable. Which had meant he'd done a lot of pondering. And one lucky day back then it was when he'd had his breakthrough: turquoise. Everyone was going to be exactly the same shade of turquoise. They couldn't complain about that, could they? It's a lovely colour; just lovely it is. He'd done up his entire house in it. And with turquoise, you couldn't get a sun-tan, and you couldn't be looking run-down and a bit off-colour (not that anyone was going to, once the week was up). But he still wasn't quite happy. You see, it looked just a bit bland, and it didn't really go with body hair. The hair was easy - he just got rid of every last bit of it, except on the top of the head and round the eyes (and btw no-one was ever going bald again – he'd suffered quite enough from that, thank-you). Anyway, he wanted his people to look spectacular. But once he'd decided that the colour of everyone's hair must be the same (well, you couldn't let difference creep back in that way, could you?) it struck him what was needed.

So he made everyone's hair gold. Not blond, not yellow, not flaxen, but proper shiny gold bullion colour. Because it was gold bullion: his people really were going to be precious in his sight. It just went with the turquoise in his opinion – and his was the only opinion that mattered, after all. And that got him to thinking, and he got the final touch. People needed circles of gold all over them. No variation of course as to where the circles went – each person had them in exactly the same places. And no variation in the number or size. All the people on earth had exactly 141 gold circles in carefully calculated patterns arranged over their bodies. And gold eyes. It all looked classy, a quality product. And nobody could ever wear jewellery again – he hated all jewellery except thick gold chains – since nothing would match. And he fixed it so that tattoos were impossible (the ink wouldn't stay in the skin for more than thirty seconds), because he wasn't having anyone trying to improve on his design, thank-you-very-much.

Now, you couldn't have everybody looking identical, since they'd never tell each other apart, but equally you can't go to all this trouble and still have ugly people. So he made everyone look beautiful (though not as beautiful as him, of course) but each in their own way (and this was going to come in useful later on in the week when he dealt with relationships, because he certainly was going to sort all that stuff out, but good). Nobody was fat, and nobody was too skinny, and nobody was short (5'10" was the minimum) and nobody was too tall (up to 6'3"), but within those limits anything stunningly good-looking and drop-dead fit was perfectly acceptable.

So now, he's got the plan ready, and he knows what everyone is going to look like (and, being omnipotent, sorting out the individual quirks of a few thousand million people is far less tiring than you'd possibly guess), but he's got a handful of problems left. Memory's easy – you just fix it that everyone remembers themselves growing up turquoise and gold – but what are you going to do about all the films and the photographs and the paintings? He didn't have any qualms about altering the photos. I mean, if you were looking at your wedding pictures and you weren't turquoise then that would not be very nice, would it? And since he didn't think much of fine art photos (just glorified snaps in his opinion (and remember – it's his opinion that counts)), there was no problem with those. Films didn't take long to decide about either – he wasn't a film buff, and he saw no reason why any of the stars could possibly object to having their looks improved, and believe him, they could only think it was an improvement, if he ever let them in on the secret of what was going to happen – except that he wasn't.

But he was just a bit perturbed about the paintings. Would the *Mona Lisa* look right in turquoise? What would Michelangelo really have thought about putting gold circles all over the *Creation of Adam* or the *Last Judgement*? And all the Giottoes and the Vermeers? And as for Gauguin and Van Goch, he dreaded to think what the result would be. But what must be, must be. And he thought that, well, if the *Gioconda* had been in actual fact looking enigmatically turquoise then that's how Leonardo would have depicted her. And you could always alter the background of the Sistine Chapel if it didn't come out right, and then, if all else failed, you could just make people believe that Van Goch was exquisitely beautiful. And they would. After all, they did.

As for the history books and all the racism references – he just deleted them. It was easier than trying to find substitute reasons. Anyway, it was only going to be a problem for a couple of days at most.

So at twelve noon GMT on the second day, he changed the way people looked. And since they had no choice about it, they just carried on as if nothing had happened. Which it hadn't, of course.

Mind you, that wasn't all that didn't happen then, either. You can't go around getting rid of all these distinctions between people, and still leave them talking different languages. Of course, that meant no more Shakespeare or Dante or Tolstoy or Goethe, well, at least not in their previous form. But if you're going to create the perfect world, then changes there must be, and multiple languages were a no-no, so really when you think about it, that meant that Shakespeare et al weren't quite up to the mark really, because not everyone could understand them. He'd thought about using an existing language but that would mean something like French, which he wasn't going to stoop to. And then he'd wondered about a dead language, an ex-tongue, say perhaps Latin or Greek – Linear B would be fun – but that was a bit prejudiced and classist, not to say classicist, so then he came back to the present and thought about one of the obscurer ones. Perhaps everyone should speak Basque or Finnish or Nivkh.

But in the end, he saw that only a completely new language would do. And since he'd never liked learning languages, even though language was fascinating, because he was English which explains everything, he decided that this one would have to be very special.

So he did away with all distinctions between nouns and verbs, so that everything just depended on the endings. And then he had dozens of separate cases, more than Finnish even. But there was no redundancy anywhere, so letters like c and q and w and y all went, since k, s, u, and i could do everything needed there. So the alphabet was just a, b, d, e, g, h, i, k, l, m n, o, p, s, t, u, and a glottal stop – he couldn't never not get by without one of those glo'al stops - with which he created all the sounds worth worrying about. Then he picked all the stems out by generating all possible combinations on his computer and matching them to a dictionary via random numbers. So it was no particular tongue ever spoken before.

The other thing was, he wasn't going to have any dialects, and he wasn't going to have anyone changing the rules or the pronunciations. It had to be exactly the same in every part of the globe. That meant fixing it firmly in the head of all the people, but hey, if you're omnipotent, you're omnipotent.

The real job was going to be getting everything written since the beginning of time translated into the new tongue, but then he realised that he didn't need to worry overmuch, since no one could tell whether anything was beautiful or not, because if he made them think it was, then it would be. So he kept all of literature, but it just sounded a bit different, and really it was going to be the thought that counts. Therefore when Hamlet comes on stage and soliloquises about being and nothingness, and this question of whether mihspat is better than not mihspat that he's got to decide, then the audience was still wonderfully moved, and agreed that it was just the most pressing issue.

Not that it was Hamlet now, since names had all to match. But he had no qualms over that: there isn't that much difference between being "John Smith" and being "Ahpesis Hsedak'ah" once you get used to it. Which people wouldn't need to do anyway, since that's all they'd have ever known.

So all of that got done at exactly the same moment. With which he'd had quite enough for day two, thank you, and it was going quite well, and it was going to be very good when it was finished, and tomorrow he'd got to sort out the problem of evil, and though he knew exactly how it was going to be, having worked it out long since, and being omniscient meant that he already knew what he would be going to decide if he had still had to work it out, which he hadn't, but there we are, he still thought it was worth taking the afternoon off, and sitting in his garden working on his tan, since he was the only person in the world who still had one.

Day three, then, it was. He'd long been of the entirely right and proper view, and he wasn't at all right-wing, just realistic, therefore right, that there were far too many people in the world that the world would be better off without. There's all those murderers and rapists, for a start, I'd never miss any of them, and then there's the tyrants and the extortioners and the blackmailers. And them fundamentalists. And bishops. They could all go, and we'd be much better off. So go they were going to.

But even then, there'd still be far too many people around, what with over-population and everything and people trying to live in places where it was perfectly obvious they'd never really make a go of it. So if you're getting rid of unnecessary people, you might as well do a good job, and sort that out too. And clearly, since it was going to be the end of the problem of evil, once and for all, it had all to be done with perfect justice. He'd got no problem, not as such, with just making them drop dead, but it could look a bit arbitrary, and anyway he'd feel happier if the death of a couple of billion people wasn't on his conscience, so he'd decided it was one job he wasn't going to do himself.

And it wasn't really fair to create some new plague to kill off all the right, which is to say the wrong, and none of the wrong, which is to say the good, people. There'd be no problem in doing it, but what had the virus or bacteria which he hadn't invented yet but would have if he had needed to ever done to him? Why should it get the blame? And, of course, people might think it had all happened by chance, instead of by absolute, absolutely-perfect justice.

Accordingly, he was clear that the only proper way was to get people to do it themselves.

Since, as you know, suicide is just the coward's way out, they couldn't commit suicide, and they couldn't go round killing each other. Because either the police or someone would investigate all this massacre, which would be inconvenient, timewasting and pointless, or else they wouldn't, which wouldn't put them in too good a light, and would look as if the world was lawless, which rather took away the point. Because of this, you had to have a more elegant method.

And he had it. Self-conviction. Early on the morning of the third day, everyone in the world became aware of their moral status, whether they wanted to or not, and knew that their self-knowledge was flawless. But that's not enough, since plenty of people know they're evil, and quite enjoy it, since it's the sort of one-upmanship that always gets you noticed. No, he made them judge themselves with perfect justice. At which point, an awful lot of people had no option but to realise that they shouldn't be living. At all. Absolutely. Not to be. So they executed themselves.

Now this, had it been done precipitously, would have given the undertakers rather too much work. So he staggered it out, and people popped into their friendly local funeral director to book themselves a funeral slot and to acquire a coffin. And at the appointed time, they went along, climbed into their coffin, and just died by their own free-will. You'll gather it was quite a long day, but then it was going to be very good.

Now, in some parts of the world, morticians aren't too easily available. So in those places, people just got together and someone would say, "You know, what we actually need round here is a really big mass grave, 'cause it might come in handy some time." And the others would spontaneously reply "Strange, I was just thinking the same thing: a mass grave would really improve the neighbourhood." And they all set to work, and dug themselves the grave. And then someone would say, "Well, now we've got it dug, it'd make sense to check it's the right size." At which obvious prompt, they all lay themselves down in neat rows – and, of course, it was just the right size. And you know what happened next.

Being a caring kind of guy, he wasn't going to let people not have the kind of funeral they wanted. A basic one, obviously. But decent enough. And therefore in the appropriate places, it was a more than handsomely sized funeral pyre that they decided to build. But it all worked out the same.

What's that? What about the ones who weren't criminals? Well, you see, the people who weren't really evil, but just in the wrong places, or who were overpopulated, convicted themselves of being in the wrong place or overpopulated, and therefore that they were no more than a drain on the world's resources, which is proper criminal it is. So justice was served everywhere, and billions had died, and it wasn't down to him at all.

On day four, now that it was plain that it was all going to be very good, it was time for religion and science.

He'd observed that people weren't ever capable of being happy unless they believed in something, whatever it was, but equally they weren't happy if their neighbour believed in anything different. And none of the existing religions – Christianity, football, ambition, etc – seemed quite to deliver the goods in terms of the promised reign of peace and tranquillity. There had to be a better way. And therefore there was. On day four all the old models were completely obsolete. So obsolete that they left no traces behind. The priests and teachers all taught the new faith as if they'd been called to it, and all the people received a new spirit and heard the word – without exception. No freethinkers. The religious texts were no more, for this faith was written in the people's hearts and minds. And the buildings were all in the new form – plain boxes with no tricks. Just nice landscapes of trees and sky and rivers on the walls, and some chairs here and there so you could sit and think. Nothing else – no pulpits, since there would never be another sermon; no altars, for there was no sacrifice to make but a contrite spirit. You just went to the place, sat for a while in silence, thinking about nothing at all, and came out feeling renewed. Really, it was all anyone had ever needed out of religion, and it struck him as very strange that he was the first person in all creation to have arranged it that way.

With everyone in the right frame of mind, it was time to sort out learning, and science, and all that sort of thing. Has it never occurred to you how much trouble people get into from wanting to know stuff? I mean, if you want to find out how to cope with your rheumatism, someone has to go off and do lots of research and make discoveries and invent treatments and test them; and then you have to go and have some fool examine you and tell you that you're not very well, as if you weren't quite well aware already, and inform you you've got rheumatism, which is what you'd told them, and prescribe you some tablets; and then you've got to go and get them and take them, and find out that they don't help that much anyway. Of course, he could just get rid of rheumatism, but that wasn't due for another couple of days.

Or else, for no sensible reason, you want to know what the rings of Saturn really look like. And that means learning physics, and building rockets, and waiting for years until the satellite gets there to send the pictures back. Or perhaps you want to know something useful, like what your aunt actually meant when she sent you that gift, or whether your girlfriend really loves you. And that takes even more effort.

Then there's the really big problem – whatever the answer you come up with, someone will always tell you it's wrong, and there's bound to be a row, or else they'll tell you the truth, and you can't believe it, or you do believe it and they want you to be grateful.

Wouldn't the world be ever so much better if you could cut through all of this and just find the answer and have it be the right one? Of course, it would.

So he made the book: the Totally Acceptable Book of Answers. Whatever you wanted to know, you just opened the book, and it would tell you exactly what you needed to know. No more, no less. No knowledge you didn't need; nothing you couldn't handle; no questions left hanging in the air to torment you. And since it was always right, then, even if it told you one thing and someone else another thing, you never needed to argue, since it must be right for each of you.

For something that was going to contain everything that the human race ever would want to know, it was surprisingly slim. Just a pair of board covers and a single article, illustrated as profusely as needed. Well, there's no point in having to carry round knowledge that you don't need just then, so the book just presented you with the immediate stuff. If you have a second question, then close the book and open it again. The answer will always be there. Even if you don't know what the question is, it doesn't matter: open the book anyway and it well tell you the answer to the question you can't quite put into words.

This, it hardly needs saying, means everything else ever written is no longer needed. If you did want to know what was in act two of King Lear, there's no point in actually looking at the script any more, since you'd have to find the right page. Anyway, you only want to read King Lear because of the effect it has on you, and that means there's something that needs fulfilling, which is answering a question, so the book will tell you what the answer is. Which might not be in King Lear at all. So all the other books in the world vanished in a moment, and no-one even noticed they'd gone.

And no-one was ever going to need to write anything ever again. No books, obviously. But no letters either – if you want to read what the folks have been up to: the answer's in the book; if you want to know why the new fridge hasn't been delivered yet, and what are they going to do about it: the answer's in the book; if you want to know whether I'll come to lunch on Friday: the answer's in the book.

The libraries and the universities were no more; the schools were no more; the newspapers were no more; the novels were no more; the textbooks and manuals were no more; the internet, the e-mails, the mobile phones: all were no more; the diaries were no more; for the answer's in the book.

Life would fundamentally be so much better with the book.

And since it's all in the book, schooling isn't going to take long, so he can accelerate growing-up. He wasn't having anyone going through bits of life that aren't essential. So nought to five gets sandwiched into six months, to the relief of parents everywhere. Then there's the nice part of childhood, or what ought to be, which he keeps. And adolescence gets the speeding-up treatment, and twelve to sixteen gets sandwiched into another six months. A bit tempestuous, maybe. But let's face it, it's best got out of the way. Well, most of it. So to get to sixteen actually now will take half the time. Which means you can be adult for that much longer and still keep the same life span.

So, it's day five, and everything is going to be very good. But he still wasn't happy; in fact, nobody's happy yet. There are these things called relationships, and they never go right. Even if you've found the perfect partner, they'll always disagree about something, and if they don't, then you realise you've married a doormat. No, relationships definitely needed sorting.

Now, there are three problems with relationships. Either people want one and haven't got it, or they've got one and don't want it, or they've got one they sort of want but it's not right. So it's simplicity itself to solve: everyone will have one, just one, and be completely satisfied with it.

And there are three problems with getting relationships. Either you don't know how to get one, or you know how but can't succeed, or else someone else is telling you what to do and you don't want them to. And the answer: everyone will get one without needing to try.

So the first thing he does is put in a new bit of brain-stem which has the job of making all the people who've got relationships deliriously happy with them, so that no-one will ever so much as fantasise about wanting anyone else ever, and make them all treat each other with perfect kindness and understanding and adjustment, so that everyone knows that not only are they happy, but they are entirely right to be happy. But just to make sure, he alters people's circuitry so that once you're in a relationship, you actually can't desire anyone else. The happiness caused by falling in love releases lots of chemicals in the brain, as clever-clog scientists have discovered. So he just added one. That it was also a neurotoxin and killed off the part of the brain responsible for forbidden lust, well now, wasn't that a thing?

Which just leaves the unrelated. Now, actually proper love isn't a feeling: it's an act of the will, and feelings just get in the way. Will, desire and satisfaction is all and all one. So everyone who's unrelated, on this morning of day five, falls hopelessly and irrevocably in love with the first unrelated person of appropriate age, gender and outlook they see that day. And they realise that this was the person they've been looking for all their life, etc, etc. This he sorts by making unrelated and available people give off an electromagnetic field which can be picked up by a special, new and really erogenous organ he's just invented and implanted in everyone. Once the mutual recognition occurs, then the new organs atrophy because they're never going to be needed again.

Those who are too young at the moment develop the organ on the morning of their eighteenth birthday (or its equivalent in the speeded-up version, but it's the same thing). It's done its job completely and successfully, and then atrophied, without exception, by sundown.

And he builds in birth-control, so no-one has more kids than the world needs. And people die in couples from this moment on, so there's no widowhood.

Everyone's happy; there's no more adultery, divorce, domestic violence, abuse; and he's feeling really good about himself. But there's more. Since everybody's happy, and since they've all been moral for the last two days, nobody bothers even with petty crime, and nobody wants to watch TV or listen to the radio anymore. What's the point, when you can be curled up in the arms of your beloved? And definitely no more war and conflict. Just wastes good cuddling time.

Things are nearly ready for the final day, and things are going to be very good, but there's a bit of tidying up to do. I mean, there's still disease, pestilence and natural disaster, and that would spoil the effect, so they've got to go, and they do. Age isn't too nice either, so he makes it so that physical youth lasts right up until old age, and all of old age just takes just a final couple of hours before a calm and peaceful death on your seventy-fifth birthday, and that's day six accounted for.

He's got a world in which race, colour and language are no longer barriers, where the evil are no more, throughout which all belief comes from a pure heart free of rancour, that has all knowledge necessary for life assured, free from overpopulation, whose people need pursue happiness no more and can live without fear of disease, age or disaster. So everything is going to be very good.

But day seven is the one for which he has kept back his masterstroke. It's an idea of such elegance and simplicity that he can't get over it. Why had no-one done it before? You see, it's all right giving people free-will, in fact, it's quite a good idea. And it's all right giving people the knowledge of good and evil, and implanting a conscience in every one; in fact, that's quite a good idea, too, and all he did was turn the volume up to full, like he always did in his motor. But none of this will ever work unless people are sensible. So this morning he creates them sensible: male and female makes he them sensible; to old and young alike gives he sense. And then he just waits.

It isn't recorded where the idea first entered the minds of the people; it couldn't be since there was no more writing; and, in any case, at almost the same time the idea was taking root everywhere else too.

"I say," said one of them, "wouldn't it be sensible to stop using all this unnecessary energy, and wasting all these things, and eating the wrong foods, and getting drunk, and building houses we don't really need and cities that are crowded, and doing jobs that don't need doing, and stuff? I mean, if each us just did what we actually needed to live, we'd be much better off, and could spend lots of time just enjoying being. And we'd take nothing from the earth except what was essential, and give it all back again, and live in harmony with the universe; you know, like we always said we wanted."

"I suppose that means I'd get landed with looking after the kids, doing the washing, cooking the meals, and all the other chores," said his wife, who was just being realistic, since she knew he meant well.

"Well," said her friend from number 32, "we could go the whole hog. If we just eat fruit and nuts and berries and leaves, there'll be no cooking. And if we go and live in warm places, we wouldn't need clothes, especially now that none of us needs to feel ashamed getting undressed. And the men would find they enjoyed sharing the children."

And the more they talked, the more the idea appealed.

So that's exactly what they did. And the earth was peopled by little groups of naked people made up of loving couples, doing only good and never evil, sharing everything, and living in perfection without disease, pestilence, famine, war, violence or even petty squabbles over whose turn it was to pick the fig leaves – since there aren't any being used.

And on the evening of the seventh day, he coloured himself turquoise with gold spots, and joined them again.

And now it was going to be very good. For he created paradise. He's destroyed all of civilisation, all that was ever valued about civilisation, true, but nobody is ever going to notice.

The forces of heaven looked down and saw what had been done, and set up a committee. For there was just three thousand years less one week of this reign of wonder until they could get to work and put things back to something more interesting. And this time, no-one would be able to unravel it. And it would be really good – as they decide.

So Luther was telling this story too.

Then the butterfly said to him, "You must tell me further yet a story, and if it does please me you shall indeed live, and if it does displease me, I shall sever your head from the body and you shall die and what shall be will be."

And here we have a problem. For cats have no great fund of stories; they make no history, but content themselves with many pleasant things. And then, if you've told the last story I've recounted for you, what further stories can there be? But Luther found one last story.

She was Caterina, commonly known as Contadina Caterina, and her hair was Raven-black, and if not improper, Hawking-black, since once you caught sight of it, it slowly dragged you in and you had no way of not getting absorbed into her beauty, and, yes, there was radiation from that hair, straight, waist-length, framing dark skin.

Her father was a wood-cutter, descended from a long line of woodcutters, which in those regions, since there were forests for miles around, was a most honourable trade. It had been intended that his son would carry on the family tradition, but her father had no son, and therefore Caterina was marked out to be betrothed at the customary age to the most eligible wood-cutter that this noble family could find.

But Caterina had dishonoured herself, her father, her family and the very forests, for she had been found with child, and had borne a child out of sacred wedlock. She would never say anything about what happened. Whenever questioned her eyes would frost over like a January morning, and at the same time her expression made it plain that it was no dishonour in her mind to have known the man concerned, even only for one brief episode. People knew better than to cross her fieriness.

The son she bore was not black-haired, but blond, and his hair was not straight, but curly. His skin was pale, though slightly tanned from time spent outdoors. For he had inherited from her and from his grandfather the forest's physique, and was therefore swiftly put to work.

As he grew, he knew ever two things. First, from her bearing, he knew his mother was proud and honourable, and therefore he must defend her honour. Second, from the way he was treated by everyone else, which was harsh though not cruel, and from how others kept their distance from him, he knew that his existence was seen as a reproach to her, even if he knew she was sinless.

So at the age when a boy can become aware what it is to dishonour a woman, he had taken a solemn vow – not before a priest but before the trees of the forest and all the life in them – that he would avenge his mother. Though the man who was his father might have given him his body, his mother had given him the spirit and she must be made honourable in the sight of men. So even if he had to kill his own father, he would avenge his mother.

Now, though he was not accepted, nor could be, people were very well aware that he was a very handsome youth, and the best-framed of the forest, and the fittest, and all the rest, and it was therefore expected generally, not without consternation, that sooner or later, and all hoped much later, some beautiful girl of the forest would become his woman. And what colour hair would the children have?

But as if he knew what they feared, he never so much as looked at any one of their girls, and this made them very glad, though they called him proud, too proud to look at one of their girls. But it was not for any reason they would think. He knew that he wanted something that it was not wise even to think to attempt to pretend to seek. And he knew how deep was all the violence within him.

On the very day of the beginning of his twenty-second year, he announced to his mother and to his step-father (of whom nothing needs to be said, except he was the sort of man found fitting to marry a dishonoured woman) that it was the time to go to fulfil his vow. His mother was filled with foreboding, for she had known of his vow, and knew therefore that the thing must be done, but she did not want it done, for then she would be dishonoured indeed, by being revenged by her own son. For only a woman who must be revenged has been judged to be dishonoured, and only a woman who has been revenged can never deny dishonour did lay upon her, and dishonour once admitted is never forgotten.

But how dare she seek to stop him? For he sought to do that which he believed honourable. So she perforce kept silence as he departed. Of her silence, much was said, but none of it needful to have been recorded.

Need it, though, be said, too, that ere long he came to a big town, perhaps even a city, the first such gathering he had ever seen in his life? And that in this town, he soon saw a man, aged in the early forties? And that this man had golden, curly hair, and was beautiful as men can only be beautiful who are wholly male?

Now that which cannot be expressed but must be, can only grow until denial must be denied, and thus all caution had so to vanish, and gave he his heart to this man. And this man, though he was what such a man must be, he had never yet seen himself one who was fit for him, to make him to be complete, to be an eternal truth. So that night, was it not glorious?

And in the seldomness meet contentment of shared arms, that which makes all sense of life, and troubles worry into ease, they talked the talk of such hours, and the young man told the older his story – of his upbringing, his mother, his vow and what he was there to do, and how now that he had found such a hero he had the strength to perform a vow, and had already sworn another to be true for the rest of life, because he had seen in the eyes that had looked down into his that the other had sworn the selfsame vow.

Do you need still to be told who this man was? And that he had, yes, sworn that vow? And that therefore he had no choice but to tell his truth, and of how he met Caterina and how she of all women in the world was the only one ever to have caught him for an hour, and that he was full of wonder, even glory, even as he told this tale of who and what he really was?

So now our blond wood-cutter is trapped like the birds whose hunger leads them into the wicker baskets that they use in the forest to catch birds, for food so that hunger sates hunger. For he has sworn a vow of revenge and he has sworn a vow to love for ever, and no-one can ever go back from a vow, and these are vows of immense mass and stability that he has sworn, with gravity inescapable.

There are, of course, the usual glib solutions of murder and suicide, or just suicide, or just murder, or fighting to the death, or elsewise finding his death at his father's hand.

But none of these would he contemplate. For whatever else he was, he was an honest man, honest as all men and yes as such men as these two have to be in order to be men at all. For there is a truth which is all that can ever be had to be a friend. For between one so and any other there would always be some slightest breeze certain to catch sights and sounds and move them a little away from knowing or being known, until that day when they have to be known and to know had run its final hour.

At dawn, accordingly, they could agree only to part until sunset, and to talk again of what might be done.

So the wood-cutter went to find a priest. For while in the forest priests are not regarded, the trees being finer for those ends, he knew that in the town they have to serve to grasp onto the life that the forest rightly holds. And so, finding one in a temple, he asked him what a man who had worn two vows but whose two vows were contrary to the other could do.

But the priest, well, he rather hummed, and then he rather hawed, this not being one of those things he had been prepared for. Sure obligations should be fulfilled, and vows definite. But these were pagan vows not prescribed by faith's said-true mother, for only certain particular revenges were ever encouraged at her bidding, and these were not they. Yet how do you tell a man his vow is a false vow when it is his truth? So the wood-cutter got no sure answer for anyone's understanding.

Now as he was leaving the house of this priest, down-cast, there was a beggar sitting by the porch importuning and holding out his hand to all who passed by; but he had not seen him in his eager entry. But he heard the beggar cry out, and went and sat by him, since now he too belonged to that place and posture.

Beggars know when there will be money forthcoming and when not, and make marks accordingly, for others to see as they travel their circuit of seasons. And they know when there will be drink and oblivion and a little closeness towards desired extinction. And they know, for they see through all falsity, having fallen from the world by falseness, when is delusion found invited in the minds of all them that pass by.

So, being utterly mad and of no account, he asked the wood-cutter what his vow was. And was told revenge. So he asked what the vow was. And was told of the restoration of honour. So he asked what vow that was. And in the puzzling of the silence following, he asked if the vow had not been fulfilled before it was made, by being intended. And he asked who had dishonoured whom. And he confessed, and did not deny, but said plainly, there is no-one to slay.

The wood-cutter knew for sure that this beggar was throughly mad, because he hadn't said a single thing that made any sense, and the wood-cutter had not understood one solitary of the utterances of the beggar's mouth. So he stood up again and walked away.

And as he walked away, the thought came to him from nowhere that everything was somehow all right, and there was nothing to do but accept his salvation. And the rest, you will be understanding, child, Luther had no need to complete.

Now, the King Butterfly saw that Luther knew no more stories, and he looked to his right and his left, and Luther noticed that the wings of seven butterflies about the King looked rather remarkably closely like the gimped gowns of Oxford dons.

"That seems enough to conclude a Viva, I think,", said one of them, "and overall I give a beta plus."

"Beta plus plus.", said the butterfly next to him.

"Beta plus minus", said the next.

"Perhaps overcautious, those marks;" said the fourth, "I'd go quite definitely for beta plus plus question plus."

"No more than beta, I think.", said number five.

"Well, I'm going for an alpha minus.", was number six's view. "I was definitely entertained, and even mildly enlightened."

"That is a mark I can only call courageous.", opined the seventh Doctor. "I find it beta question plus, and no more."

"Are we all staying with those marks, or are there any amendments?", the first asked.

89

There being no response, he summed up. "Well, putting those together and averaging, then it's almost exactly a beta plus plus minus. A little higher than I thought, but close enough to call it consensus." He turned to the King. "Our judgement is that you could be, should you graciously choose so to be, almost quite, quite pleased, but definitely not very pleased."

The King Butterfly nodded with sagesse apt, and then with pleasure evident, put a leg into his mouth and whistled to summon the Old Red Queen.

This was a real queen, who dressed in velvet and fur, and was driven around with a certain carriage, and was very fond of taking head, or at least of beheading people. You could tell she was a real queen because she looked like a tea-pot. "Off with his head!", the Old Red Queen absolutely screamed, my dear. And off his head came.

So now you know how Luther had to go to heaven. Cats had long ago debated the existence of heaven. There were the conservatives, who believed that heaven must exist, because unless you said it did, then you couldn't persuade kittens to behave properly, and if you said it did, then you must at least pretend it did, and once you get to pretending something exists, then, by the ontological argument, it must necessarily exist. The rationalists, though, argued that it was immoral to think that anything should gain infinite satisfaction from doing any finite good even if one had done nothing bad. And the modernisers pointed out that you would never get anyone to accept that you should have an unceasing reward just for believing in something. So after arguing for a couple of thousand years, they came up with a compromise that everyone didn't agree with just enough to accept unanimously, and pronounced that heaven probably existed, but that if it did, it was undoubtedly empty.

So to get there, and just for not being able to tell a story, was a little surprising. Yes, quite right, because I can tell stories it proves both that I am not a cat, and that I shall never go to heaven. I've no intention of ending up in that awful there. ... Howbeit. ...

CHAPTER 6

The pilgrim oft
At dead of night, mid his orison hears
Aghast the voice of Time, disparting tow'rs.
John Dyer
The Ruins of Rome

We meet again, I believe. One day, you know, one day since we last talked. And after this time you want to continue, to hear the rest of the story. It seems an infinitude of time, this day: you, certainly, are a different person. As for me, who can say? I am different and not different, which is how it should in the perhaps world be. Things are less automatic now. I have to struggle to get my words out. There are two many words that fight to stay in me, refuse to be expelled out of my fantasy its mind, that have to be tricked out. And when they are uttered, they take their revenge on me. Old age is a regretting or a celebrating, but not very often a living. Neither dead nor alive, breath so gentle it leaves the air quite still. What remains is a focus, an vanishing point of concentration where one sees the lines don't finally meet but simply blur into a wash. A focus where you can see nothing but yourself with a history that, sorry, I was miles away.

So, Luther's head had just come off, a few seconds since. And he had pounced his way through the first two heavens where there was nothing for him to comprehend.

The third heaven is a multiple. Every moment your life severs one possibility from another, makes one thing real and condemns who knows how much to remain in the nothingness of what might have been. So, if you are ever to be complete, ever to be finished, it must all become real. In the third heaven, you do not contain, you are multitudes. Here you are an architect, a doctor, a painter, poet, murderer and saint. And every architect you might have been you are here.

Ah, but the final heaven, the seventh if one can still count. There is a kind of binomial series that determines how far into the heavenwards a person goes. With each degree there are coefficientally fewer to go to the next in the series. Half get into the first heaven. (Not nearly as many as anyone would guess, but that's divine mercy for you.) Then one eighth of those get to the second, and one sixteenth of those to the third, and five one-hundred-and-twenty-eighths of those go to the next. And then it's seven in two-hundred and fifty six, twenty one in 1024, 33 in 2048, and 429 in 32768. Not in the slightest that you wanted to know that, but a little theological exactness is always a rarity to be preserved. In fact, out of every 720,202,335,418 people to be born on earth, exactly thirteen, without remainder or fraction, get to go through all the heavens and reach into the empyrean.

So, here was Luther in the seventh heaven. And there was this house of his last awakening, and so he went into that house. And there was a little gate. Curiosest!, thought Luther, as by now he was entitled to, How odd to have a gate inside a heaven, as if you still need to keep the neighbours out. But there it was, and through it he entered. And inside he was.

Well, it's strange to describe. Nothing was different anywhere. You see, first everything was exactly the same even colour, a sort of khaki - the shade you got that afternoon when you mixed all the paints in your paint box together -, so that there were no boundaries between things, and you couldn't tell when one thing ended and the next began, and certainly couldn't mark where a person ended and the void took over. There were no highlights and no shadows, and the light came from every spot at once - there was no source of light: the light just was. And there was this, well, not a sound exactly; I mean, it was a sound, but it never altered, just a perpetual chord of C major in root position, played on something that sounded a bit like every instrument you ever heard of, but wasn't actually similar to any of them. And it didn't come from anywhere: so there was no point in turning round to find where it was, not that you could tell if you were turning round, since there were no reference points. No, you didn't hear it and you didn't not hear it: it was just in the air. It was like you breathed this one equal harmony without any rhythm. And nothing happened: nothing began, nothing ended, nothing changed. Even your arrival hadn't made any difference. So you couldn't tell how much time was passing, or whether any time had passed at all.

And weirdest of all, you had no particular emotions: you weren't sad, or happy, or afraid, or hopeful, or anything; but at the same time you weren't empty of feeling. You felt, but you didn't feel something. It was like all your emotions were settled in an equilibrium, which meant you had something which was nothing. And this unsensation filled you.

Now if you had a mind left to perceive with, you would have gone mad, with the absence of everything, and the absence of absence. But that wasn't possible either: madness would be a definite something, and nothing was able to be individual. You couldn't even get away with being a cabbage either.

Now, Luther, being a real protestant, a someone who wouldn't even conform to non-conformity, was a kind of anti-matter in that place. Utterly the opposition of its essence. Not the opposite of any thing: since there couldn't be any opposites here. He was the type of the innateness of opposition, a perpetual motion which knows neither order nor chaos. So he didn't need to do anything. Which is just as well, since doing anything was not possible, just as not doing anything was impossible too.

He was just incompatible with being there: his existing or not existing in that nowhere was logically inconceivable of being confirmed or denied. So he wasn't there: indeed, he never could be there, therefore he never had been there. Despite all we know. And so he found himself elsewhere: poles away, miles away.

He didn't mind this one scintilla or photon: since of the empyrean, Luther had long since computed what must be. The elect, the 13, the verymost perfect of people, those whom even saints long to emulate, they are admitted to the pinnacle of religious longing, to the true contemplation and loving of the godhead that is beyond every

God, where not even the name of godness is known to be changeable. And there, for ages of ages, where once you have done a million years of praising you have done as it were less than the first second of the first minute of all eternity, you are enwrapped in your own foundation of love, the ground of all your being, to pour out salutation and praise and exaltation and laud and worship and honour and adoration and glory and acclamation and tribute and a few other things beside until you could burst with the rapture of it all. But the poor fools are so engrossed with their veneration that they never once, not for one instant of an instance, ever notice that no sense of this godhead is given to them, no awareness or touch or perception. For they are still creatures, formed out of nothing. And godhead is utterly transcendent to all that has been created.

So Luther, having been being forewarned of all these things one undreamed day, told himself that he had decided that like the sagacious angels he must go straight to hell. Not passing the dragon, and certainly not collecting 200 plenary indulgences.

CHAPTER 7

There is no excellent beauty that hath not some strangeness in the proportion.
Francis Bacon
Essays

Of Luther's many philosophical achievements, the one for which he entered the unhistorical record, since he was dead when he first proposed it, was in the field of paradoxical syllogisms. There are, he asserted, arguments whose conclusions are undeniably entailed by their postulates, yet which cannot logically be derived from them.

Consider, he said, the following two steps in a syllogism:

> No cat dislikes smoked salmon.
> This mammal dislikes smoked salmon.

Logically, the conclusion to be derived is:

> This mammal is not a cat.

However, the only possible correct conclusion is:

> This mammal is an unspeakable wretch, beneath contempt.

And, Luther pointed out, not only is it plain that is this so, but also it is plain that no other postulates are required to achieve this sole conceivable conclusion, and further that no additional postulates could ever modify or negate the conclusion.

Now, while everyone concurred that the result was certainly correct, at first no-one was ready to accept the implications for logic. Aristopsy, acknowledged by all to be the greatest philosopher of all time, being not only the founder of the Acatemy but also creator of the original and only true theory of syllogisms, was outraged that Luther should dare to show such presumption. So he said that Luther was just hiding a postulate, somewhere. Unfortunately, his first attempt to identify the postulate was facile, for he held it to be:

All mammals which are not cats are dogs.

This caused uproar amongst the other philosophers; but it was held that Luther gave the most elegant riposte. As Luther said, was it not Aristopsy himself, correcting the egregious impostor Aristotle, in his discussion of humans - a topic which simply to discuss showed such boldness of mind on Aristopsy's part -, who had demonstrated that there were hierarchies of beings amongst those mammals not able to be counted as cats? Amongst people, human ones, Aristopsy had identified:

zoa politika	humans appearing to understand basic philosophy
zoa suburbica	(properly zoa parapolitika, qv)
zoa parapolitika	commuters, therefore devoid of intelligence
zoa paralitika	drunkards
zoa apolitika	rustics, capable of what appears to be speech
zoa katapolitika	protesters, solitaries, theologians, the insane, etc.

And had Aristopsy not said that even the very lowest two ranks of these pseudo-rational beings:

zoa adikiaphilia	incorrigible criminals
zoa atima	politicians

were still worthy of theoretical contemplation and therefore were transcendent to dogs, who were incapable of being considered by any rational means? So if Aristopsy was to be believed, as he must be, there were mammals between cats and dogs. And since Aristopsy had considered them, they were not beneath contempt.

At which Aristopsy, secretly satisfied by the complement, but still publicly none too pleased, said there was undoubtedly a hidden postulate, but it needed more careful definition. Before, however, he could continue, Spinoverandover tried to contribute.

This led to greater uproar. Spinoverandover had argued once that all things were derived from or, indeed, even were, a monad, and therefore in some subtle sense there must be qualities shared by all things, including cats and dogs. This idea was not to be tolerated, and so all philosophers had agreed that he was never to be heard again in all eternity.

This gave Can'tandshan't his chance. Since, he argued, we could have no awareness of what really was, but only of those categories by which we sorted our experience, and since only cats could have true judgement, it was impossible for any other species to appreciate smoked salmon. Luther was thought to have the better of it when he pointed out that while this was undoubtedly true in all absolute senses, there were categories which might be termed animal and which thought, or appeared to think, that they could appreciate smoked salmon. That being so, they must deserve some consideration, and were therefore not automatically unspeakable wretches, beneath contempt.

Moreover, said Luther, sensing that Humesweethume would be next and would just go on for ages getting nowhere, his syllogism's conclusion was plainly not analytic, that is, derived logically from the postulates, but equally no rational person could regard it as synthetic, contingent or empirical. Therefore, he had also shown that there was a category of propositions that were unquestionably true, but had neither logical nor experimental basis.

Ah, said Bishop Barkless, if they don't like smoked salmon, they never experience it, so they don't know that it exists, so they can't know that they don't like it, any more than I can know that I do like it when I'm not eating it. At which Luther said that he thought he might perhaps have had some smoked salmon in his travelling bag, and might not have finished it; the drool coming from the good Bishop's mouth prevented all need to go further.

The mood, by now, was turning hostile, since if there's one thing philosophers hate, it's another philosopher looking like he's getting the better of them. And too, Catsonguard hadn't said anything yet, which added to the general anxiety and tetchiness, though not as much as he would do if he did speak.

So Luther pulled his master stroke. He gave each person in the circle of philosophers the most enormous bowl of smoked salmon topped with clotted cream and no strawberries, and then said that each of his most esteemed colleagues, whose wisdom he could never hope to emulate, had contributed an idea which he would attempt to synthesise into a possible theory to account for his discovery. (Afterwards he could never account for how he got the bowls of smoked salmon – they just all were there as soon as he needed them.) Might it not be, he said, that there was not a hidden hypothesis or postulate, but a postulate which was both ever-patent and ever-ignored, built into the very fabric of the universe or universal mind, so that it would always function even though it would never be spoken or even recognised, because no one would ever think it needed to be brought to mind? And might this not be, as it were, an element towards the much-needed Prolegomena to all possible metaphysics? - the postulate being the proposition that:

All creatures who do not share the fundamental good taste of cats are unspeakable wretches, not merely beneath contempt, but embodying the form or platonic essence of being beyond contempt itself.

Amidst much licking of lips, sucking of whiskers and cleaning of paws, Luther was immediately elected unanimously as an Acatemician, and, as such, one of the immortals.

Seeking leave to go and put on his robes, he slipped out, resolved never to have anything more to do with that bunch, and at once met an oddest of even odder creatures.

"Ooh, 'ello dear, welcome to hell." It was wearing a pink plastic sprayed-on body suit, with thigh-length black leatherette bootees (touchingly finished with mauve pompons), had cropped green hair, far too much magenta mascara, aquamarine lipstick which provided just the right degree of complement to his maroon teeth, and the mark of a rubber stamp on his hand. It, for that was Luther's first thought, twirled a fake fur boa constrictor through his fingers as he talked.

"Now then love, what we usually do is give you a bit of time to wonder round and see what's on offer, and then one of the personal trainers will work out an individual timetable for disciplines with you. You could start with Mrs Bagley who does whipping on Sundays, Mondays and Thursdays, or then there's lion-dancing, or you could try the boiling ghee baths and volcano saunas, they're both on Tuesdays. Or you can have time-out in the reminiscence pits on a Friday, or not meet your relatives in the communication suites, every Saturday that is. Then there's the queues if you're feeling lazy: you can get those most days, except Wednesdays. There's just lots to do. Which reminds me, pillars of salt are off just at the moment. A sea-monster had one of those little accidents. Anyway sweetie-pie, here's your street-map and your complimentary vanity bonfire case. Got to dash, it's time to have a manicure. I just love having my fingernails torn out. Ooh, I nearly forgot, just remember you've got to abandon all hope in here."

Now Luther, being a philosopher and all, thought hope was a very strange commodity. You can buy it, when you have to pay far more for it than anything's ever worth. But if you sell it then it's worthless, and if you try to give it away then nobody wants it. Yet the best way to find it is through a free offering of love, even though they'll make you pay somehow. If you're a real cheapskate, you can try making some for yourself, but it never turns out right. So most people just keep the little they've acquired along the way, in a vase on the mantelpiece, and look at it now and again, and remind themselves that it's still there, and just dust round it. The only time hope isn't just merchandise is if it justly appears, and then it stays with you for ever, even if it gets taken away by the authorities. Whoever they are, they do seem fond of confiscating illicit drugs. But abandon it? Nobody ever abandoned any hope. Luther thought he was going to like hell: it would give him plenty to think about.

He was therefore about to ask the creature for some directions (direction being essential in hell), when there came something that was not quite a sound, but nothing other than a sound, implicative of wings rustling themselves into place. And out of nothing, there came to be standing behind the creature's left jewel-encrusted shoulder, the figure of an enormously-built man in evening dress. The man cleared his throat. At least, he would have been clearing his throat, if he'd had a neck to house a throat to clear, but he hadn't. He had traps instead.

The creature looked round and his features contorted with panic.

"What have you been told about the dress code, Simkins-el?", said the man.

"That my duty is to dress soberly and suitably for all occasions.", replied Simkins-el.

"I'm not actually going to reprimand you," the man said," but you will perhaps wish to reconsider your choice of vesture. Perhaps a quarter-century in quiet contemplation will help?"

"You are truly merciful." said Simkins-el, who immediately transmigrated back to his office, where he had some comforting paperwork to focus his thoughts.

"You must excuse my colleague.", the man addressed Luther, with just a little too much emphasis on the second word for Luther to feel comfortable, "he's recently been promoted. Perpetual problem, you see. Reward them for doing well, by making them up into archangels, and it goes straight to their head: they think they're supposed to be arch. He'll get over it, they always do; might even do well in his new grade. But for the next couple of centuries, he'll only be good for paperwork.

"However, you don't wish to listen to the problems of administration. Let me introduce myself. I am, and my full title, and therefore name, is: His Everlasting Transcendence's Domination (Hell) (Induction, Preparatory Tortures and Minor Punishments). You may call me Domination. If you wish. As you do.

"I am one of the senior angels responsible for the outsourced management of hell, and Deputy Chair of the All-Hells' Steering Committee. So I'm officially enormously busy. But I thought I'd take charge of you myself." Luther, quite properly, understood this to mean that his own arrival was the most interesting thing that was available to give the chap something to do. And you will, Child, be understanding that Luther had met an angel.

Angels are not much understood by mortals. Even worse than dragons. And actually dragons and angels can make very good friends if they're ever allowed to.

Forget all the mimsy you've heard about angels, Child. Angels are to terrify us, out of their splendour. Imagine, if you can, though actually you never will succeed, but try anyway, something which is totally immaterial yet harder than steel, which is all-spiritual but as present to you as an asthma attack; a Something you can't comprehend but which you make out to look much like more than a man.

Give him thickest-strong legs of patinated bronze, a serrated belly made of ancient ivory, a chest of blazing blue fire, and powered arms of diamond wider than a head; top that with a face as bright as the sun you dare not look at; and then if that were a shadow that had passed for one moment in front of a corroded mirror, that's how close you've got to the unaccustomed triumph of an angel's being. And to add as a backcloth wider than the very horizon there are its wings. Two with which to fly; two to shield its brilliant face from the beaming of the consuming heat of the sight of God, which not even the cherubim can bear; and two to cover its feet:- Feet that are the proof of...

Well, in point of fact I'm not sure I should say this, but angels are all rather emphatically male. And it's not actually their feet that they cover up in God's presence because of how inadequate they feel before his.

So you'll understand that in the insignificant bits of heaven and hell that *homo sapiens sapiens* is ever allowed into, the actual sight of angels would be a just a tiny bit intolerable. What they do, out of consideration, is to fold their wings close round themselves, and colour them to look like whatever takes their fancy or suits their purpose, which, being angels, tends to be much the same thing.

Now, angels come in three groups or choirs, each with three ranks. First you have your cherubim and seraphim, who look after God, and you have your thrones. Then there's dominations, virtues and powers. And at the bottom of the pile are principalities, archangels and angels. Only archangels and angels actually deal with people, which rather shows where we fit in the scheme of things. So Luther, it must be acknowledged, was getting an unusual level of respect, in being spoken to and appeared to by a Domination.

"You need a badge," said Domination, "otherwise you'll be taken for an inmate. No, you're not;" he replied, having read Luther's thoughts, "we've brought you here for a purpose. Now, here we are."

In the air appeared a range of visitor's badges, all golden. Luther had time to take in that they included ones saying: Just Beholding; Registered Services' Visitor; Temperature Engineering Visitor; Recreational Visitor; Non-Earthbased Brother, before Domination pulled out one that said simply "Authorised Visitor" and fixed it carefully round Luther's head, so that it circled it nicely. At which, the many others vanished.

"No-one will question that.", said Domination, "It shows you're here on official business."

"Yes, you are." he went on, and added in response to Luther's next thought, "I'm sorry if you don't like my reading your mind, but it's what we do up here most of the time. Since none of us has thoughts that we ought not to have, there's no possible proper objection to the rest of us knowing them. The angels, I mean, not the inmates. We read their thoughts, of course, for our work. And consent certainly doesn't come into that. But they can't read ours."

Luther didn't think about it. Well, he did. But only after he'd made the switch. He wasn't having anyone reading his mind. So he started thinking in qkqatt, which is understood only by cats and by God – who needs both to remain inscrutable and to be having people he can trust to bounce ideas off.

Qkqatt is both the most logical of all languages, and the most difficult. You see, they can't be doing with mixing up consonants and vowels. It's messy. So all the consonants go at the beginning of the word, and all the vowels at the end. The vowels are then merged into a single multiphthong, unpronounceable by any other species, while the consonants are each articulated separately but incredibly quickly. So a word might read something like bdmlkeiaoauoi or kbsptoeiiaouu. And if you try pronouncing one, you'll realise you've heard the language spoken many times and never recognised it. Which is just as well, since cats only use qkqatt to humans when swearing is qkqwite definitely required.

Domination looked at Luther incredulously. "That isn't supposed to happen. It just isn't allowed." But Luther merely said, "Well, it has happened, so it must be possible, so it must be allowed. At least for me. And therefore for all cats."

"Oh, I see.", said Domination, who was rather concerned about losing his position, "It's because this is one of the human hells. I haven't been prepared for cat hell."

And indeed he hasn't. Nor could he be. For such a place cannot exist by definition. I mean it, Child, not even God has the power to create a hell for cats. And I'm sure you can work out why.

"One of the human hells?", Luther mused.

"There are separate heavens and hells for each sentient creature in the universe. You can't put them together in heaven, because they would just be rude and start pointing at the other species, which means they'd all have to go to hell, which rather spoils the point. And they all need specific punishments suited to the world they've come from, so separate hells is easier. As for the humans, it was even more essential. If you put the protestants in together with the catholics and the orthodox, they all start arguing about which sort is having the more beatific visions and the purer heavenly delights. And if you put two faiths together, you get the same thing, more or less. So we keep them all apart. It's for their own good really. This place, for example, has Afterlife Code HPECP21LM – Hell, Preliminary, Earth, Christian, Protestant, type 21 – Liberal, Mild.

"Each hell is overseen by a Virtue. We think it's a nice touch. The Dominations have broadly generic, cross-hell, policy and administration oversight responsibilities. And there's a Throne who covers everything hellish.

"It's all very different in the heavens. I mean, you weren't even properly received when you arrived there, were you? And no-one had organised a conducted tour for you? It's all right them going on about the glorious freedom of the children of God, but it does not get anything done. We do things much better down here. Order, law and justice, is what we stand for, and in that exact sequence moreover."

Luther had never really thought about the mechanics of the afterlife – who does? Not even theologians ever consider how it actually gets administered. But like every effective system, Luther realised, it all had to be managed. So if there are angels with celestial MBA's, it's only because it's necessary. (Mages of Blessed Administration, since you ask.)

And, equally, that explained why he'd met angels in hell, not demons. If you want the thing to run according to specification, then you have to have reliable souls in charge. And on the whole angels are reliable: much better than humans anyway.

"Let me come back to the issue at hand." said Domination, who had recovered his composure a little. "We've brought you into the afterlife for a reason. So what I'd like to do is show you round, so you can see something of how we operate, and then I'm certain you'll agree to help us."

"What's in it for me?", said Luther. He was now rather angry. He'd agreed to help a dragon out of the very goodness of his heart, with the result he had gotten his head cut off, and now it turns out to have been prearranged?

Well, actually angry was what Luther was not. Being the greatest of philosophers, he had overcome all ignoble passions long since, and had emptied himself of even the capacity for anger. But equally well, he knew it did have its uses. So once he'd reached perfection, at the age of about three months, he'd then practised looking as if he was angry. He imagined the fiercest and ugliest of dogs and then let it transmute, like base metal into gold, into a mouse that was within easy reach, and then responded accordingly. Practice had been more difficult than he imagined at first, and there had been an embarrassing episode when he'd leapt into the air and administered the death-bite *con fuoco* to the arm of a sofa, but persistence had been worthwhile. He did a very good angry. It was as good an angry as ever was seen or deserved to be seen.

"What's in it for me?" I mean, he didn't actually repeat himself, he's too clever for that, but I put it in again to pick up the thread of the story for you, since you're none too good at cat's-cradle, are you, Child? But since I've put the narrative on pause, let me just add that Luther isn't being selfish. There's a big difference between being selfish and wanting justice for yourself. Isn't there?

"What's in it for me?"

CHAPTER 8

Network. Anything reticulated or decussated at equal distances, with interstices between the intersections.
Samuel Johnson
A Dictionary of the English Language

No, I haven't forgot about the dragon. You can't forget about dragons, that's the point of them. If you could forget about one, it wouldn't be a dragon any more. That's right, it's a bit like fairies, only you don't have to believe in dragons. And dragons have got a great advantage over fairies; while fairies evolved so that if you say "I don't believe" then another one gets to take a curtain pratfall, dragons, on the other hand, were far more sensible, and got people to do the evolving instead. No-one's quite sure how they did it – that's there, secret, and they're certainly not telling -, but it they certainly did. So human beings have evolved over the millennia just in order that they are utterly incapable of forgetting any dragon whose acquaintance they've once made, be it for ever so brief a moment's awareness.

So the dragon was still sitting there amidst all that horrible illumination, in the instant that endures beyond any endurance you might have. In times like that – it was not the best of times, it was the worst of times -, you fall back on the older things, the chthonic, even the realm of the mothers. And our poor dragon didn't quite remember. Yes, they're allowed to forget each other; they have to in order to survive. Didn't quite remember a time when some one that called itself mother suggested he took himself off and have a good cry. There are cries and cries, of course. There's the crying that seizes hold of you, and shakes you down with sobbing, and then there's the crying, for those who use it, that says simply that you've been horrible to want your own way and not agree with me and give me my slightest whim whatever it might be. That one's truly terrible. I saw it often enough, and was so horrified that I've never been tempted even once. Not even to see what it was like and then get addicted, you know like one of they godless cigarettes.

But this dragon had got beyond proper crying. He could feel the being torn apart, or the force of the one that curls you up into a little ball, but the crying itself he didn't do. He wasn't going to give anyone that satisfaction. So his habit on these occasions was to go into the privatest part of his cave, and lie down on a bed of feathers or stuff, and not go through the motions. And it did seem to do him some good, for afterwards, he'd get up again, and behave as if nothing had happened, and get on with whatever it was that he was supposed to do, to the point where people would admire his courage and wisdom. Though, as far as he was concerned, it was just what had to be done to survive through the length and breadth of that god-given, devil-damned day.

Now, yes, it is true, he didn't have ready access to his cave just at that moment, but when needs must, you do. I know, needs always must; when did you ever hear a need that just might, or that needs could? Frightfully pressing things. So you do what you can, which is, must. And in his inwardest part, beyond anything you might call a soul, right down beyond that limit where there's anything even to be unconscious of, he let himself know. Dragons do have one thing in common with people: they have the same instinct that it is not a very sensible thing to let yourself know what you know for very long, in case you can't come back from it. So he let himself know for a millionth of a trillionth part of a nanosecond. And then he just switched off for a couple of months and spent his time playing silly games in what passed for his brain. And then he repeated the knowing for just a little bit longer, and thought he might as well get on with it.

So he shook his rheumatic neck, and pulled himself up to his full height – something he was usually loath to do because he didn't really believe, feel that is, that he deserved to be that tall. He wasn't what you would call an impressive dragon; he'd been anorexic before there was anorexic, and he'd been seasonally depressed before that existed too; in his daydreams he was a brawny hunk of a dragon, though in his real dreams he was rarely aware of what he was like. He hated being looked at so much that he'd convinced himself he was in fact invisible, just floating round observing the world, and when something happened to wake him up to the fact that he was real, and had mass, and that other dragons could see him, he'd get terribly upset for a moment, and curse them for their impertinence, and go back to not feeling not inadequate. But sometimes, and he wasn't quite sure that he did it – but then little frightened things that look like dragons rarely are aware of doing this -, he would say something in a very quiet, very calmly firm sort of voice, and monsters many times his size would quake with fear, and become very afraid that he was going to do something so terrible to them that they'd rather that someone just cut something vital off them now so they could get it over with. He never did that, it needn't be pointed out, because he wasn't that merciful, even though he didn't have a vicious bone in his body, and at those moments, if he did know he was doing it (though usually, he'd realize afterwards), he quite enjoyed it.

And he did again just as he'd done before in our story. He just started walking. Yes, I know you thought that was very brave and beautiful before, but it isn't really, not really. If the only place you have in the world is a cave somewhere that you don't really like leaving, even though you want to get out of it all the time, you still have to get through each of the days there is, despite it being one of those days when you've arranged it so that you don't wake up till mid-afternoon and are intending to get an early night that evening because you're feeling tired. You still have to do the walking around thing. It's what life comes down to really, just getting on with it. To have the patience to wake up and potter around, that takes just as much bravery as anything else you can do. That's why anybody can be a hero when the time comes. Because you're used to it. You've been doing being a hero every day since you have anything at all to remember or forget, and you will go on doing it until that day when you become nothing again.

So our dragon was quite brave, I suppose, but not particularly brave.

What the dragon knew is that there are wounds that can be healed, wounds that heal themselves given time, and wounds which abide for ever. Of the number of these last, there are a very few which bring honour and a few more that bring some sympathy if it not be asked for, and with sympathy often comes respect. These ensamples, though they remain as wounds and bear to you the pain of wounds, can be borne with acceptance.

Some wounds can be quietly endured. Not a few are very noisily endured and so transfigured into assets that are precious and guarded. But some wounds will not be accepted, for they refuse to be. It is ever in them not you where stands the refusal. And they demand your silence, for they cannot be shown to the world, for very horror flows ichorous-slowly from them hourly. Therefore it is needful to hide them from all. And you are of them all the first who must have the shield engineered behind which it shall be encased. So you do forgetting as your morning exercise. Even before your eyes are opened, the shield is put in place, and the blessing of today's amnesia is invoked. Let the oozing pus in the corner of the dozy eye be metabolised into what can be made of it. And sometimes, when you perhaps are happier or perhaps more like to forgetfulness of all self, the shield and the amnesia too are neglected a little. Then you will see it, that wound, and you will know that you are still screaming and that you have that teasing agony as your burthen unto the last day. And you are ashamed.

Shamed by owning it, shamed by not associating with it, shamed by allying yourself to people, shamed by hiding you from people, shamed by being a nothing but just your wound, no matter how much else there is of you.

A shameful deed can be repented in a simulacrum of penance for guilt, and at long last its shame be quieted by your humility. But for a shameful wound, the one that was doled out to you to choke you from your birthrights, a moment's pleasure for the torturer who knew he constrained you for all time and more, what offering can you bring before your own soul's altar? You were burned there long since. You were left as ash, and how shall ash and dust expiate this undeserved nullity of injury and laceration? There is nothing to undo shame from these wounds.

Why are you ashamed of that which you did not do and could not undo? Because they succeeded. Because they did wound you. And you should have had strength to beat them. And you did not. Because you were weak. Even if you were only a day old, even if you were but a six-year old child, stranger in a still-strange world, you were weak. Did you not see them laugh?

I once knew a man who could not laugh. Not because he was not allowed, or did not allow, or never met with funny, but because he was born without it. But he had learned the rules. He watched what they did, and taught himself to copy. So when there was a sound like maybe it was this thing, he looked to see. If they smiled, he grimaced; if they chortled, he gurgled; if they belly-laughed, he threw back his head and howled. It must be confessed that he did it well. He was thought a good chap and a good laugh. He didn't know what they meant, and comforted himself with his ambition. But he did the shameful deed, not understanding that he was wounded, and there was a reckoning. I know I should pity him. But he did that shameful deed. And later Mammon gave him glory, as it must. Empire called to empire and gave him a Spartan village.

And you, dragon, you were weak. Even hatred is beyond you.

An acquaintance of Luther's master had made themselves into a millionaire in a very little time by opening the world's first Hating Agency. He realised that Dating Agencies were more properly speaking Mating Agencies, and that a fair proportion of their clients had no prospect of ever acquiring such a thing as a mate, and so had grasped that what these poor unfortunates did have every prospect of finding in each other was someone to truly loathe. I mean, just look at them; who do they think they're kidding? From then on it was simple. Initially there was a little clever advertising (if you make it sound perverse enough then people will queue up to join, just out of curiosity you understand, to find out what it's really like). This was rapidly followed up with developing a portfolio of profiles, each stressing the person's physical, spiritual and moral ugliness, their vileness and their weak spots, and listing what the person hated most in other people. Matching these profiles was a doddle. The lucky duo would meet and find that here was someone that they really couldn't stand, and that this was success! Having beforehand been carefully briefed how to conduct the first encounter winningly, they fixated on the features of the other which most got up their nose. The friend's genius had consisted in the realization that there would always be something. From fixation came innuendo, innuendo led to insult, and insult to injury. Initially this was normally psychological, although the contract was worded to allow for all possibilities.

Realising that most social venues are devoted to catering to those who go there wishing to appear to look like they want to be with each other, the friend branched out into establishments that were socially truthful. That this led to much increased profitability could not take away from the moral propriety of encouraging honesty. In these places, the crockery was meant to be broken. The chefs became renowned for how delicious their food was when thrown with force, and for how its texture was of just the right degree of glutinosity to slide down the face inelegantly. The wine, though it was necessarily of high alcohol content, was all chosen for its capacity to stain clothes beyond the fantasies of the most outrageous of detergent commercials. Since dissatisfaction was guaranteed and delivered, the venues were wildly successful, and their place as a *de rigueur* part of the smart social scene was crowned when, in the same week as each other, a right-wing MP and a liberal Bishop both condemned them as degrading, as destructive of the fabric of society and as undermining the sacrament of marriage.

It was that serendipitous event which prompted the completion of the friend's *oeuvre* with the introduction of the Committal

Ceremony. The unhappy couple, glowering at each other from opposite sides of the nave, kept apart by hired muscle at the posher observances, took solemn oaths - to loathe, dishonour and defame.

As the minister asked the woman the stirring words, "Wilt thou take this man to be thy lawless monstrous obsession, to hate him with grievous ordnance in the hellish estate of fixation? Wilt thou loathe him, discomfit him, dishonour and keelhaul him, into sickness out of health, and enlisting all other, adhere thee only against him, so long as ye both shall live?", and the man the same, tears and more than tears (though sturdy fabrics were a good idea at these events) usually followed.

What was most notable, though in retrospect it could be seen to have been utterly predictable, was that this was one commitment that people had no difficulty maintaining over the longest life-spans.

Luther's friend finally licensed the business to a multinational conglomeration, which franchised it across the globe, and then retired with much more than enough money to devote himself to philanthropy. For his many contributions to significant charities, he did, in due course, naturally receive all the usual honours, and so came to be looked up to universally as a shining beacon of generosity and care. He was, however, very careful never ever even to consider sampling any of his own products.

All histories, child, are nothing but lies. Take yourself out of an even truth into narrative and it is at once no more. The point of such a story is to turn away from reality to reality, to create a new, a replacing of what is. Never narrate. Speak plainly and you cannot tell a thing. Eschew discourse. If you want to demonstrate the things which are real, you can only show them, never tell them. I do not mean you cannot speak them. Speak them you must. Only you cannot tell them, not as histories. The best a story can do is point. And to point at anyone is only a rudeness. I mean the unformed.

But of our course what do we but tell our histories? It is the character of us, of some of us. We do not all tell such stories. There are who have not that wit. These are not pleasant people, not ones to be chatting to. There is no small talk with them. There Yes is Yes, never perhaps. If you are wrong they will tell you.

They have no past. They have memories in abundance, but never are formed by them. They have been eroded and weathered by the reign of time. Which is precisely why dragon and Luther complemented each other. For dragon had no cosmetic of story, no face-pack of fantasy.

Therefore you must be careful what you pray for, and remember a certain Jemima, for when she was little once she prayed to be really, really beautiful when she grew up. And her wish was granted, you see. Only, by then she'd forgotten she'd ever prayed for it, because she'd gone down a particular path. But a prayer granted can not be ungranted. And she was really beautiful.

Now, the burlesque may have fostered the talents of many overly-loved artists, but Jemima, when she began her appearance to the world, was plainly of a different rank to all who had preceded her. She was by no mundane convention beautiful; her skin was slightly pasty, her nose a little too much for feminine expectation, and her teeth were admittedly crooked. Yet she was really beautiful, beautiful in all and only real senses, so that when the chorus insinuated itself before your stage-drawn eyes, it was on Jemima alone that you could focus.

It was not that any of the other girls was less strikingly, athletically and otherwise-variously talented; if anything Jemima was a little more than nearly imperceptibly less forthcoming. It was that, well, she meant it. That she was no better than people thought she ought to be may be at once allowed; that she earned her little gifts cannot be gainsaid; that she knew all she needed to prosper in her trade is definite. Her marina was for vessels not vestals. But in her, it was not sordid, it was glorious. Her manner proclaimed that she was not constrained to do it; her carriage that she knew it honourable. Whatever was required of her, she was not demeaned.

So, amongst the objects given for your eyes upon the dais, for Jemima alone could you have attention. When she was haughty, you were exalted with her. When she smiled, it was like the warm dayspring giving you your innermost soul as young and fresh as you never remembered it. When she pouted, it was the shocking thrill of finest young true Dutch gin warming your core. And, Ah, when she smiled, her teeth were the contours of all our charm, so that straightness would be the fault to enchant you less.

When her foot was raised above her head, her legs were compasses to divide out sincerity; when she kicked, she pricked only your conscience; when she flounced, you were rocked by the mother of all earths; her head-dress would serve as a compass line for life. And for Jemima, this was all very convenient, for she could ordain all desired releaseful contentment without any laying on of hands, and yet you would reward her so that she truly loved a cheerful giver. Such was Jemima.

So when, in that city where she was first manifested, men of a certain age were suddenly and particularly solicitous to their wives, a reaction was only to be expected. Yet to the sustained interrogations there was no attempt at denial or evasion, but only glowing eyes that were focussed both far-off and solely on the questioner. This not being in the troubleshooting section of the on-line help file, as many peeress-to-peeress network telephone calls simultaneously hysterical, flummoxed and determined soon established, it will be understood that it was not with smilies that these happy men were greeted after they had been sighing "Oh, Jemima" repeatedly in their sleep.

Consternation became *terra incognita*, however, when to the seismic question, "Who is this Jemima woman? Don't deny it. I know you're seeing her!", there came only the placid reply, "You must meet her for yourself this very night, dear. You'll love her."

Well, of course, they did. To be entertained by Jemima, they soon knew, was to be transfused with a strange life that made you twice-betrothed and nuptially borne-again. Their own thick rolls of fat were now beyond even Ruben's power to celebrate, and the migrating thatches of their husbands, wandering all ways down from scalps to bellies, were strands fit for the Haywain. Potency was in need of no purchasing of magical blue diamonds. Instead husband and wife went to their trysting-house as for the first time, carefully washed each other's gravely-flattened feet, gazed wonderingly on each radiant corn, kissed the jewelled bunions and anointed velvety calluses with raptured tears.

Now, though no name but Jemima's was spoken in all that town, the artists who were her fur-graced peers were not jealous; their ladyships were content to learn from her noble ways, for so they did profit greatly. The management, too, were overflowing with the gilded rewards of her grace and virtue.

To every shrine there must come pilgrims drawn by susurrations of sanctity passed from initiate to willing catechumen. And with them came Barons, drawn from commerce and industry and of whatever other bloodlines provided the plentiful notes acquired from their prophets. Now, it is an immutable law of physics that as a massive body is raised up further from its original, and thus presumably true, level, it must acquire potentials of derivative energy. And it is certain that the sudden discharge of the greater is more dramatically noted than the slower of the lesser. So when the sight of Jemima caused these men to be moved, they moved; sans incentive. They didn't need committees to persuade them that no remuneration would be enough to gain exclusive rights to Jemima, and that this could only lead to fewer executive tussles. She alone was all to the good. The bulls were bared, to their very souls.

And likewise in them the bejewelled turned from crystal, and towards new trading positions. Cartels were abandoned, monopolies went unsorted, deals were equitable, and unions were amicably desired.

It needs no saying that it is a still deeper law of physick that where the bodies are, there must the politicians be also. A chance meeting of Presidents, Prime Ministers, Kings, a General Secretary and one or two other Dear Ones, who all found it pressing to undertake urgent but pleasantly informal fact-finding missions in an atmosphere that grew increasingly cordial had the predictable but nonetheless serendipitous effect that as their temperatures optimised, they found ways might be found of doing the same for earth's. And if Jemima could conquer all yet be acquired by none no other methods of assured mutually blissful death and destruction were needed.

As Jemima was so plainly the fruit of the age-long fervent prayers of so many clergy, both men and celibates and virgins alike, the Pope himself knew that he must find his way into, is it to wrong to say?, her grotto of healing. And he was so far impressed that the next night he booked the entire theatre, filling it with cardinals and bishops both arch and ordinary, protesting and orthodox and fundamentally liberal alike. You must be left to imagine the consequences of the ensuing fervour, of the odour of sanctity and of so many pious ejaculations. Precative it was with possibilities.

It hardly therefore needs to be said that that was the last performance Jemima ever gave. The following night's scheduled spectacular had to be cancelled and the invited audience of all the worlds great religious leaders together with the dozen or so people who really do the holy work of running the world never were exposed to Jemima's potentialities.

For that afternoon, God, who had been increasingly irritated with all these improprieties, decided to reward Jemima for all her supererogatoriness. And the highest reward that God can endue any mortal with is Sainthood. And Sainthood requires you to be dead.

On earth, her cult vanished as quickly as it had arisen and she is all but forgotten, but in one of the more tenebrous chambers of eternity there is a woman dressed in weeds and lace and spangles who does her allotted tasks, of course with utmost joy; the tasks which she knows are hers, only hers, because she was given what she asked for when she asked for what she really wanted.

So don't powder your face with wishes, child.

CHAPTER 9

Indeed the tears live in an onion that should water this sorrow.
Shakespeare
Anthony and Cleopatra

What's in it for you if you do this little job for us? Well, it does rather depend on whether or not you do it.

It usually does, said Luther.

Indeed, replied Domination, we find it helps.

You could, of course, refuse to do it, which is your absolute, free sovereign choice, completely unconstrained. But you would have to stay here, without any particular privileges, not really belonging, for all eternity. Though we would keep the little job open for you; an opportunity can never end in eternity.

And if I agree to do it?

Then you go back and do it, and then, when you've done it but not before, you can live out the rest of your life-span until it's time to return. But then you'd have what we would hope would be the satisfaction, but anyway at least the experience, of knowing you'd helped, which might make you to have the feeling that you belong somewhere in this realm.

And would I, you know, belong?

Actually, I have absolutely no idea. That one really is down to you.

So, said Luther, I have the option of a working trip back to earth once and once only, which might or might not make me feel my existence had not been utterly futile.

If you put it like that. As you do.

Then the only rational response is to put it off indefinitely, since so long as I haven't done it, I have the expectation of it, but if I've done it, then expectation has gone for ever.

But you would have the experience, and in here memory and reality aren't so very far apart. What is remembered is what actually was, and what was is eternal, and so it still is, in a certain sense, don't you see?

Mm, said Luther, but any gap at all, even if only barely tangible, is exactly big enough to matter. So all gaps are identical as between what I remember and what I live.

You think so?, said Domination. Really, it's only your memory which makes you conscious even of the present second. Unless you are already remembering this second, it doesn't exist at all. So every gap is essential. Which provides your real choice — to have or not have a gap between memory and experience, between it being dead and you being alive.

If that's too hard, let me give you another decision instead. Shall I show you the workings of heaven and hell? Which is an offer that nobody in their right mind ever … what?

I'm not human, said Luther, so I can certainly see that much.

As you will, said Domination.

It might be amusing, said Luther, and there's nothing better to do.

There's never anything better to do in here. Whatever you're doing. But it's still your choice which causes you to be doing it.

Then I choose to learn how it works.

Then first I shall show you the mechanism for operating the universe. It has to be placed here in Hell to function smoothly and without a mind of its own. Punishments come later, once you understand how they fit in.

Wherefore and immediately Luther was in a corridor. It was so long a corridor that it appeared to have no end in either direction, which indeed it had not; what it did have, though, were doors, stout mahogany doors, each with shiny brass handles and shinier brass nameplate, at absolutely regular intervals on both sides for its entire length.

Welcome to the Universal Ministry, said Domination. You won't need to see all of it, which is just as well, since it's infinite; two or three Departments will show you all you need to know. This is the Corridor around which all things created revolve. As you see, it is infinitely long, but only of finite width. And you will recall that a finite divided by an infinity is always?

Infinitesimal, said Luther, effective zero, non-existence.

Precisely, so this Corridor, where everything is governed from, doesn't actually exist. As you would expect, of course. But, on the other hand, if you divide an infinity by a finite you get an infinity. So by putting doors at regular intervals along it, then the space between any two doors is infinite, which gives just enough room to fit in the bureaucracy.

And, said Luther, catching on, although each door is uniquely labelled, it is in fact the same as every other door since in an infinite set of definite objects each one must be repeated an infinite number of times.

Exactly, said Domination, which means?

That you are always outside the door you want, which is in fact also the door you've just left.

Perfectly understood, glowed Domination, who like everyone else was proud of a bright pupil who was smaller than him. So here we are.

The offices are manned by a mixture of angels and saints, explained Domination. The saints are a mixture of volunteers and escapees from heaven, not that there's any difference. There's an earthly saying 'You can run but you can't hide', but here you can run and you can hide but you can never escape. So if you think you've escaped, you've volunteered.

He opened the first door, on which Luther read the name "Department of Planetary Weather (Inhabited)."

You know how it is when your ma is at taking you to see that aunt of yourn in the tower block, you know, the listed one, where she lives. You get into the lift, and the stench hits you both at once, that someone's used it for a really nasty bodily function, and your ma tries to ignore it, but the stink is just too strong and something's got to be said. So she pokes around with the tip of her umbrella and shows you all the discarded things lying on the floor, and gives you the lecture about how only depraved lowlife use them, and why don't they do like normal people do and just take a pill or use a twenty-pound note to take a snort, or just inject like civilized people? So you say that you'll never do things like that, and at once you want to grow up and find out what smoking's like.

Well, the first thing Luther was aware of was a reek like that, only it wasn't the burning of dried leaves; it was incense. Now you know how that after your da he's knifed off the hair from his face each morning like God may or may not have commanded, seeing as how He put it there in the first place, he's thinking it would make the world like him better if he splashes himself with some after-shaving scenting-stuff, not that it stops anyone knowing exactly what he's like the moment they take a single glance at him, but there we are. Well, your average working angel is prone to the same sort of thinking, only in heaven there's no shaving and incense is the only fragrance as is allowed. And since each angel is a complete species to itself, no two of them can use the same scent. Which means they each concoct their own little fancy. So if you go into a room and there's ten thousand angels each with their own particular incense, you'd recoil a bit at first. But Luther's a polite sort, so he goes in and lets himself have this lot introduced to him.

This, says Domination, is the Weather Room. Where we control the weather throughout the Universe. Obviously. And that, he says, pointing vaguely to a gentleman in Morning Dress with a myrrh, acacia wood and brimstone aura where the Top Hat should go, standing all by himself doing nothing at all, is the Power of All Weathers. But he'll be far too busy to talk to us. So we'll show ourselves around; he won't notice with all the work he has to get through. If you'll follow me I'll show you the Earth. Luther, meanwhile realising that Domination now has a quite definite quality of olive wood, sulphur, cedar of Lebanon and bitter chocolate about him, glances back at The Power, notes that the angel was still just staring into space, and for the first time in his life feels he's been outdone at masterly inactivity.

So, anyway, he gets led through a throng of orrories to some far corner, where there's a blue and green globe and three angels standing round it. The first was wearing a coat of many furs with a label saying "Team Leader"; from him emanated a gentle odour of raspberry, liquorice and hyssop. Next to him, with a label saying "Assistant Team Leader", and a wafting of rotten eggs, coal tar and attar of roses, stood a rather skinny figure with a pair of lens-less pince-nez floating just above the tip of his nose. Seeing Luther trying not to stare at this feature, he explained "They pinch horribly if you actually wear them; much more comfortable like this", in tones which conveyed that he was at least being logical. Finally there was a typically spotty youth (lavender water and boiled spiders, since you ask; invention wasn't his strong point) whose label read "Operative Deputy Assistant Team Leader".

The ODATL (it was of course acronymic, considering they were situated in a long-established bureaucracy) had by him a table, whereon were laid all the instruments of his masters' trade. There were, *inter alia,* a beautifully-painted folding fan, and a spoon or twenty, and a variety of bellows, and watering cans of all sizes, and an atomizer, and a couple of Meerschaum pipes, and a curious contraption of batteries and wires leading to terminals that well were looking a bit like a defibrillator. The Team Leader and Assistant Team Leader stooped over the earth, each with a large magnifying glass in one hand, and a combined thermometer, windmeter and flowmeter in the other, which each occasionally dipped into the atmosphere, while they muttered to each other.

Do you think the roaring forties could do with just a little more roar?

Not really, I'd suggest we just monitor it, but the Atlantic definitely doesn't look depressed enough.

Mmm, Yes, it looks that way. Let's lower the pressure a bit. ... Hair dryer, please, ODATL, minimum setting.

So the ODATL picked up a travel hair dryer, switched it on, tested the heat coming from it with the back of his hand, and passed it to the ATL. The ATL received it blow-end first, so the handle was free when he proffered it to Fur-Man. With a gentleness and sureness acquired from aeons of doing just this very thing, he held the hair-dryer a few inches above the atmosphere. Not so close that it caused winds, but close enough to warm the mid-Atlantic. A few seconds later thick clouds appeared, starting over Norfolk and spreading out over the North Sea.

Not quite the right angle, perhaps I've veered when I should have backed, or backed when I should have veered. What's your view, number two?

I get those two confused myself all the time, Sir, said the ATL, who knew how promotion works in the Civil Service.

Careful, Sir, interrupted ODATL, in that tone of nominal inferiors which implies humility, contempt and superior knowledge at the same time, but which can't actually be regarded as anything but properly deferential. ATL glared at him from over his pince nez (they conveniently moved out of the way to make it easier), while his superior just didn't actually look at him. You're going to set off a sirocco. So ATL grabbed the fan, and waved it across the Sahara. A few dunes got moved, and an oasis was obscured, but no real damage was done.

At which the senior two turned their attention to some glaciers. The ODATL took a measuring rod, and checked the depth of the ocean in a few places. "Fairly leaky it is, in places, Sir", he said very quietly to Luther. "So I just have to make sure it's kept just about exactly wherever they've decided the level should be." He glanced at the rod after each dip, and then wiped it with a grimy rag. Yup, just like daddy checking the engine oil.

"Could do with just a little top up." So he reached over for a bucket, and filled it from a tap marked "Salt Water (unblessed)(polluted)".

One must be fair to Luther. He had been trying very hard. He'd tried to rise above the atmospherics; he'd tried breathing through his mouth; he'd tried holding his paws in front of his nose. But he could not block out the, what we have so properly called, perfumes. He did try to stop himself, but there comes a point where it is just not feasible. So it did happen.

He sneezed.

With great force.

The shock unbalanced them all, throughout the room, but the only true casualty was the ODATL, or, to be more precise, and when dealing with the management of the Universe that's a fairly good thing, the bucket, or, more exactly still, the water therein. For ODATL gave a start and his arms jerked, and though he did not actually drop the bucket into the ocean (which, as The Board of Enquiry agreed later, might have been embarrassing), he was unable to stop the entire contents of the aforesaid vessel being added to the volume of water in the oceans.

You will have gathered that Fur-Man and ATL were not the sort to be exactly quick on the up-take, so the tip of Mount Everest was just disappearing beneath the extra water by the time they'd noticed. And by the time they actually reacted, there was no dry land anywhere. Absolute deluge there was. Covering the whole earth. Drowning it in fact. And every living thing that lives on dry land, or, at that moment, used to.

"Oops.", said ODATL.

It is to be noted, child, that there are some states of affairs, as situations should ever correctly be described, in which something has to be said, but in which, equally, there is nothing that can be acceptably said. There are always things which can be said. Yes, like "I was so glad to hear that your wife had died. You never did get on.", or "Dreadful news about your granny getting rabies. Mind you she was always one for saying Hello to strange dogs, and I suppose she just thought it had been at the washing-up liquid.", or "Deirdre's just told me that your Janice is going to bring it up on her own. Still, one more bastard in the family won't notice.", or "Do have one of these delicious Belgian chocolates. Oh, I'm so sorry; how is the diabetes going?", or "Is it really true your Uncle Rodney did all those murders?". But nothing you can say which isn't just a tad off. So "Oops", all things considered, wasn't doing too badly.

It was strange, really; I mean you'd expect people to leap into action and all that, but they didn't. Fur-man simply said, "Somewhat unexpected, ODATL, that. Inconvenient, you know. It will require an intervention." But that last word, quietly uttered, had a remarkable effect. The entire rest of the room, which it will already be plain was somewhat on the sizeable side, and had been pleasantly buzzing with official activity, instantly became utterly silent, and all eyes (and many of the workers were well-supplied with them) turned towards the aura of the Power of All Weathers, as this august, even septemberal, figure, moved, as on wheels, and without any expression, towards the blue and green globe.

Luther noticed that Domination was shaking with fear, and not-quite-muttering to himself. That is to say Domination's lips were moving, but he wasn't daring to break the silence. Even so, it was plain enough what he wasn't saying.

An intervention... There aren't supposed to be any interventions... Everything is in the plan... All the miracles were carefully foreordained... Even the changes of mind were pre-written in the script... for dramatic emphasis. Free will, yes, but only because we know what gets chosen. Nothing like this ever. Not since even before the beginning. What will He say? What will He do? How many millions of years before He calms down? Power will get us out of this. Say what you like, Power knows how to solve things. That's it. Power will solve it.

And quite a bit more besides would not have emerged from Domination's mouth, were it not for the fact that the Power of All Weathers was ready to pronounce.

Perhaps if we deal with this quietly, so there's no actual consequence, then we can restore the impression of competence. A straw, I think. Mister ODATL, you actually poured the water, then it is only just that you suck.

So suck he did, filling the straw, which he just happened to have in his mouth, and thus the aforesaid mouth with the seawater, in great gulps, before spitting each one back into the bucket. And bit by bit, the sea-level did decline. The tip of Everest was followed by the rest of Nepal. And after several hundred spittings, ODATL managed to produce the little islands of the pacific that are the markers for the right level.

But of course, you couldn't actually talk about dry land. It was just, well, soaked land; muddy, even. And the vegetation was wilting and rotting from the roots upwards. And there were all these corpses floating about.

" 'Air Dryer, please.", said Power, and, putting the instrument onto its highest setting, proceeded to demonstrate how to coiffeur an entire planet. The skill required to put the quiffs back into the Sahara should not be underestimated.

"And now some Dry Ice, for the glaciers and poles, if you would, please." No cocktail glass was ever frosted more beautifully than the tip of Mount Fuji, or the peak of Kilimanjaro. And no ice-sculptor ever shaped anything neater than the glaciers which were waiting ready to break off the Arctic and Antartic caps under the influence of real, historical global warming.

"And if you'd all care to shut your eyes and all other entrances to your psyches, please." Of course, one rather insufficiently embarrassed feline absolutely did not care to. Which is how I am able to tell you that Power just got hold of the hands of the Earth Clock and turned them back fifteen minutes. Which is also how no-one on earth ever knew there'd been a great flood. And why there was no run on the market in Gopher wood.

"Fine. Panic over. You can carry on.", came a voice from the centre of a room where a gentleman in Morning Dress now stood, staring into space. And the buzz of voices refilled the room as work resumed.

It need not be said that there are a few certain workplaces, which for very good reasons indeed, are completely devoid on occasion of all gossip. So Domination just thanked Fur-man for his trouble and led Luther back out into the corridor.

A change of theme, I think, thought Domination, forgetting that Luther could overhear. We'll do the rest of the administration, when I've got my heart back to not beating again.

Domination waved vaguely at a range of doors.

Those are the judgment courts. But I'll omit them. See one judgment and you've seen them all. Don't understand the point of having them, to be honest. I mean, arrivals know their fate no sooner or later than they would any how.

Nonetheless, Luther held a door just ajar.

The Judge was addressing the prisoner.

"Prisoner at the dock, it is my plain duty to sentence you to eternal damnation and infinite pain, without possibility of parole, for offences as heinous as any I shall ever hear. Which done, the jury will now pronounce its verdict."

A bewigged Clerk was now on his feet, addressing the dock.

"You are Arthur Henry Vox Humana Tremulant."

A surprisingly strong voice replied, "I am".

"It was not a question. You will be told when to speak." The Clerk continued, "Will the foreman of the jury please stand."

A stout burgher got to his feet with a determined flex of the knees.

"Have you reached a verdict on all the charges?"

"We have, m'lud."

"How do you find the soul?"

"Of all forty-five million, three hundred and eighty nine thousand, six hundred and twelve charges, we find the soul Guilty."

"And that is the verdict of you all?"

"It is."

"And do you make any recommendation of mercy?"

"None, m'lud."

The judge turned to two counsel sitting in the front row before him.

"Are learned counsel happy to dispense with closing speeches, evidence and opening outlines?"

They both half-rose, bowed and resumed their seats.

"In which case, the Clerk will now read the charges."

A trolley of thick bound volumes was wheeled in by a heftily-built porter. Each was labelled "A H V H Tremulant". The Clerk, picking up Volume One, and beginning at page One, started to gabble.

"You are charged that at the age of nine months, two days and twelve minutes before your birth, your parents did carnally conceive you in original sin, with lust and desire. How do you plead, guiltiernotgilty? You are charged that at divers times from that time forth you did bring your mother to a state of nausea. How do you plead, guiltiernotgilty?..."

Luther closed the door. This was going to take some time, and it wasn't exactly suspense-filled. A reverse thriller: you knew who'd done it, but not what, and you weren't going to find out how.

He caught up with Domination, who to be candid had been glad of a moment alone.

This is the sort of thing we do with renaissance Popes, said Domination, opening another door. The cell within was hung in gold and silver silk drapes, and contained nothing but an unmade bed. A very expensive unmade bed, admittedly. The sort you might want to show off to people.

Alexander VI is in this cell.

The father of Cesare and Lucrezia Borgia, I think?

The very same. He kept his own establishment of 40 courtesans throughout his reign, so we thought he'd like to keep them up here as well. But, of course, we think he too should keep up to the mark, and have regular knowledge of each of them.

Appropriate, said Luther, he has to keep at least some of his treaties.

Quite so, each one, each day, each minute. So for quite a lot of time to come he has to perform with a fresh lady - and these are ladies worthy of the name – every 36 minutes. Once each one has finished with him, or he with them, then the next one is ready. Re-virgined; we think these little touches make all the difference. Hell should be elegant.

Doesn't he get, well, just a little weary?

Of course; world-weariness is mandatory hereabouts. So we arrange it that if he doesn't commence work within ten seconds, then his privities balloon to enormous size and ache as if he'd been on the receiving end of a donkey's kick. But if he gets on with things, then that stops, and he has the beginnings of certain feelings of enjoyment, and just enough stamina to complete this one act. You can watch, if you like. Or don't.

Luther noted a naked 500-year old man, with one organ alone that hadn't aged, climb, with the weariness of a once-high mountain being ground down by the millionth drop of morning dew, onto an 18-year old nymph and begin. Beside the bed, absent-mindedly eating bunches of grapes, was a row of similar nymphs, each looking as if just prepared by all means usual for a Saturday night in a northern English city and as typically eager for the customary joys to be found there.

What's he doing in a Protestant hell, by the way?

Are you saying he was Catholic?

Point taken.

Alexander was accelerating a little and beginning to sound as does a cow in need of milking when the farmer is late.

This is his 7,409,839th time, you know. We do like to keep an accurate record of these things. If you look over there you can see the meter.

Luther, having glanced at the number shining out of the cell wall, began to perceive changes in the maiden's flesh; there were undulations appearing in the skin, each, O, about 3mm wide and perhaps 2cm long, starting from her navel and rapidly spreading to cover every part of her flesh. The room's definite, shall we say?, musk began to become putrid. Alexander, however, seemed not to notice, continuing his efforts as if counting out reps on a recalcitrant gym machine.

The dermal undulations developed a life of their own, beginning to fidget and then to wiggle and going on to acquire, quite plainly, what may only be named a squirminess. Writhings were soon enough going to be inexorable. This increasing range of dermatological movement was accompanied with a change in texture, as the skin became mucous and then frankly slimy. His Holiness had been staring blankly ahead of him, focusing on some internal iconic fragment of memory, so far as his brain's oxytocin level, which was in the range mundanely associated with a little less than not yet moderately intense pleasure, allowed. Now, though, his attention seemed to shift to the current partner, and his face expressed no particular emotion other than intensity itself.

The writhings arrived, and the glimmering chits of flesh separated promptly into things frankly vermicular. Maggots. And the maggots began to crawl over him, and to explore his orifices. His mouth, open from exertion, was just one of their goals. Alexander's grunts were perforce muffled by these new little friends of his tongue, who no sooner than they had passed the time of the day with his palate, and cheerily embraced his adenoids, pressed on towards sharing reminiscences from their last meeting with his vocal cords. The consequent muting could not, even so, sufficiently effect an occlusion of significance: Alexander was screaming with revulsion.

His hips, however, were now committed to their course of action. He could no more stop thrusting than he could be charitable to his enemies. The process still had some augmentations to take him through, but it will suffice to say that whatever occurred between his legs, and it is not likely that he was here to be spared that, he vomited copiously over the transfigured and spreading maiden.

At which, instantly, each maggot having gone through this episode of its development, became the efficiency that is the housefly, and took flight. Alexander, deprived of his support, fell heavily onto the bed, bending that part of him liable to land first on the mattress, which was itself of now-departing insect origin, and rolled directly onto the floor. The next maiden threw aside her half-eaten bunch of seedless grapes and positioned herself for today's contribution to the divine economy, the bed having meanwhile remade itself in the perfect untidiness. And it became plain that the Pontiff's ten seconds began with a sharp awareness even of the first of them.

Domination glowed with satisfaction.

Augustine was so right, don't you think?; the joy of the blessed *is* made perfect by their awareness of the punishments suffered by the damned.

Luther thought it better not to say anything. It could so easily be misinterpreted. Though "Oops" did come to mind.

CHAPTER 10

The best number for a dinner party is two - myself and a dam' good head waiter.
Nubar Gulbenkian
Daily Telegraph, 1965

What am I doing? Well, I'm sitting here playing Spider Patience, and if I win this game then I won't kill myself, and if I lose then I shall let myself live a bit longer.

Actually, it is a real choice; there's a big difference between not killing yourself and living a bit longer. It's all in the endurance. They say we can't take a lot of reality, but when you're in my state all you get is the hard stuff, undiluted realness, 'cos fantasy isn't around any more, walked out on me years ago.

I tried, I really did, to stop us splitting up, pointed out all the nice times we'd had, the way I hadn't tidied things up, so my head was the kind of place you could really relax in, but it was no good. Said I was too sorted, whatever I pretended to other people; apparently you could see that on the inside my heart wasn't in it any more. And then there was some guff about wanderlust, about how it doesn't matter if it's the same scene every hour on the hour, so long as you're not pretending. But I wasn't putting myself into it, was doing it out of a sense of duty. Well, you can't really argue with that, and you can't ever really keep someone once they're going out the door, not without violence, and fantasy had never been cruel to me, so I didn't do nothing to stop it happening.

Can't say I was that cut up; I'd seen it coming, - well, you would do, wouldn't you?, under those circumstances I mean -; so it was no great shock. In a way it was quite nice to have the place to myself. You know, set to and clear out all the clutter, re-arrange the furniture the way you actually do want it, live simply, all that sort of stuff. And that's how I've carried on, you see, really ever since. So I get all the reality that's going, can't see anything else, never get to listen to another tune. So when you know that you're like what I am, sorry, are like to that which now I am, then you get to understand a few things about endurance. So the idea of suicide helps you stay alive.

Sometimes people really do want to die; that's rare that is, wanting non-existence and the end of the body. Then there's those that execute themselves from shame; and it's no kindness to stop them, which is why they ought to be stopped, of course. As well, there're the ones who just want a good long sleep, and forget about the rest. And never forget the ones who didn't want to see it through, were just crying out with pain, and wanted the pain off them and off them right now. Of course, you never get to forget that there are the stupid ones who do it to punish someone else, but act it out on themselves. That way no-one gets to feel any better.

And then there are the ones for whom it's life-giving. You see, if you know, and I mean really know, no fantasy, you've got to be ready to do it right through if the time comes, that you can die later on if you decide to, then it's easier to put up with what is here and now. So that's why you find your Grandpapa sitting here playing patience with the cards and fighting for his very life.

What? Well, this is a second degree game. First degree is shall I make a few plans? Second degree is shall I live or not die? And third degree, do you need me to explain what that is? You don't do third degree patience too often, in case you get addicted - Oh, it's Very addictive - and you never play it, just do it. It's one of the things that make me such a good psychoanalyst. People who ought to know tell me I'm the best there is. And I suppose they're right. I am. It's to do with authority. I speak with authority not like their own teachers. Because I know.

It's certainly important. Think now, if you had to go and get, Oh, your liver seen to, you'd want to go to the man, the top one, so that when he said you've got idiopathic necrotising hepatocellular chromosynthesising syndrome, but it's benign and nothing much to worry your pretty little head about, you can really believe. Because he knows what he's talking about. Of course, he's probably never had it, which in his trade could be a bit of an advantage (might not be, of course, but that's not the point) but he's seen plenty of it, and handled as many livers as any one could ever want to of them that have got it. So he knows.

Same in my trade. People come to me, and they say, Doctor, am I going mad? And usually I can say, No, but you're not a well person, and they trust me, because they can sense that I know. But in my trade, there's no biopsies, no blood tests and lab technicians, no having a quick shufty at the inside of their substantia nigra to see how it's doing, because it wouldn't help. You can't touch consciousness like that. There's no needle biopsy for guilt. So the only way to know with truth and authority is if you've been there. And I can, here and now, hand on heart, say that whatever it is, I have suffered it and gone through it unable to blink and explored it 'til it's ready to fall apart in my hands, and then I've come out the other side, designed the tee-shirt and ripped it to shreds.

That's how my patients all know. You can tell when someone's visited the same hotel as you. Does cause a bit of a problem with ordinary folk, who've never gone travelling, because they think you're a bit odd, but probably harmless. Occasionally you do get a generous one who says, he's probably some sort of genius. Doesn't make much difference to what I think of them. I tell you true, child, ordinary folk give me the willies; they are capable of anything. Just anything. There won't be many of them get into the Kingdom of God, I can tell you: the obsessives and the self-harmers and the depressives will all go in before them. Which is exactly how it should be, if you ask me.

Anyway, we're not here to talk about me.

So this is the beginning of the story of a Christmas eve-eve, that is two days before Christmas, when an old man, well, sort of old-ish but not as old as he was going to be, had nothing whatever to do, so decided not to not have fun by doing something meaningful, but instead just to do a thing which would mean nothing at all. For that would neither be fun nor not fun, and that suited his mood perfectly.

So he thought of all the things that had happened to him in recent times, because he knew he'd have to succeed in putting them out of his head, otherwise meaning would creep back in unannounced. Now, lots of things had happened to him, like making all sorts of realisations about what was never going to happen in his life, but he decided to think of two things not in particular.

In virtue of which, I need to tell you they went into another punishment room.

"In here are some announcers from a thing called Radio 3; it bears some relation to what used to be the Third Programme.

"These fiends decided in the early 1970's that they were so refined, and so influential, that they could change the way a whole nation spoke. "Baroque" used to rhyme with "oak"; there was none other correct pronunciation." (He made six syllables of that.) "Starting late at night but then spreading to other hours, they began to make it rhyme with "block". Their employer's reputation was such that people hearing them thought these fellows must be right. Within two years, the change was complete."

"Is that really so terrible?", asked Luther.

"We're angels. We like baroque. It suits us. It's what we do. And we like it uncontaminated by anything after the 18th century.

"So we've set each bloke to write out lines. On a stone block, with a chisel. If they get it wrong...."

Domination pointed to the back of the room where a group of angels stood, looking decidedly on the tetchier side of crotchety, each holding a fearsome tool.

"Those look a bit like electric cattle prods."

"That's because they are. When used, the recipient is awarded a gentle reminder of something else that rhymes with "blocks"."

On the wall, Luther saw, there was that sentence so little actually used in English elocution training: The rain in Spain falls mainly on the plain. The miscreants, none of whom looked strong enough to lift, let alone wield, a chisel, were carving this on to the stone. Despite the lack of formal training, they had by now achieved a regular and pleasing style.

One of them put up his hand and said, "Finished, Sir.", and a moment later lay on the ground, hands between legs, desperately trying not to groan.

"Idiot," said the angel-in-charge, "is that what is written on the board? Look, and tell me what it says."

"It says, Sir, 'The reigning heads of Spain felt often rather plain.'."

"Indeed. And is that what you have written? No, it isn't. So you will all just have to start over and do it again until you get it right, won't you?"

The umquhile announcers looked most carefully at the board, and addressed themselves again to their pristine granite blocks. As they did so, Luther saw the sentence reform itself.

'A strain on the spine can form major pain.'

"That'll teach'em.", said Domination.

"Now this", he continued, not bothering with doors, "is the poets' and playwrights' room. They're all doing a paper. You can look for yourself if you want."

The first, rather martyred-looking, figure had 'Write a comedy in the manner of Feydeau, using only the following three characters: King Lear, Hamlet and Titus Andronicus." Luther noted it was going slowly, as if he was waiting for inspiration, or something, perhaps.

Next to him, a Mr Keats had as his task 'Write a Petrarchan Sonnet beginning "Thou art comparable to a steal tea-tray.'", while at a third school desk, a Lord Byron had been given 'Write an Ode dedicated to Gracie and 'Ern.'

The atmosphere was that of an examination room, with its many rows of wobbling desks at each of which there was uncomfortable scribbling. In most such rooms, however, the black-gowned invigilators do not carry red-hot pincers for twisting ears, nor do they stop their paradings at random and shred the candidate's efforts. It is also fairly usual to allow the use of non-disappearing ink. Glancing again at some papers, Luther saw there was but a single rubric: 'You SHALL complete a whole question.'

Domination took Luther by the shoulder, and guided him towards a cupboard.

"I must just point out this little annexation: it's where we place all those who misuse the word 'egregious'. We hang them up by thumbscrews, and make fun of them, until they feel throughly atramentous of spirit."

"I don't need to see inside," said Luther as Domination made to open the door. "Let them have some privacy; in any case, I think I get the general idea. Bizarrely, aptly inapt, unending mental cruelty."

"So does that mean you don't want to see the rest of the suite?", said Domination, looking as sad as he was allowed to. "Then you'd better see more of the gubbins."

Luther had another idea, that he hadn't expected to think, and thus interrupting my chains of thinking as well.

Punish me, said Luther.

I beg your pardon?, replied Domination.

Punish me. If you're showing me how it all works, then you should punish me in order to give me the full hands-on hell experience.

It's not really allowed; punishments aren't for fun, you know.

But this wouldn't be for fun, it would be educational. And I'm not here under the usual rules anyway. You yourself have said it's part of my special task. I shall need to understand how it all works. So punish me. Something philosophical, obviously. Go on, you know you want to.

Well, of course, Domination did want to. First, it was built in, since he was an avenging angel. And second, he hadn't been pleased at being allocated to mind a cat. And third, someone, mentioning no names, had just mentioned philosophy.

So Luther found himself on the escalator going towards the entrance of the tube station in the middle of the British Museum car park. There isn't one there in real of course, but in a punishment, anything's possible.

He was in a hurry to catch a bus.

Luther went to buy a newspaper, from the man at the kiosk by the bus-stop, as you do when you're in a hurry to catch something. He knew it was expected, though quite why humans need them was all but incomprehensible. I mean, do you think that the Magpie that just landed outside your window, just the one, sorry, wants to know what the five Magpies that got together in the next street yesterday were up to, or in the next county, let alone, saints ever-alive help us, foreign lands? But then Magpies don't trade in worm futures, they just decide them. And they need no help in choosing hedges.

As he got back onto the escalator that formed the queue for the bus; it does often enough doesn't it?, Luther was stared at by all and singular the ones of the passengers, who were each descending into the earth. All were as if dressed in a single blue suit, darkish-blue, not perhaps of the best cut, but the sort of thing the supermarket would sell you fit to work in, ready for you to personalise; you know, add the crumples in the small of the back of the jacket yourself, all set for you to drape the jacket over your chair and the trousers over your shoes. It was, all one, a suit to make you feel safely always the same, so you didn't have to think or worry, not what you looked like, nor that people could see you, nor that you might stand out different.

It being the not-rushing-hour, this place was stuffed-up with them, going up and going down, and the streets of the surface were likewise full, numbering them in thousands of equal, in milliards of uniformity. All peers.

Coming out of the station, which debouched exactly at the foot of the stairs that lead up to the British Museum, within the great National Gallery it holds, Luther thought to make a brief visit into the museum. It would be nice, just nice, to go and commune with a marble or a bronze, or a great painting, say of a horse, and feel like them that you really belong on that spot, are wanted just where you are, rather than some foreign city. The steps, unusually, were clear of tourists. This day there was only the blue-jackets, a vibration of them, all looking purposeful for the course of their oscillating from a pole to another.

But as Luther got the door, an attendant, blue-of-uniform of course, came out.

"You can't come in 'ere. Not the likes of you. Who do you people think you are, showing yourselves in these parts? Why don't you go back to wherever it is you do come from?"

Luther, who had been too engrossed in watching his surroundings to suppose he looked any different from normal, politely asked him to explain.

"Explain is it? Explain?" A fist and a boot explained, and Luther was sat on the ground, more neatly than would be the imagining usual for it, and next to a tramp.

"Ere you,", the attendant ever so politely screamed to the tramp, "tell this geezer wot's wrong wiv 'im." And the tramp, who had a voice as mellifluous as might ever be heard and for this while used it, explained. Luther, it emerges, has most glaring faults, growing more unbecoming by quick steps.

He was dressed in a darkest of charcoal-grey suits; three-piece, not two; sewn with silk seamings; as well as this, Luther was wearing a patterned red and yellow tie.

There was, his preceptor struggled to say politely enough, another thing: there was a little something not quite right about Luther's nose. He had a black spot, hardly a pimple really, but it was nowadays inherently disfiguring, hideous, monstrous and disqualifying, hardly to be thought of, as it might be it impended death. Or something plaguy. A boo-boo, anyway. That was what Luther had. If the suit had not been sufficient, the spot must constrain Luther to alien status in any realm where the signs of mortality were not suffered to be suffered. And if the spot had not so indicated, then the suit would. Luther has both, it is explained with even more politesse.

The tramp then suggested, possibly a little less wonderfully politely, by words we need only *précis*, that Luther might perhaps choose to take a walk, so as to proceed to impress his person elsewhere, as it might be. The alternative, he seemed to be quite sure, was not one his interlocutor would wish to contemplate.

Luther chose to walk.

He knew that, were he to chose, he could acquire a regulation blue suit in seconds, even if the charcoal-grey was of far finer cut, having been very-well bespoken, but the spot, he thought, might be a different matter. Just possibly.

Now as it happened, immediately opposite, in the midst of Bloomsbury as it long had been arranged, standing beside the Royal College of Music on the one hand, and the Royal Institution on the other, there was the place where shelter and repose *sans pareil* might be had.

It was the Royal College of Patients.

The Royal College of Judgment may be more refined; the Royal College of Patience more renowned; the Royal Institution for Haruspication more penetrating, the Royal Academy of Apprehension more misunderstood, but within none of the manifold Royal Colleges, any of them, some two hundred and fifty of them in that street alone, and straitsful of them all around, was it more difficult to achieve Membership.

Now, child, you must, you are to, understand that the Royal College of Patients is, to the same degree as its iatrogenic compeers, devoted to the relief of suffering and to the promotion of the necessary altitude of standards amongst its professed.

Probands are first admitted to Affiliate status; assigned backless robes on which but a single bow, the one between the shoulder blades, is left intact; and placed on nil by mouth for a week. That first night, as every, while her charges are lying in their pristine and starchy beds of pain, Staff Nurse comes around every twenty minutes between lights-out at 9.52p.m. and reveille at 5.38a.m., to shine her bright torch in each face to check it is not asleep. Indeed, she looks to see that the putative patient either is lying rigidly afraid to move a single thing because of the agony it will cause, or else is slowly writhing with the agony it is causing, "it" being as yet undefined. After breakfast, which in their case they do not have, the tests begin. These, if passed in enough quantity and regularity, qualify the postulant to be admitted an Associate. While this is to the medical profession a lowly qualification, it does at least bring with it a set of letters, entitling the one who takes hold of that status to append to their name the mystic acronym ARCPa.

To be an ARCPa is to enter the College's training programme, and so to set one's aim at the highest ranks of patientdom.

The College is also much valued for the training experience it provides for medics. "You can always tell a College chep.", it is said. And it is true; you can. If when a patient is complaining in aggrieved tones that something is blocking his nasal passages, "It gets right up my nose, it does.", and that this is causing additional cranial symptoms, "It's doing my 'ead in, it is, 'no wot I mean, do yer?", you can reply that "That must be deshed uncomfortable for you, ild chep." and be received as possessing *echt* sympathy, "'E proper understands me, that doc' does.", then your qualities will be regarded as invaluable everywhere from Kensington to Canning Town.

As for the nurses, a stint at the College is also meritworthy. Certain is it that arduous is their life. Between departing and arriving of patients, the nurses strip the bed, incinerate all the bedclothes, and fumigate the mattress and pillows with sulphur candles, right down to the last straw, before they proceed to steam clean the bed frame. Each day the floors, walls, ceilings and all other surfaces, of what accessibility so ever, are to be disinfected with carbolic, and every patient, without fail, is given a most thorough bed bath with strong antiseptic. And gotten to go.

Amply, omptly, willingly and promptly, yet without sign of stress, strain or excess. An eliable go.

The trainee nurse learns the many rules rapidly. No line is permitted to have within it the smallest bubble of air. No injection is but within one thirty-second of an inch of its target. No cannula is ever misplaced. No catheter ever comes out. The starched cap, all fifteen inches height of it, is exactly vertical at all times. The silver-gilt belt-buckle ever has the proper soft glow.

And each day every bed occupied or not shall have new linen. This is starched, of course, as already indicated. The amount has perhaps not been made clear: within the College, if you lay down your weary, aching head on a pillow, you are sure to discover what it is for linen to be starched as stiff as a board, for, be sure, your head will make no impression in your pillowcase, try how much you may. Not will, do, can or may you leave your bed, except with nutricial permission and assistance of nouriceship.

In these wards, patience is to be learned, and the patient to be gently assisted in understanding that charters are solely for staff use. The patient not will but shall subject themself to long hours of discipline, in the interstices of which, as do the students in medical schools ubiquitous, they strive to study what they need to know. But first, there shall be discipline.

And where there must be discipline, obedience shall flourish and authority blossom. In these wards, a Staff-Nurse can raise or lower temperatures with a glance; here, a Sister (Charge-Nurses there are none) can quell epidemics by lifting an eyebrow; and here, Matron...

Space permits it only to be said that Matron is traditional. Before entering her kingdom, even the recording angels check they have clean underwear, and hope to keep it so.

For this level of devotion the nurses are, needfully and naturally, well-remunerated. A Staff-Nurse after five years or so will be sure to have accumulated enough to rescue a penurious noble house. A Sister can measure herself above the run of millionaires American, Arab and Russian. As for Matron and her Assistants, they accrue wealth on a scale which ensures they remain unmarried: it is so great in quantity that no-one of sense could contemplate giving others hopes of sharing it; nor has one Divorce lawyer ever, by what means we need not speculate, ever moistened any part of their anatomy by dreaming of such sums.

It will be plain therefore how urgent is the need of each ARCPa to ascend the ladder if they are willing to fund all this.

The ARCPa, their status having been marked by a second string to a bow on their gown, is required, as at Oxford, The Inns of Court and Cambridge, to keep a set number of terms, and not to consume a prescribed number of dinners in each. Unlike those Institutions, however, examinations come at the end of all terms. The twice-weekly tutorials from the Senior Members are some help, but there is a real terror attached to every paper, since to fail but one brings the expulsion irrevocable, as surely as major surgery or a great social *faux pas* does the cut direct. In the bloody universe of Patients there can be no resits.

The essence of the paper is invariable, only the topic varying, with the thoroughness of scrutiny increasing hyperbolically each term. The examinee, *viva voce corpeque*, must each time accomplish two things with distinction: no test administered may return a positive result; but the examining doctor must nonetheless be utterly convinced that there is something really wrong with this patient and that not one symptom is feigned. The number of possible candidates would be huge were the College not so stringent in its examination procedures.

After what stretches as long years (the College, like all hospitals, has in its heart a machine that stretches time till hours is days, and days weeks, and weeks, well, you don't think about weeks [it always amazes me that physicists don't investigate how that's done in hospitals if they want to get to the basis of space and time {it was sorted years since}]), the ARCPa is rewarded, and becomes MRCPa and, thus, respected by everyone in the medical profession as their peer in skill, cunning and professionalism. They are allowed a Dressing Gown.

The Fellows, naturally enough, keep to themselves the criteria for election to that most blessed of states. The sole thing known for certain is that to have a dreadful, incurable disease which has been named after one as patient, which no-one else in the world has or ever has had or ever will, while yet appearing to all around as if there was nothing at all the matter, is one of the minor though literally vital criteria. The misfortune of one particular Fellow suffering a not-immediately-fatal heart attack and desiring to clear as much of his conscience as was possible in the time left to him, while it didn't accomplish much of that aim, did permit this one snippet to escape. The rules were at once tightened to ensure that there could be no repeat.

Luther was a Fellow. He had no memory of ever becoming a Fellow, of ever having any lesser status, of any training nor of any examination, but a Fellow he assuredly was, with all the privileges thereto appertaining.

One of which was the special outfit of robes. On his arrival, the concierge, a man so ancient as to make Methuselah feel skittish, had escorted Luther to his room, assisted him to remove the suit that had brought him to this place, which suit was then not hung, but folded and laid in draws as are a gentleman's clothes traditionally and properly, and then vested Luther: first in the subfusc of a gown back-less in conception, but to which the addition of extra folds gave an all-enclosing capacity, tying by numerous bows internal and external at the sides, and of ankle-length; then in the gown proper, of black (scarlet on high-days and holly-days) with glove sleeves embellished with much lace, embroidered on the left breast with Luther's name, degrees, title and rank, and held together with strings in the Cantab fashion; and finally with the bonnet, grandma style, of black velvet gathered with gold bullion cords. Whilst the centrepiece of Luther's room was certainly the bed, only a little more commodious than that of Ware, but with fresher brocade hangings, rewoven and rehung daily, there were also several large mahogany tables, a pair of leather armchairs, a commode for every hour of the day and night, and a mediaeval bookcase lined with books - of lightish reading - that had evidently escaped the Kelmscott press, for there each had been made but of them no catalogue of that press's work had ever had notice.

Luther bespoke him no treatments other than seclusion (with esclusion and ceslusion to make it utter), rest, retirement and good food and drink. It being near the time of that letter that stands between S and U, a selection of savouries and good coffee was brought him.

The Fellows, by means as arcane as their election, had removed from the College every instance of the colour blue. I do not mean that they had justly thrown out every blue object in the place, though that they had, but that they had forbidden the colour itself to enter. Within those walls, the rainbow had no such shades, light no such wavelengths. The spectrum stopped at green and continued with soft X-rays (for the learned, pedants and train-spotters, all wavelengths from 500 nm to 3 nm had been disposed of). The removal was not effected by filters, prismatic deflection, interference or any method which allows that the relevant light existed in the first place. The Fellows had caused the laws of physics within the College to be such that those putative wavelengths were incapable of being.

Blue was depressing and caused suffering. Therefore it must be extirpated. So had the Fellows reasoned.

Now, if a blue suit gives off blue light, and that blue light does not exist, then such a suit is incapable of being even imagined. The *soi-disant* science, if even that it be, of psychology offers demonstration that an eye presented with an image which would otherwise make sense, but from which some part is missing, fills up the blanks. Accordingly, to look out of the windows of the

College was to look out on a world without people. Unblue vehicles might drive themselves down the street, but of people they were empty. Doors might open and close, but no-one ever went in or out. All the blue-suited people of that city, be they ever so many, might have no visible existence. Human life could be seen to exist only within the College. Of patients and their attendants did culture deal exclusively.

The Fellows, however, had never accomplished a like feat with sound. Wherever, therefore, you went in the College, despite the quintuple glazing, there was a background of human noise, a massed whispering from voices that had no source. Sometimes a phrase or sentence would be clear, but mostly it could not be said what was said. Yet there it was, never utterly absent, but more present in the daylight. All told themselves that these sounds were just noise, but were disconcerted e'en so.

The fear was that some day a door might be opened, and nothing would enter in, and would speak with utter clarity. So the doors must be guarded at all hours, and relaxation could not be had, not truly, though it was still safer within than anywhere without.

So Luther realised there was a different amissness when a very blue-faced Domination interrupted him mid-sip, saying, "I've just had strictest instructions that I am not even to pretend to punish you. I am to further your understanding instead."

So they were back in the corridor.

CHAPTER 11

"Ipse dixit." "Ipse" autem erat Pythagoras.
"He himself said it.", and this 'himself' was Pythagoras.
Cicero, De Natura Deorum

Very few people have any cause to know that angels' wings are prehensile, indeed are made able to prehend whatsoever they need. Which is one reason why it would never occur to Luther to go looking for a certain door in the corridor, and Domination had no need to demonstrate it.

Had he had entrance, Luther would have beheld a river running in the midst of a desert landscape; the river rose and fell periodically. Enough to sustain, dare I say it, a corridor in the desert. And at the shores of the river there grew rushes in abundance.

And he would have beheld an angel seated in a deckchair. Two of his wings were arched over him, with the feathers arranged to block out just as much of the sun as he wanted. I mean, if you're dealing with the transcendent, the sun-rays are literally something else. A third wing was engaged in wafting aer sufficient to make the gentlest and locallest of breezes, and a fourth was tending a table on the angel's left side. There was a glass, a cylindrical green bottle of export-strength gin (or what would be export-strength were there any exports), a bottle of tonic-water, every bit as opalescent as if it had been confected from actual opals, which, for aught I ought to know, it might have been, and an ice-bucket. The wing having made a very large one earlier, that aspect of the angel's comfort was assured.

In his hands, he held the newspaper he was reading. Given that there isn't news as such in those parts, that a certain degree of seriousness hardly needs to be made mandatory, and that the power of thundering is ubiquitous, it could only be The Aeons he was absorbed in. It's a very thick paper, of course, but has the decided advantage that there were and are and will be no supplements.

The other two wings, to which he was paying not the slightest attention, since they knew exactly what to do by themselves, were performing for him his day's work. One plucked out of the rush-beds a selection of the very finest of those sharp, triangular leaves, and deftly skinned and flattened them, leaving perfectly rectangular lengths of pith. These it laid edge to edge on the remaining wing, which was held out horizontally. Once the active wing had formed them into an A3 oblong, it went back for more pith strips, with which at right-angles it overlaid the first set. The two wings clamped together, turned through 90° to let the juices drip out, and pressured the strips together with force that would make hydraulic engineers weep until the fibres were fused incorrigibly.

Returned to the horizontal, the wings separated, exposing the plant remains to the drying heat from above, and once they were dried, the active one lifted the sheet off and flicked it, with more panache and sheer wheeeee than any frisbee can ever know, so as to land on a pile of exactly similar sheets, perfectly aligned, so the whole would need no adjusting or shuffling when the ream was done. For it was a sheet of papyrus that the angel had made.

After giving themselves a most thorough rinsing in the river, the wings repeated the process, and after another two hours a further sheet was thus added to the pile. The angel, having thus completed his morning shift, had earned an hour of rest. The afternoon would see another two sheets made before it was time to knock off for the day, guv.

It will seem an uncommon slow process. However, given enough of infinity, even one sheet a millennium would still create an infinite number of sheets, and so, in fact, the angel was under the strictest instructions to work to rule, and not cause a glut in the papyrus market. For had you looked behind him, you would have seen warehouses beyond counting, all packed to the rafters with the reams of papyrus sheets he'd made.

Papyrus is of necessity the only writing material the heavenly realms know. There are no rags available, obviously, and cutting down trees is a total no-no, so paper is out. Clay had, quite early on, been reserved for a more creative use. Chalk and slate might have been on until someone asked why go to the effort of laying them down in strata, only to have to dig them up again. As for vellum, well, just how likely is it that they could ever contemplate using lamb-skin?

It is perhaps a mark of just how smooth in functioning is the celestial realm that a sole angel reading the newspaper (strictly, the newspapyrus) and sipping G & T can meet all of the stationery requirements of the Civil Service. But then they do organise things rather well in those parts.

His work however was vital. The Celestial Service is of necessity a moderately large organisation; but within it two Departments above all others have need of written records, of which one is the Office of Prayers, Petitions and Obsecrations, otherwise known as OfPray, or as OPPO. (The other is the Office of the Recording Angels, OfReal.)

Some buildings, such as Saint Peter's basilica, are so proportioned that their size is not apparent at once. OfPray had this feature: you knew it was large, but not that it takes hours to walk across.

Into that Office, Domination now escorted Luther, and introduced him to the Registrar.

Although the Registrar must perforce be taken to be a Saint, he was a peevish, suspicious man, pernickety about his own work, little though that was, and hyper-critical of his sub-ordinates' efforts.

It was not that the Registrar did not trust his aides; it was just that in the increasingly unlikely event that they came up with the suggestion, the irresponsibly novel suggestion, that two and two make four, he knew better than so much as to dream of giving it serious consideration unless he heard it, unprompted, from a more senior and reliable authority. Meanwhile he daily noted how his assistants' declining rate of suggestion-offering was plain evidence of their increasing incompetence.

So it may be regarded as probable that he made known to Domination his displeasure at having to show a visitor round. Domination accordingly pointed out that on returning to his desk, the Registrar would probably want to double-check what his minions had done in his absence. Suddenly the Registrar was for Luther. Indeed, he sent for tea and biscuits.

Domination could do nothing about another characteristic of the Registrar. A few hours previously, while excoriating an underling, he had pointed out that on earth his wisdom had been of such a degree that he had acquired a special cold-weather garment with attached fur-lined hood, originally used by the natives of Greenland, who wore it with their mukluks, and which had first been noticed by Europeans in 1924. It was, he said, called an anoraq, sometimes spelled instead with a k, which is the eleventh letter of the alphabet. In consequence whereof, taken with the size of the office which takes fully several hours to tour and explain, the following account has been necessarily abbreviated. In other words, I've shortened it. A lot.

"First, catch your prayer. Just my little joke, that. You can see where they come in."

Luther looked. There was, in effect, a working museum of listening devices: ear-trumpets, stone circles, semaphore signallers, ticker-tape machines, Bakelite wire-less receivers from the days of 'listening in', through to mobile phones, and thence to unreversed baseball caps with attached ear-pieces. These were plainly as far as progress could go, and accordingly were quite popular. Each instrument, whatever its type, was staffed by a listener, stylus in hand, and with a pile of papyrus scraps within easy reach. Every so often a listener would scribble something down.

"Between them the listeners systematically scan all of space and time, and whenever they pick up an incoming message they jot it down quickly in shorthand and put it into an In-Tray.", explained the Registrar. "When the Tray is filled, a messenger collects a batch together and takes them over to the Scriptorium. Scriptorium Alpha, that is. We have several Scriptoria, each with its own task, of course.

"The slips are separated by a clerk, who then attaches to each a blank prayer application form, PAF1, and fills it out properly in long-hand, adding all the necessary background information. The Scriptorium Supervisor looks the form over for mistakes, and when she is, eventually, satisfied it needs no further amendments by the clerk to achieve a state of correctness, she puts in the Out-Tray ready for the messenger-on-duty.

"Then the messenger-on-duty takes the form into the General Archives, which are next door and join this office to the Office of the Recording Angels. We have to work very closely with the Recording Angels. If someone does something that earns negative points, and we give them forgiveness, it would render their total, that is their total according to the Recording Angels, erroneous, which would not be desirable. So each office is scrupulous about record-keeping. That's why they are arranged as they are, you see, in parallel, so we can share one common set of records.

"In the General Archives, therefore, the messenger-on-duty requests the person's ledger, which is booked out to him, once it is available, and carefully tucks the form inside.

"Once the completed application section of the form is therefore matched up with the person's ledger, the messenger-on-duty brings it to my section of the office for initial processing.

"A quite extraordinarily large percentage of prayers don't require any actual decision or response, so we weed them out. Obviously praise and thanksgivings and blessings are very nice to get, but we can't actually do anything with them once they've arrived, except make a note of them in the person's ledger, and not always that if they aren't going to make any difference to the person's final score.

"Then there are the prayers for world peace and understanding, and wise politicians, and goodwill amongst all men. They're all down to the human race and free-will, and we've already sent out the rules and all the grace anyone can ever use, so there is nothing we can do - other than use them for quiet amusement, naturally. Each scores ten points for the intention, if it's genuine, and minus ten for stupidity, whether the intention is genuine or not."

"Excuse me interrupting," said Luther, who wasn't sure just how serious the Registrar was being, "but doesn't that mean that you can never gain any points by making those prayers, but you can sometimes lose points?"

"Shush.", said the Registrar, who was attempting to giggle. "We don't usually let people know that one; for some reason they don't like it. But stupidity is stupidity is sinful, so points do have to be deducted. It's a major reason why bishops should be most careful: there are some of them with huge minus scores from nothing else.

"Quite similar are all the prayers people have been instructed to pray, where you can earn five points for obedience if you really are, but do earn minus five for not exercising full and free judgement. So don't be religious unless you're really going to pray. That way, it might make you a better person, and that would get you a net gain in points, probably. But otherwise it's not a helpful activity.

"And," he continued, "there are the prayers we can't do anything about even if we want to, such as when you ask for a friend to pass their driving test and they've already crashed the gears five times. So all of these forms go straight to the Scriptorium to be copied into the personal ledger, and scored, and then the form goes for recycling.

"What is left, therefore, quite obviously, is the material that needs a reply. So for each of those we need to open a decision form, PAF2, and tag it to the PAF1, ready for the decision processing integrity team.

"What that means is that it gets sent on to the saint responsible for the relevant category of prayer. So you can see how important my section is."

"Indeed.", said Luther. The Registrar always liked to get a straightforward agreement from an interested listener. So he smiled. Even perhaps apparently.

"So then, as I say, I send the joined forms, together with the relevant ledger, on to the pertinent patron Saint. Such as Anthony for lost things, and Jude for lost causes, who are the best-known two. The busy ones, like them, delegate most of the work to one of their under-Saints; as you can see, Anthony has about two hundred desks facing his.

"On the other hand, we do have some section heads who don't get called on too often, like Saint Kentigern who is Patron Saint of Salmon, the fish, yes, though obviously not the fishing because of potential conflict of interest. Regrettably these saints do therefore tend to put their feet up and read improving literature.

"Now actually, Saint Kentigern has officially got Glasgow to look after as well, but after he said it was giving him headaches, and just stopped doing it, he was given a deputy and a small army of underlings to take on that job. I'm not sure how a saint can get a headache in the afterlife, but since he is a saint one can not possibly doubt his word." Luther refrained from asking if the Registrar had ever been to Glasgow in the bad times.

"Added to them, there are others who get work referred to them, but can't actually do anything with it. Austregildus over there, Good century to you!, all well? excellent!, is an example; he has lawsuits to look after. If he ever did intervene it would be either to make an unjust trial just, which he can't do because of free-will and needing to preserve judicial independence, or else to make a just trial unjust, which we're not exactly likely to do, are we, ha ha, which rather makes him a little short of options. So he just has to file all his cases, and he spends his days helping out on other desks, when he's feeling so inclined. He can't really go on vacation, because it has been designated as his position, so he has to be here, since we can't not keep an eye on justice, even if we can't do anything about it, which we can't, but there you are.

"Now, while that does take care of most things, since we're not short of Saints, Patron or otherwise, there are a fair few things that haven't got a Saint assigned to them, or else that have but the Saint's required for other work, like Saint Peter or someone, and needs a permanent arrangement. So all of this work comes to Saint Whomever, who is the Patron Saint of everything else. Miscellanea, if you will.

"Saint Whomever is the nicest and most unflappable of all the Saints there have ever been - that's how he got the job. You see, if it hasn't been assigned to a set saint, then it, whatever it is, is likely to be quite tricky, and need careful thought. So there's not much he can delegate. So he just has a couple of Under-Saints and a lot of Researchers. But he has never failed us yet and never will. Although everyone in the Great Corridor enjoys their work - because, as you know, they're either an Angel or a Saint - Saint Whomever has been given more job satisfaction than anyone else, in recognition of the fact that he is the busiest sentient life-form in the Universe. And as you know, if you want something done quickly and well, it's best to give it to a busy person. So we do.

"Now, whoever the form ends up with, it has to be gone through with great care, to make sure no detail has been missed, and all the implications are clear. And whenever they need, the designated

Saint can check a Precedent Book - you can see each one can bring it up on screen when needed - to see what was done in the past or will be done in the future. Then they decide whether the prayer is allowed or not."

Luther interrupted; "You have IT?", he asked.

"Of course we have IT.", came the answer. "How could we not? We are IT. We are the Information and we are the Technology. Without us there is no information to process. Anywhere. But, of course, we have got to keep busy through eternity somehow, and we're not allowed bugs. Our source code never needs fixes."

"So you deliberately slow it down as far as it can be.", said Luther, trying to look as if he had only just worked this out.

"Certainly not!", came the riposte. "That would be self-deceit, which we're not allowed either. But we are allowed, that is, required, to ensure perfection. Whosoever writes, necessarily perfects. Since we exist, existence is self-writing."

Luther decided not to go for the killer argument. It wasn't really the place for it, somehow.

You'll be noting from the Registrar's words, child, that that's why prayers need answering.

The Registrar took up his account. "If there's nothing in the Precedent Book, the Saint usually sends it to a Precedent Committee, particularly if he or she chairs the Committee, which argues all the pros and cons through, and after a millennium or so usually reaches a recommended judgement, and lets the Saint know the outcome.

"If the Precedent Committee gets deadlocked or wants advice, it can refer to a Consulting Seraph, who can, well, you know..., which rather settles matters promptly, so the Consulting Seraphim don't get referred to very often. Committees do like to have their allotted amount of talking fully used up.

"Eventually, one way or another, the relevant Saint makes his decision, records it in the proper space on the form, puts a note in the Precedent book if needed, signs it all off, and tucks the form back into the individual record book. Then another messenger takes the file over to the Scriptoria. Scriptorium Beta, actually.

"In Scriptorium Beta the scribe enters the decision in the individual's record book and passes it back for filing, and then the signed-off form is taken, by a third messenger, to Scriptorium Gamma to be illuminated as Letters Patent. Those get signed by the Virtue who is in charge of the Office; it gives him something to do.

"Then when we've got the decision made, and all the records brought up to date, and the precedents noted and the document has been finally drafted and illuminated, it's published for twenty-one days in case a member of the public wants to object."

"Where, exactly?"

"We have a notice board at the end of the corridor, where anyone can read it."

"And how are they going to do that, if they don't know it's there?"

"Precisely. So when there have been no objections, we transmit the result back to the petitioner - that's those chaps over there with the microphones and parabolic reflectors, and the document goes for recycling, unless anyone wants it for sentimental value or something, which they don't.

"This is one that's just ready for the shredder."

It looked finer than the *Tres Riche Heures*, but as the Registrar pointed out, in the sublime realms, the sublime is just the ordinary.

Luther read.

TO ALL AND SUNDRY,

of what kynde, degree or species soever these letters seeing,

The Vyrtue of prayer sendeth all due and humble greeting.

WHEREAS the soul benamed

JOHN SMITH

an human in form, sapient in appearance and lawfully bearing the Eternal Security Number 5256786666nkz 567123qpa59, being at all relevant times located in the region known as y'Erthe, by petycion bearing the date, time and epoch below-written or thereabouts

Dyddest Represent with zeal, much urgency and great emphasis unto the most blessed Saint Anthony, named of Padua, these dyvers facts, in the said soule's knowledge and immediate awareness and seeming consciousness, followyng,

That Is To Say:~~~

ITEM, that he had lost his damned glasses (otherwyse properly in th'Englyshe language of those tymes called spectacles),

ITEM, that he could not see a thing without them, and ITEM, that his lyfe would not be worth lyving if he had not found the dratted things by the time his wyfe, Gawd bless her, got home from doing the shopping and syche-lyke, on account of how she would say he was going doolally, which he was not in his opinyon, and surely after fourty-fyue years of devoated marriage he was entitled to his own opynion every once in a while;

AND by great numbers of prayers with fervent and frequent imprecacyons, pious ejaculacyons, ardent entreaties and great wailings together with much penitence and many self-accusacyons for his countless admitted mental failings (they beeing cheefly those previously alleged and encouraged by his said most uxorious partner and help-mete)

Dyd Then And There entreat that most blessed Sayncte Anthony that by all means the said objects, namely to whit the glasses (otherwyse properly called spectacles in &etc), might be found,

And Whereas the blessed Saint did look favourably upon the said soule, well-knowyng how many and fowle are the terryble payns of purgacion already awaityng the said piteous soule, of th'whyche things we are to say nothing,

Know Ye Therefore, by the tenor of these presents that out of his especyal grace and auctorytie, dewly commytted unto hym, and by hys certayn knowledge and mere motion the blessed Saynt diddest wondrously and swyftly procure,

Convey and transmit threw the aether such an measure of efficacious grace as he had in hys partycular mercy determined

To Have And To Holde unto hym the said Soule with quyet use and enjoyment

To Th'effect whereby and whereat immedyately the said humble soule afore-numbered 525678666nkz 567123qpa59, called &etc, dyddest hym with greate amazement find the aforesaid missing objects, namely to whit &etc, exactly where he haddest left them, being amydst yesterday's racing pages whych were on top of the telly so they were, **AND THAT** in pious thanksgiving for so marvellous an act the sayd soule dyddest with much feeling audibly utter the words "O thank God, there they are! I'm saved.";

And Know Ye Further That all the foregoing has been dewly recorded in the dyvers Bookes and reccordes thereyn for it proper to be wrytten;

In Testimony Whereof WE the Vyrtue afore-specyfied have caused to be affixed hereunto Our seale whyche We do use in this case and have subscribed that One of Oure many Names whych We do deign to use in a matter of thys grate, whych is to saye not muche, ymport, thys eleventh hour of the forenoon in the thirtyfivethousandeighthundredandseventyfirst year of the fourth Epoch of the Aeons and of Our turne of duty the third, being but a Century untyl Our coffee-break.

(sygned) *THE VYRTUE OF PRAYER*

Gyven in Ower House and Office of Workes in the
Great Corrydor
At the Axis of AllThings.

Luther handed it back, and watched the manuscript being turned into shreds. Sic transit.

"Most impressive.", he said. "But if there is omniscience, why the bureaucracy? Surely it could all be done in the twinkling of an eye."

"That", said the Registrar, now rapidly changing his opinion of his guest, "is the sort of defeatist attitude that would result in mass unemployment, and the diminution of good honest toil. Good morning to you, Sir!"

As the Registrar walked off in a state of much-enjoyed high dudgeon, Domination let Luther in on a secret. "He's not actually a saint. He's here as a first punishment. After he has spent all of created time feeling blessed at being allowed to shuffle paper, we shall give him something which makes the truth literally and painfully obvious."

Luther began to approve of the logic that operated in these regions.

Coming from OfPray, Luther spotted a door different from all the others. It was stainless-steel, for starters. Behind it, Dominion explained, dwells Saint Muros, yclept the Pharmakopygous, and so far the most wondrous of saints that his name has been expunged from history. Hitherto.

Muros ought to have been a hermit's hermit. Yet more than somehow he was not. Sinful it might be, but the other hermits for tens of leagues about were united in hatred of him. Some expressed it in simple dismissiveness, "I suppose he does count as a hermit."; others denied any knowledge of him, though the tension of their jaw muscles told otherwise; a few went so far as to accuse of him of desiring to be a saint, therefore famous, therefore not unworldly, therefore not a hermit; but most used hints and ellipses to make it quite plain that he was unsound.

Of all this, Muros was, literally beatifically, unaware. Being by disposition both retiring and ardent, serious and ruthless, once he conceived his vocation to dwell in the desert, he knew no other way than to do it whole-heartedly. At Lent, the forty days of the Western Church was to him just effete backsliding. The seventy days of an Orthodox Lent might suffice, but surely a serious hermit would want to fast just so soon as Epiphany was done? At Advent, he began at the autumnal equinox: was it not a symbol that the sun's power could fade from the world? Even in the most festal of weeks, Wednesdays, Fridays and Saturdays were still for fasting.

The greatest feasts saw him have only one meal, as on every other day, of vegetables, but the festivals were still indeed marked, for holy Church requires celebration on those days. He allowed himself an extra mouthful of water above his standard cupful.

His Office? It was to say each day the whole Psalter, all 150 songs of it, from memory, while balanced on one leg, followed by one full book from the Old Testament and one from the New. This all being done, he was then free to begin his more serious prayers and mortifications.

Never did he sit down, much less lie down. At night, he roped himself to a stake for a single hour of sleep. That stake, a cupboard and a table were all his furnishings.

Since meat might not pass his lips, certainly neither might skin or fur touch his flesh. All woven cloth was vanity, so knotted reeds provided the covering for his hateful, cozening body. It went without saying that washing was wicked, weak self-indulgence.

He might not, so he reckoned, have as much luxury as would be provided by living in an actual cave; hourly he did penance for his inadequacy in needing so much shelter as was provided by a hollow half-way up the sheerest cliff-face he could find in that mesa-lined wilderness. Of course, as he passed from novice to journeyman hermit, he exchanged his sybaritic rope-ladder for a solitary rope (more knotted reeds), and often accused himself of indulgence in having so useful an aid. Must it not be holier just to climb the cliff? His failure to locate either hand-holds or any other route of ascent, he had, after much scarification, therefore taken as a sign of some grant of great favour to him, and this had quieted his conscience, though never by so much as for him to suppose that heaven might even find him passably good.

In those parts, all this should have gained him admiration. So it would, were it not for his choice of diet.

The seed of that one of the Phaseoleae that is p. vulgaris - otherwise known as the kidney bean - was the only solid that ever entered his stomach. Having, before his call, studied both maths and nutrition at uni (as his sort called it), he could carefully assess the exact amount required for a successful hermitic lifestyle.

This came out at exactly 1lb 7.31oz of raw beans per diem (a quantity objectionable in itself, let the reader understand). Add a quarter-pint of oil (extra-virgin, since the theological consequences of any other type are too wicked even to think about) and the juices of a dozen thoroughly crushed whole heads of garlic (n.b. heads, not cloves), and you can, in fact, survive indefinitely on it. It isn't even necessary to add coriander or balsamic vinegar. (Be it noted, however, that on fasting days the oil was wholly replaced by a pint of vinegar - malt, since you enquire - which since it contains water rendered drinking unnecessary - to which was added twice as much garlic juice.)

It is said, and perhaps even scientifically reported, anecdotally one presumes, of the guts of those who eat food which actually does amount to a whole hill of beans that in time they do adjust, and a certain, let us say effusive, consequence diminishes and then in (even more) time disappears.

In him, it had not.

For whatever cause, his guts not only did not adjust, they misadjusted, maladjusted and counter-adjusted. The aforesaid consequence had become worse, and progressively more worse. (If you think "more worse" to be bad English, do please accept that those were bad guts.) The first few years were of no consequence to his neighbours, given the distance at which even the nearest of them dwelt, and those who came to avail themselves of spiritual advice (the provision of which, despite an obvious and sometimes worrying lack of quality control, is part of the eremite's job description) simply learned to stand upwind, and not to seek counsel in the absence of at least a stiff breeze. But that was just standard when consulting a seriously holy man.

As the early decades of his discipline advanced, so did the rate, quantity and toxicity of his emanations, and therefore the required distance for dispersal. Accordingly, there came a day when, if the other hermits throughout the region were heard to cry loudly and in unison "O my blessed Lord", it was not from some shared act of piety.

There are mortifications and there are mortifications. There are consequences and there are consequences. It cannot therefore be said that the brethren were themselves entirely ignorant or innocent of the distressing phenomenon. Desert-based diets are part of what the seriously holy must face, and which the devil uses as opportunities for distraction. Yet ever before, it had been a predominantly solitary matter to be learned to be overlooked. It had not spread often, and never far enough to interfere with one's neighbour, who in that state of life one does love, as much as, if not always more than, one's self. This was novelty of degree unforeseen and unforeseeable. One of the number, indeed, who from a diet purely of berries had a particular, similar but localised problem, had cause to complain that he was utterly unable to get the right rhythm going when whipping and beating himself, so consumed was he by involuntary retchings.

It is, of course, entirely true that men given to holiness are never given to gossip, and utterly that they never, never say a bad word about another of the same, in this case lack of, cloth; yet it is also true that when they meet formally in synod, council or convocation they are not only allowed, but positively encouraged, to condemn and anathematise those of their colleagues who have been unwise enough to become judgeable as heretics. So, a synod general it had to be. And was.

It was at this synod that Muros, who had abandoned any name along with all his other possessions on fleeing from the world, was first called by that name. "Muros" - "the perfumed one" - by itself would have been as charitable a name as any men in their predicament could be expected to find. Yet, as the Synod, over which the autonominative miasma still continually lay, passed hours in conversation, it was resolved to add to Muros an additional, sobriquetical, descriptor. From thenceforth, he was Muros the Pharmakopygous. Work it out for yourself.

Eventually, it was resolved the youngest and fittest of the company be sent to suggest to Muros, not that he should change his diet - God forbid such a thing! - but that his example was great, and would be greater were it not for his habit of indulging himself on so rich and nutritious a bean. Might there not be less savoury ones he might use? By means of stuffing his nostrils with sand, the delegated one, almost a lamb to the slaughter it was admitted, managed to achieve his task.

It was music to Muros' ears. How could any hermit have resisted the siren-call that his peers had constructed? Praise for his asceticism, yet tempered with rebuke for indulgence, and suggestion of greater deprivation had all been confected together as a pill for his delectation. So swallow it he did.

The haricot was too grand. Muros accepted the knowledge with joy. He was being blessed, that is to say punished, by the blessed.

On returning to the Synod with the news that Muros had responded so well, the messenger was, on this occasion, rewarded. It was unanimously agreed that on Christmas Day next he might sit on, yes, a cushion for a whole hour. It was an excessive reward, but these were desperate men.

Alas, alas. They had not even guessed how flawed was their plan. Having spent many years seeking to get rid of all traces of their personalities and characters, in their very desperation they had forgotten that it is never possible totally to undo who we are.

For Muros had ruminated upon the news, and decided that if the haricot were too luxurious, then some other bean must be less so. As a nutritionist, how could he abandon the bean family which had served him so well? The haricot gave way to the mung.

The guts of Muros, those ultimate authors of this tale, did not like the change. They rebelled. This time even Muros had an inkling that all was not as minimally right as it should be.

The mung gave way to the lima. The guts gave out more rebellion.

In turn, there were used the moth and the azuki, the arad and the tepary, the jack bean and the sword bean, the soy, hyacinth, velvet, winged, Kersting's, pinto, red, black, pink and yellow beans, beans broad and beans string, and, if there be any other, they too were employed. Every one had but a single effect: the effusions worsened. By now, Muros had come to see the worsening as a grace. Week by week his bodily malfunctions were growing, and therefore his spirit must have been improved in inverse proportion.

Finally, he discovered the lupin. In an angelic vision (*anglice*: hallucination) he saw a great bunch of them being lowered to him out of heaven. Such a grace commands acceptance, and from that hour, the fruit of the lupin displaced all other legumes. He could not but rejoice at the impact on his digestive tract.

Meanwhile, his peers progressed from scheming to complaining, thence to greater grumbling, from whence to penance, prayer and plotting, otherwise known as serious scheming. This progress was interrupted, of course, by the periods they spent lying on the ground, groaning and involuntarily emptying their own guts. Birds were seen to drop from the sky, stone dead; the region became free of hyenas; camels' expressions showed they knew they'd been upstaged; clouds and dew both were reluctant to form, and lizards wished their blood would freeze.

It is most unlikely that a body of holy, humble hermits would combine to form a homicidal hunt and wholly imperil their heavenly hopes, so the aspiring and generous monks of later times have always believed that the end of Muros was intestinal suicide, by auto-eruption and not, as legend insisted, a *pre-mortem* or *vivipsy*. It is recorded in the chronicles of that desert, albeit written at least a century afterwards - but some memories are never lost from folk - that those who found his remains were struck dumb and only could explain what they found by gesticulating wildly. Sceptical scholars have interpreted this as some form of hysterical fit. Only geologists have provided one certain fact, from otherwise inexplicable layers of fossils covered with muddy sediment, which is that some mass extinction was followed by prolonged rain in the very year tradition ascribes to the celebrated death of that holiest of men.

Which, actually, is just where the real trouble started.

Child, I have brought you up properly, with creed and catechism and the usual lessons all well learned; the alphabet used; you ought to know the proper fate of bodies. Once they die. They are changed. The corruptible flees. Innocence is used instead for ever. As I have raised you up so you are made mine, or so many think of those good men with whom the care of children is by birth well placed, for customary, common wants take form within their minds, to shape, caress and hold their pretty charges deep within for life. What good parent has not groomed their child's hair? But, child, I only do the things you need to make you know the rules we say are good.

Anyway, you see, when you die you get a new heavenly body, and it's perfect. Not necessarily the perfect body as such, but perfect for you: one you'll be delighted with, I promise. At least if you do get to go to all the right places. Then you can relax about being one of the beautiful people.

What with the state of the world being wicked as it is, and people letting themselves go something rotten, or being let gone, the process of change had to be automated long ago. From the start, really. Best management practices just anywhere they use, obviously. So when Muros arrived, with his guts so attuned the way they were, he comes out with them having been perfected in that particular, and now he is absolutely toxic. It was the angels collapsing round him as they prepared to take him to his rest that first indicated what had happened. Being where all this takes place, and all, there's no question of anything gone wrong, plainly, but all agreed it certainly was a different kind of ideal flesh. They put the whole reception zone into total white-alert lock-down, and sent in the special stem: angels with purpose-made (well, even more purpose-made, since you ask) non-breathing apparatus to detain him in a sealed chamber, while the afflicted (*recte*: dead) angels were resuscitated, all on a need-to-know basis.

Now, whatever happens in the heavenly realms is for the best, so they, the duty angels that is, had a conference about how to realise this. And you do have to admire, at least I think you do, the audacity and elegance of the solution.

When the herald-angels explained things to Muros, and outlined the strategy for making him a positive role-model, he was, supernaturally, as you would be, just a bit disappointed that he wouldn't share the glory of the other saints. But as it sank in, the extra-special task they'd got for him, he realised that everything, all of it, the being hated and the rest, had been totally worth-while. It would be a service to everyone past, present and future to express himself with ultimate pungency.

It did niggle that he had to wear a really nice set of white robes for the nonce, but it was all in a good cause, so must be endured. Since it was such a good cause, he even volunteered to do all the preparations himself, which was genuinely appreciated. He is, indeed, the only sentient being anywhere who ever has had unmitigated pleasure all the way through the joyous chore of writing out a very large batch of invitations.

It was for a tea-party.

Invites such as these are the sort that are too important even for the middle classes to display on the mantelpiece. You only want people to hear about it afterwards, when you can just gently drop it into the conversation that you were there, all right. It makes the neighbours that jealous it does. Every single one, therefore, was swiftly accepted.

Why the devil all the fallen angels thought this party had been put on for them is not recorded, but arrive they all did, dressed in their weekday best, and made polite conversation. Then, when they were all there, and for once everyone was prompt, and Muros knew the doors had been sealed, he started pouring cups of Earl Grey out of not-bone china, and passing round plates of cucumber sandwiches with the rinds cut off and shaped into neat triangles. Equilateral, in case you were even thinking of asking.

The effort for Muros of keeping perfect composure was immense, but for such a cause he'd suffer anything, and he made sure that the whole roomful of guests had all got some sandwiches before he essayed one himself. Cucumber, they were.

The impact of that substance, vegetable though it is alleged to be, even with all the rind gone and tempered by the finest butter, on innards that had been tempered by a life-time of beans and then been transfigured accordingly, Muros himself confessed afterwards, he had been dreading. But a Saint's gotta do what a Saint's gotta do.

He did.

One can expect no less of a well-run event than that the host considers the guests' likely reactions to all eventualities. That the guests would collapse, aetherially asphyxiate and die swiftly had therefore been accurately predicted. That the superflatus, when it came into contact with these rebellious souls, would cause their utter and instant disintegration into non-existence had not. But as a stray Buddhist later explained, he had revealed what they had all ever aspired to, for non-being can be reached through corruption as well as any other path. It had been a second invitation there was no refusing.

Hardier ones - thicker horns and hooves perhaps - made it through the cucumber, and were simply told that some had had to leave early. A good tea-party, howbeit, passes on to better things. The scones with here-made jam and clotted cream were too, I do apologise for saying it, heavenly to resist. Muros followed them up with slices from a fruit-cake so rich that the sultanas and raisins clung to each other for comfort.

You know how, at good parties, initial tension is followed by pleasant relaxation. Muros relaxed more than he had ever done, and of the devil and all his works nothing remained to need renouncing. You do know too, though, that now you've heard this tale, if you want one of your parties to go with a bang ever again, you have quite a standard to reach.

Muros the Pharmakopygous knows he has no further tasks to perform. He knows full well that if he were ever released all life would cease. Yet Muros is perfectly happy to spend all eternity alone in a sealed room. It's his idea of heaven. He has the assurance: he was right to become a hermit.

I would say, child, that it just goes to show that it takes all sorts, etc., but I'm not that crass. I have been strictly instructed, however, to point out how all things can look planned to end well.

CHAPTER 12

With your body between your knees
William Cory
Eton Boating song

Death, O my child, is nothing to sever the unsevered. Death is all nothing. You can make in this world a relationship, a union that will endure longer than the cosmos. Choose it together, this minute, and it is formed; be tender faithful to its needs and never shall it fail. For I tell you not the gates of heaven, nor no squadrons of cherubim, not the old sky-father himself have power to prevail over it.

And the miracle, the unbelievable true creed, is that such a bond is offered to you just once in this life. And then but more. For and if you refuse its first coming, there will be some unbidden day a second calling. And if you will feign deaf to that, because that it will disturb what you have formed out of yourself into yourself, still it will return. It will call you to the repenting, demand you be dismembered by love and flayed by affection and rebuilt by acceptance into a being alien. It always must. But say Yes, and it is yours for ever. And so it is all one in asking. One bidding.

Only by the making of that day of wrath, the one of your killing of your soul, does it know never to try more.

For them that have killed their soul, hell is God's only sure, only feasible, mercy, the one only way he can show he still loves them. For all of the ages, he forces them to hate him; he will not have a single dead soul. Sure he keeps all things in life.

People, those, talk of the problem of evil. There's no such thing not nowhere. There is just sin. And sin had to be given in order that you be created.

And again, "The old forget." Not so. It is the young who lose not having done or learned, and, being taught, let pass the content thought not worth attending. The old, they value memory as finery more gorgeous than gold, for all their tales, that's where there's only now a place to hold their jewels: they can talk them still into worth.

And therefore wise and old while the change is still before is that rare juvenile, who, but for care take you sure only, befriends these treasurers, who will love to love to give away all within the storeroom, until you'd certain be weighed down beyond the bearing of, child. But come you back, still, for now the pricest gems are in inconsequential boxes, overlooked and hence only lately to be found. Even the oldest, fondest fool has junk in plenty that's worth the sifting. With judgement stiff, stiff as first its making a half-century since, can there lie still some sense, observed custom and things you'd not had else for twenty years to come; for even these lonely, loathsome leeches have been where you must go, although no inkling of where is in your handsome pretty wits.

Beware just one lesson, which has nothing but self-failing. When old ones hurry ever they'll choose the hound that pants the most, and likes enough their petting, but'll count too spare the time to examine frame or joints or teeth, the sharpened teeth. Too dim of eye to watch the race, or see where are the hidden goods and costs, they can only totter quick as can. When such a pet shall lick 'em, pray God to help the world.

And eschew, beshrew one other. If they see a leech, they'll bleed, and not them. Shed blood. They've done it beforetimes, remember.

Bleeding, floating, or perhaps better, bob-bob-bobbing, from somewhere down the corridor came a set of sounds of what was not not music; a sour music. Luther decided to go and listen, for maybe sweet harmony was not the only rule of this axis.

Domination caught him up outside the door, and put his hand on the door, making it thus clear that opening was not going to be.

The sound, now loud and more untuneful, was so obvious that it could not go unmarked. Like when you're on the train and it's late and the announcement comes, "Friendly Great South Matron Mega-Trains regret the late arrival of this disservice into your final destination station stop.... this was due to... a delay.", and the least you can do is share a look of disgusted disdain with whoever is near to.

"It's the band. They're practising for the Last Trumpet."

"I hope they're not taking the stage too soon."

"Not until. Anyway, they've only got to get through one performance, and once people realise what it is, they won't be listening. The most contemporary music ever.

"But rules is rules, and it has to be as perfect as can be, giving as how it is the dissolution of all things.

"I did warn them that letting composers and big name conductors and virtuosi in was not the way. The military band from one of the more forgotten losing regiments would sound much more disciplined. But no, they would go for 'New Harmony'. I mean, Beethoven's deaf (we decided after the ninth never to cure him for fear of what might follow), so he doesn't do much for ensemble; Mozart insisted we recruit The Queen of the Night for an obbligato; Haydn keeps walking out; Wagner won't take direction from anyone but Cosima, but she's not included; Bruckner won't use Italian while Verdi recognises nothing else; Handel and Bach both say they've done it already, but can't agree what. Then you've got Dufay and Palestrina on horns, Berg and Stockhausen on trombones, and Berlioz on twelve separate trumpets all played by himself, so try getting them in tune. Not easy when Toscanini and Beecham are joint conductors. Then Josquin keeps getting attacks of the hockets. If a decent sound came from that, even I'd believe the age of miracles was not over. As for a certain person who will insist on playing the Devil's Trill on the bass tuba, it doesn't go down well hereabouts.

"Mind you, of course, we did foresee it and we'll be using plan B. Official plan B, that is; it was always Angelic plan alpha."

Luther didn't bother asking for elucidation; it would come anyway.

"There's a synthesiser and a hundred thousand amplifiers programmed ready in the room next door. This crew have no chance once we switch that mother on."

In another part of the corridor, Someone Else was not in a harmonious frame of mind. He was psyching Himself up for a certain guest. He'd tried reading one of the Revelations, which brought back fond memories of holding the saint's trembling hand and making him form the Greek letters one by one. All of the Revelations were true in every detail; every word was utterly inspired. He knew. He'd done the inspiring.

All of the texts were like that, of course. Equally of course, to understand any of it you had to have the key, which deliberately had not been made a substance included in the outline. It was all too obvious why. It was a nice consequence: whoever thought they understood the message, didn't.

Somehow that led to other fond reminiscences. Proverbs had been nice. There were still some of the unused ones that were worth thinking about. 'A wise man does not teach a crocodile to swim, but the unwise trains them to wrestle.' 'Be the river broad or narrow, the pike can know the whole width of it.' 'It is good to know that the tiger and the puma are different, but only from a distance.' 'If there is dust under your feet, surely all of you is founded on dust.'

Happy days. But this doesn't get things prepared. One must remember inexorable Will.

Domination had not forgotten his agenda either.

"Now if you don't mind, I'll show you what an efficient organisation can be like. It's time you were shown the crypts. Where we keep the punishments. Perfectly performed. True punishment. Our reason for being here. It is done well. Very well.

"I, sadly, cannot go with you into those regions;", said Domination; "angels are incapable of what must be inflicted there: we are allowed but a few preparatory tricks and japes."

"So all the things Julius and the others went through meant what exactly?"

"Just the seasoning to the main course. The condemned think that that is their punishment. Until the day comes for them to be served to those who will eat them with a full stomacher of justice. It adds to their pains to know that nothing we have done to them signifies. After all, we must mirror their deeds, must we not? They piled evil on evil, so we put good on goodness." To which Domination added just a hint of a *soupçon* of smirk. "A most gracious lady awaits to escort you on your visit to the depths."

He opened the door, as before. But this one revealed behind it the sliding doors of a lift shaft. They in turn parted, and in the midst of a perfect Victorian parlour, stuffed with gewgaws enough for a Queen-Empress, all done out in maroon brocades and silks, stood a lady. Her full-skirted and crinolined dress of black bombazine (what else should it be?) was coupled with an apron of white that no alp ever sported, which had lace that was knotted better than the Celts ever imagined. Her forearms were sheathed in twenty-four button white silk gloves, while on her head was the bonnet of authority and veil of majesty that Victoria had aimed at for so many years but never quite achieved. Here was propriety; here stood dignity, here manners strove only to conceal manners. Here was charm for charm. Yet, Luther thought, there was a little too much of ease with oneself, a certain self-satisfaction which no gentlewoman, as distinguished from Lady, ever had had.

She half-curtsied; Domination bowed; and he effected the introductions.

"Holy Jemima, may I beg to present to you our guest, Luther of that name.?"

"Right worthy Luther, this is the Blessed Dame Jemima, Guardian Keeper of the Crypts."

"Rightly pleased to meet y'all.", crooned Jemima, making five and a bit words express all that any male needed to know of her. "I shall be mightily pleased to make your acquaintance and show you our humble little place.

"Surely, yous and I's gonna be right good friends. Weren't no cats in any house where I've ever been, mind you, tho' p'raps we done fill us a kitty or two".

Before Luther could respond to this with the loathing it deserved, she scratched him gently on the back of his head. It had, it must be admitted, been some time since anyone had done him this courteous service, so perchance he were predisposed, but it did feel rather good. A pleasant tingling spread itself delicately down the whole length of his spine and caused, had he wit enough left to notice, his tail slowly to stand up straight, very strait. So could he hear anything but the rushing of his blood, he might have perceived himself crooning just how delighted he would be to have her as his escort in these realms. With which Dominion took no delay in making an exit; Jemima pressed a button on the wall, and the lift descended.

Luther was ushered into another parlour, of similar decoration, but equipped with a ring of *chaises longues*, on one of which she carefully disposed herself. The other inhabitants of the parlour, all male, had stood as she arrived and waited for her to invite Luther to recline himself on the neighbouring *chaise*, before filling up the circle. All bar two, that is, who, though like all their peers in being of a build and attire which can only properly be denominated as butch, had been especially nominated to act as a pair of combined book-ends and minders. One handed Jemima a long, narrow hand-rolled simulacrum of a cigarette and lit it for her with a spill that the other had ignited with an onyx lighter. She took a long draw, held the smoke in her lungs for long seconds, and gently exhaling, gave it to be taken round the circle, before speaking.

"Praise and bless the Blessedworthy One for all the gifts of creation. Misser Luther, will you share with us in making use of these finestkind herbs of the field that are given for our refreshment? Yous'll unnerstand that the tasks we be assigned to is making a little relaxing a mighty needful thing."

Luther conveyed that indeed he understood her quite altogether perfectly, but hoped she would deign to excuse his not partaking, for he found her presence itself was of necessity more relaxing than he could by words fitly express.

"Now that's the words of a fine, a mighty fine gen'l'man. We'll jest a rest here until the courts send us down the next of the labours it is our priv'lege to unnertake."

Which as it beautifully transpired, was exactly long enough for them to finish their smoke and appreciate it, but not so long that they might have considered the need for another.

In a cone of light there materialised a man, who just had time to blink at finding himself unexpectedly in that light and dressed in white robes, before he was grabbed and literally jumped on by two of the Saints. One was wearing a pair of trunks and a pair of boots, while the other had substituted tights for the trunks.

"They were in the rasslin' business," explained Jemima, "and they knows 'zact hows to make this ree-all fun. Afore they was them-there bawdy-boulders, but they done see the glowering and glaury of the laud'num, and was converted, and did become lay-purreachers to eevandalise meny, and is now f'reverend ever jest 'rasslin, as how that done got them to these parts. Ree-all fun it is an' awll."

Luther thought that their subject didn't seem to find it quite so, as they tore the white robes off.

"We lets the subjeck wear the robes and see the light for a little moment, to make 'em figure maybe there's been sum mistake, and p'raps they's not been condemned. And then they finds different."

Given that the man was face down with one wrestler having hold of his legs, while the other pinioned his arms behind his back, forcing his spine rearwards, Luther thought that was quite probably so.

The man was spared more fun when, by another of the Saints surreptitiously emptying the contents of a syringe into the neck, he became limply unconscious. At which the two wrestlers picked the man up as if he weighed next to nothing, and unceremoniously dumped him on a stainless steel table, though they did then lay him out quite neatly on it, with his neck on a little block that was intended for it, and no part of him reaching into the gutter that ran all round the edge of the table, before they turned to the others and took a bow and a round of applause.

A group of Saints in green wrap-around robes and aprons stepped up to the table, and each adjusted the light beam, conveniently located a few inches above the head, so as to provide optimal working conditions.

Jemima took up her commentary. "Now we gets to prepare the subjeck for his little spell of perdition. Firsts, as yous can see, the celestial blood, that is there for thems as is going to the temperate zones of happiness, is all drained right out of him, and 'stead he gets filled with that there ichor, on account of how it don't freeze nor boil no matter what the tempratoor is, and it gets pumped right through to supply all his tissues.

"Now's yous can see how we remove his voice-box, since we can't be doing with none o' that screaming, seeing as how it gets to be right difficult to alisten to after a whiles. But since we can't alter the shape of none of creation, we puts in a art'fis'l one instead, jest without no vocal chords.

"And nows the eyes be done sewn open. And using that there microscope, we is painting tiny aluminously radiumant stars about on one of them, so's they'll twinkle all the time and drive him to distraction, e'ens he can still see. If there's anything for'm t'see, o' course.

"That's the prelim'ry stage, befores we makes it jest a little way painful for this here condemned sinner on his way to th'eternal pits, blessed be.

"Firsts of this stage, we sews into them scalp and neck muscles so's he's got a tension head ache likes you gets from staring at one o' they godless computuk screens orl day and night, looking at indecency an' the like, not that yous does, I mean, sorry Mr Cat. Only, this ache ain't gonna shift none. Not with no massages, not parcetm'l, nutting.

"Then a single grain of sand into the eye that ain't not got the stars, which sorta evens 'em up as yer might say.

"Now you can see hows they is drilling a hole right through one of his teeth into the roots. And nows hows they is filling it with some nice good puss, reel fine yeller gunk full of nasties, so's he got an abscess bigger than no dentist never knew weren't possible. And yous sees that they fills the hole right up with good mercurius carefully after so's none o' that stuff can come out never, and there's never gonna be any lettin' up on the pain of that abscess.

"Here's a nice touch, like I added mysel' when I got this preferment. All the juices of the mouth is dried out, and the saliva glands sewn up, and then we wipes orl his tung and his gums and his palate and orl rounds inside with a little pepper that we has skinned to expose its mighty goodness and power, let there be praise. Dun breed this 'un speshul; ain't no jalapeno or the like anywhere's got one thousandth, no, dang it, one ten-, one hundred-thousandth, the heat of this little baby. And he's got no cool refreshing bier or laager coming towards going down his throat no time soon, thet's fer sure.

"And now he is having some real-finestkind, cosmically-transmuted, continent'l'n'animal 'flu virus put ups into his nose, and jest rubbed in a little, to make sure it takes, like. And since there ain't no cause for anyone to have to have no immune system herebouts on account of how they is all dead already, dem simptoms is staying with, permanint.

"In the oth'nostril goes some dust and mites and sich-like, to make him sneeze; but sins they do be glued in, that sneezing ain't to none effect.

"So that's his head done with. An' if yous'll be excusing me, I's got my own little expert touch to give him now."

She walked the few steps to the table, and looked down on the specimen with that most delightful smile that earth had ever known, and lovingly stroked the torso.

"Oops-a-betsy! Oh mah, how ever could I been so clumsy! I done scratch this poor man's chest and belly all the ways down with my fine red long fingernails, what is sharp like talons, and I dun gone through the skin and you can see the flesh, but not like it's agonna bleed or nothin'. And, oops!, Oh oops-me-a-bitsy, I jest dun it again. Sure an I's been mighty gawky."

Luther wasn't sure whether to admire this or not. True, it was as wondrously skilful and dextrous a use of claws as a cat could wish for, but the thought of not drawing blood, well, it's not quite good form, is it?

"'Twould be awful for them thar scretch'ns to go septic, now would it not? So we'll jes soak down this first lot in some fine i-o-dine, 'special-maid so it wont never dry nor stop stinging. And this second sort, yous can see I'm protectin' with this nice thick dusting of salt, and making sure it done stick proply in them there gashes I done made, liken a nice crust'n."

Having handed to one of the attendant Saints a most elegant silver-gilt Georgian salt cellar and spoon, Jemima came back to stand with Luther.

"And now with that splendid fine needle that been inserted into his diaphragm and stomach, he be getting hiccups. Bout ev'thirty seconds or thusabouts f'r'ever.

"This next'un here's a nice little surprise for him. Yous sees how they is filling into his bladder with a gallon or few of fluid, nice and strong, that you'd painful need to empty out jest right now or long since. Only, as yous'llave gest, the exit is now orl rightly, tightly sewn up, and the inlets cauterized with a reel rhett-hot needle, so no ways is that water coming out of there, not in orl eternity.

"But seein as how there done be mo than one op'ning down those parts, we's doing the same for the back way out, or an if he been one o' they preverts, that there's folk now assaying is normal, we is doin it extra. Not for them homely-sex-manuals, what the vandalgellicals is effer gett'n s'upp'ty 'bout, they's no great thing; and nor not found offen in this chamber neither - seein' as they is made that way for speshul, eternal, blessit purposes o'Th'Gratewun -, no, it's them other folk, that I jest cannot begin to de-scribe to yous, not that yous wants to know, now des yous? Irrgashun'n'nemas'n'sech, noways, ma fundament! Coffee's fer drinking. Than-you kindly, Saint Beauregarde, that be most thoughtful of you to bring your mamma some nice hot brew.

"So's we being filling that place up with some nice nasty runny liquor til there's no space for any mores. And then some mo too.

And it's all a-wantin' to come out, so bad that you'd feel that if you don't get yerself to the place in 'bout ten seconds or so, then you's in for an accident like th'Egyptians when the waters weren't parted no more. And then you'll be figerring rightly that we's after sewing that little passage up tighter than taut.

"As you can sorely work out ba now, this'awl it's a ways of working down the body. So now's he's getting gout in one knee, and a neatly broken knee-bone in the other. Nicely sawn in two, not snapped or smashed or anything, 'cos we takes our pride we does it all well as it can be.

"And them is finest stinging nettle leaves that is being proper gently slapped all th'way down from the thigh to th'ankle, making sure each one o' them pertty little needles in that there leaf is getting fixed into that skin. And jest as there's ain't no butter in hell, there ain't no dock leaves, neither.

"And if'n yous'll be 'scusing me a moment, I is just gonna stick one 'o my finestkind hatpins under his toenail right the way in."

The "rasslers" returned, and flipped the body over on to its front. Plastic parcel strips were wrapped round each ankle and tied together, before they pulled the hands behind and did the same. A black studded leather band went round the neck. The ensemble was completed by a rigid steel rod, to which the three sets of restraints were firmly attached. So packaged, the specimen was flipped back, and lay slightly askew because of the scaffolding now beneath it.

Jemima examined every part of the work with meticulous but speedy skill, and pronounced herself satisfied.

"Fellers, yer done good; this here is a right purty piece o' work. Guess we'd best be after given' thanks and blessings."

At which she began, in a contralto so deep that the male Saints had no problems with the pitch, to sing Tallis's canon, bringing the others in on cue until it was in eight parts. It was, Luther had to admit, a not unimpressive noise. Which done, Jemima hollered (there really is no other word, trust me) for Terence.

A forcible downdraft and an audible beating of wings heralded his arrival. Terence was, Luther was astonished to find, a pterodactyl of enormous size.

"We do wake them up just as Terence is ready to bear them to the cylinders, so's theys cans sees him hanging dere in th'air overneath 'em. Jest loves it when they be them s'called Intellgunt Desine folks. Ev'singul one o' that sort comes here, on account o'how they did persume to tell their Creator as how He ought to have done things diffrunt from what He did. Specially wiv Him having left plenty 'nough and mo' signs o'th'truth for any body that cares jest to look at the world, He doan think telling Him how t'arrange things is at all right respectful o'who He is."

"Quite so;" added Terence, in a beautifully modulated, best Knightsbridge accent, the one where the lips don't move, having been starched into the thinnest of slits, "I mean, really, giving out instructions willy-nilly to the Source of all being, well, it's just not orn. If you will just let me get into position, ma'am, then we shall be ready for take-orf, as the someone said to the someone else." With which, he hovered over the specimen, with his fifteen-foot-long beak open to snatch up its cargo, and looking down at it, rather severely.

The contents of a hypodermic were introduced into the specimen's neck to immediate purpose. The teeth gaped to their widest; the spine arched as far as the restraints allowed; the limbs alternated between rigidity and impotent flailing; the face strained in horror; the rib-cage and diaphragm forced aer out and in with all their might; the head thrashed from side to side though the eyes were set in focus on the ancient beast that now used its beak and seized.

Terence soared aloft, and then swiftly came back down, and still firmly holding the specimen, like he was a trained cormorant, walked towards the lift doors.

"Orl that effort has made me right plum-tuckered tired, so maybe's you'd be kindly following Terence yoursel, for the rest of the tour. Ah needs some salad. W'some herbs.", said the wondrous Lady Jemima, collapsing elegantly onto a freshly coiffured sofa.

Terence was waiting for Luther in the lift, from which all the finery had gone. It was now just bare grey metal. Hell always has everything just as is needed.

On the wall were a little row of four buttons: Corridor, Preparation Room, Punishment Drums, Specialities (Authorised Personnel Only). Terence put down the specimen, and with his beak pressed for the Punishment Drums.

"He'll be just fine there on the floor, since it's the last solid surface he will ever feel.", said Terence. "Jemima is a fine Gel, but I do always like to add a little contribution of my own." He regurgitated something into his beak, which smelled exactly as fish does after macerating in interesting digestive juices for a few hundred thousand years, and then, forcing his beak into the specimen's mouth, squirted the mixture straight down into the stomach.

"Nausea.", he explained as he extracted his jaws.

The doors opened and they were met by another pterodactyl. "Meet my brother.", said Terence.

"I suppose he's called Dax or something.", said Luther, much as one gives an awkward giggle at the wrong moment.

"Actually, I'm called Plautus.", said the brother.

Pterodactyls don't care for other people's silly jokes. Classical humour is one thing, but.

"Please follow me."

A little procession went out from the lift: Plautus, followed by Terence with the specimen back in his beak, and Luther trailing behind. They now were on a platform with a railing before them. Looking over, there was a pair of strong metal lids, each with an inset glass.

"Beaks or tails?", enquired Plautus, looking to Luther for an answer. When Luther didn't respond, Plautus explained. "You call beaks or tails, I toss a coin, and that decides which cylinder he goes into first. They get time in both, but chance has to determine their beginning. So call." Luther didn't care much for beaks, but valued tails, so beaks it was. Plautus leaned over and pulled open the right-hand lid. Beneath it was darkness deeper than the Venetian lagoon at night, but somehow oilier. Odd, considering it was plainly a void, but there we are. Terence dropped the specimen in, and flames instantly leapt from its head.

"It's hotter than the sun, in there.", said Plautus. "I'll just put the lights on and you can see inside." The void became brilliant, but was still void, and the specimen had disappeared. "Use these, and tell us what you see.", Terence added, handing over a pair of binoculars. After a while Luther could make out bodies falling and rising in the void, all looking like specks of dust in Brownian motion, but at vast distances from each other. Luther said as much. "It is Brownian motion.", said one of the reptiles. "They just drift up and down in absolute isolation. The circulation of the aether keeps them tumbling. Mostly we keep them in darkness, but put the lights on for a few seconds every few months or so, so they get to see that there are other ever-burning candles in there. Then we put the lights off again."

They showed him the other drum. This one span round at huge rate, forcing all the bodies to the edge, where Luther could see them compressed together, yet not actually meld into some solid icy mass. "It's a dry cold.", it was explained, "There's about 100G of force on them. And even in the freeze they're still quite conscious. Every so often, we just suddenly reverse the spin. Or shake them up or down or something. We did ask for front loaders but these are what we've got." His sibling, whichever it was Luther no longer cared, took up the tale. "Every day we switch a few from each drum into the other at random. You might wait a million years, or it could happen after a single day. Bit of a lottery, really. Anyway, it's time for the changing. Excuse us a moment."

With both lids therefore open, and the pterodactyls busy bobbing for specimens in the drums, Luther crept back to the lift. After all, they had given him leave. In the lift, he hardly hesitated before pressing the button he knew he was going to.

The doors opened onto a panelled atrium with a ring of doors before him. There was the "Millstone and Ocean Room", the "Absolute Blasphemy Room", the "Sodom, Gomorrah and Babylon Room", the "Urban VIII Room" and the "?a?w?in? Room" (*sic*). The latter was too intriguing to resist, so he opened the door. Behind it was another, in steel, and of a design that banks of last resort would find inspiring. He turned back, both disappointed and relieved.

"Now you is a mischeevious lidl wun, ain't you, coming down to where nowuns but me and a few my closest holiest pardners is supposed to get entry.", said the Lady Jemima, more amused than annoyed. "Kinda gest you's ud be after seeing the forbidd'n froot o'wickedniss. But can't be dun noways. Nossir, can not be dun. Anywun but us few goes in there, dey can't never come back. So unless you'da be having a care for a refereshing mint julep, guess I'd best takes you back up to the corr'dor. Terence and Plautus can be making up to me some time soon. Not that that's anyways unlike."

It was therefore about an hour or so later that a refreshed and most relaxed Luther was given back into the care of Domination.

As Domination received Luther back into the Corridor, he noted that Luther was a little pale. So he brought out his words of comfort for these occasions. Never failed, do they.

Feelings of compassion, quoth he, for these ones are not just inappropriate and unnecessary, but essentially sinful. What you've just witnessed is people getting justice. It's perfection. Eternity sans heat, light, sound, contact or stimulus, aware only of the agony of your punishment and knowing it's your own fault and only what you deserve. It is utter beauty. You have to give praise for its clean lines and elegance.

And Domination showed how proud he was of the efficiency of the domain by bursting into song.

Somehow, Luther did not feel like joining in a chorus of Nun Danket.

He was saved from needing to respond by the arrival of a decidedly-junior angel, with a scroll. The minion went down on one of his many knees, and offered Domination the missive. It was glanced over, and the underling dismissed by having it thrown back at him.

"The tour's over. You are summoned.", said Domination. He opened the door into the waiting room, ushered Luther in, and then left.

Domination was nearly happy. With any luck he'd be in time to catch the Rugby from somewhere or other. A nice, gentle, relaxing maul and ruck or three would be just the thing.

CHAPTER 13

God and I both knew what it meant once; now God alone knows.
Friedrick Klopstock (attrib)

No jumblings for me, chitterling. I know th'enemies of my house and head and how they are, which is to say all traitors.

The madness, it comes on so judgèd, and barbèd with timeless.

Yet I still will footle with some child's tale of old until the hour is come for actions. There's no quarter with these, and nor shall it be drawn out, nor took. I shall forth with surprise and confound all that thought at me wrong, discounted my worth, put me aside from mind, as fit to walk on so and off to stand, functiònal but not present. That day, there'll no mercy for dozens of prayers, not massier grace, and no blessings, absolution absolute, but then I'll and to open a store-housing house, the which has hidden many years of every minute's small remembrance.

I've not jettisoned one once, nor ever shall.

And I'll divide not justice, yes, but worse than justice, so I'll be fair, most equitable, put all with balance. But. There's no assizing now I've measurèd and hung the papers long before. Just so carry them up, give the gifts that they gave, pile upon pile, word on word, look for look, body 'gainst body. Yes.

When that's done, forgive them every one their debt, and write then out the bill of divorce, full-paid receipts, but there'll now share no dividend, for this is how it winds up the clocks with ticks for their blood. That's the ouster.

Then the inner traitors will quick be shown those fine and loyal servants, as valiant for mine own honoured welfare, as ever they attempted, but were o'ercome. Some enemy hath done me this dishonour, not my familiars, friends. There was no sweet, no sweet counsel in a Lord's house, not then.

Is it not written in one of the greatest books of truth, "I will do my best to atone, but you must never ask me what for. My lips are sealed.", and again in the same place, "Child, child, if you come to this doomed house, what is to save you?" Never ask of rights; there will be no time to answer. You must wait for never.

Which reminds me of something I meant to tell you.

The Secretary, one of the kind, helpful kind, offered Luther a saucer of milk while he waited. He declined, not wanting to get it on his whiskers.

"He does often run a bit late, "she said pleasantly, "so we have these leaflets you can look through if you want. There's some interesting bits and pieces, they tell me." She handed him a small bundle of information.

Leafing through them, Luther noticed they covered a broader range that you might expect, like "So what's it all for then?", "Heaven and hell: the user's route map", "Evil. Is there a problem?", "Do I really have free will?", "Just what is a child of the universe, and am I one?", "Love, hope and the promised kingdom", "Faith may not be enough", "The end: will it hurt much?" and so on. The one, though, that he thought he should start with happened to be the thickest, and also top of the pile: "Your first audience with the Presence. Hints and tips on etiquette." It might just, he thought, be a good idea at least to skim it.

Opening it, he noted that on the inside front cover a box announced that the leaflet was available in all known languages, extant or extinct, and to ask if you'd like one in a particular tongue. He'd never seen the point of these notices. If you can read the box, then the leaflet you've got will do you fine, but if you can't read the box, how do you know there's a choice?

"CONGRATULATIONS!", shouted the first page of text, "you've been granted a personal audience with The Presence."

A bit obvious, thought Luther.

"We know you will want to make the best of it. These simple notes are here to help."

OK. Provided they do.

"Remember that no created being, which does include you, is able to see The Presence in Its true form. So The Presence will appear to you in a specially adapted manifestation. No two audiences ever have quite the same manifestation, because it is specially tailored to suit you."

Just so long as it's not a Siamese, Luther ruminated.

"It is bad manners to comment in any way on the chosen manifestation, because obviously it can not be improved on, and you should recognise this.

"When first entering The Presence, you may find the Light unusually intense. Do not use eye-shades or sun glasses: your eyes will have been made so that they adjust.

"Some people are affected with quite strong and unfamiliar feelings, particularly of awe, when they first behold The Presence. This is quite usual, and remembering this should mean you avoid fainting away. As this is unhelpful, and resuscitating you takes up valuable time, it is always appreciated if you remain conscious. Trembling limbs, weak knees, a temporary inability to speak, and involuntary movements are to be expected, and full allowance will be made for this. Tranquillisers should not be used, because they have no effect."

How very thoughtful, Luther opined to himself, perhaps not ironically.

"Do not under any circumstances attempt to shake hands or to touch The Presence in any way. Hugging It in joy is probably very commendable, but will result in your instant annihilation, which you may well find unpleasant, particularly as it can not always be reversed.

"Grovelling, prostrating yourself on the floor, genuflections and obeisances are permissible but neither compulsory or desired. A polite bow of your head, heads or equivalent organs is all that is needed."

Magnanimous, too.

"Audiences are never given on request, but only as summonses, so it is quite inappropriate to speak until required. The Presence will usually (but not necessarily) wave you to a seat, in which case you should definitely make use of it.

"Remember that you have been summoned for one of three reasons:
    a) to be offered reproof and suggestions for improvement, along with encouragement,
    b) to be given a blessing or grace (which should be received with humility)
or   c) to be invited to undertake some entirely voluntary service.

"It is not recommended that you speculate in advance which it is. Please recall that the ways of Providence are deliberately inscrutable, and you may have been brought here for something entirely beyond your capacity to expect.

"For all these reasons, it is strongly recommended that you remain entirely silent and listen very carefully."

Sensible enough, I suppose, said Luther to himself, flicking through the remaining pages. Before he put it down, intending to read about the problem of evil (people tend to), his eye was caught by one passage.

"Requests that you undertake a task are exactly that: requests. Your sovereign free-will is not compromised or influenced in any way. For that reason, you may very well want to think most carefully before replying. Even though The Presence of Providence in Its most marvellous foreknowledge already knows how you are going to answer, you do have the right to refuse. If you want time to consult an Independent Futures Advisor, don't hesitate to ask."

Sure I will, thought Luther, wondering about why the pamphlet on evil was so very thin, but something made him carry on reading.

"When you have made your decision and have agreed to do the appointed task, it is usual to express either unworthiness or inability, or, preferably, both. This should be done twice, and no more, before expressing thanks for the great trust that has been placed in you, wretch though you are. More than twice is taken as false modesty or panic, and neither goes down well.

"Any particular qualities or special equipment you need will, of course, be supplied, as you leave, and the Secretary will show you how to reach the Stores department.

"You are strongly recommended to read the Induction to Divine Service pack that will be issued to you. It contains much useful information, together with several vital telephone numbers, some of which are confidential.

"Do enjoy the task you have freely agreed to undertake.

"Members of our Frequent Triers scheme should notice that this task will not qualify to earn you points on your next centennial statement."

They always get you in the end, Luther grumbled to himself. Anyway, now for Evil. It seemed all the same that he was meant not to get to read it, for just then he was interrupted by the Secretary.

"The Presence are ready for you now.", she said, with what was actually flawless grammar, "His All-Himselfness actually are always ready and exactly on time, though even so there are occasional delays with the schedule, which is why you have not been delayed while kept waiting. But it is Its will to see you now. So please do just go straight in."

Secretaries are, it is well known, all members of what is probably the most successful Secret Society in all possible histories. By dint of making public just a very few of their customs, they keep 99% of their activities totally away from prying eyes, and utterly secure. For example, you will know of Copy, Audio, Shorthand, Confidential and even Personal Secretaries, but, hand on heart, can you say if they have more or less than 33 types, or whether they have Secretarial Inspectors General? You may know of their Colleges - they even advertise them - but of their Sororities and Sanctuaries you are utterly ignorant. That, of course, is exactly as they planned it.

What terrible and blood-curdling vows they take have never been described in print. No-one who has ever foolishly interrupted one of their covens has ever come away with clear and unscrambled brains. I mean, do you ever remember whether a Secretary has actually promised to do anything? And if you did manage to get a stapler, do you now recall anything else that you wanted? The design of the Secretarial Obfuscation Ray-gun is desired by the security services of every government everywhere, but is still unknown to any. Their success is beyond compare.

So it must be taken on trust that if one of their number has reached the high rank of Private *and* Confidential most certainly she must have sworn to hold in absolute secrecy all that is known to her.

How therefore, not five minutes later, it was bruited about in every room off the Great Corridor that something unheard-of had happened is impenetrably mysterious. Yet cries of, "He never did!", "Strike me!", "I mean to say.", "You're not joking are you? Crikey.", "Cor blimey O'Reilly!" and such-like were the order of the day. And in each case, since in the empyrean there are no problems of messages getting distorted in transmission, the content was common. As this cat-thing, no better than he ought to be, if that, was closing the door behind him, there had emerged from The Presence's Chamber not just clearly, but loudly, the words,

"Wotcha, me ole mucker! ' Ow yer doin'? How'se they hanging? Orright?"

The majority was that it portended change, and not for the better. But then, when was it not?

As Luther closed the door, and so put the angels behind him, with the dragon before him, he relaxed from two legs onto four, and discovered that 'they' were indeed hanging, a sensation novel, since he had been deprived of them at five months old - for the very best of reasons, and on professional advice -, and *pace* Freud, who knows what such a loss is at that age?

He trotted over, noting merely that a room indefinitely large had been made definitely cosy, after a fashion. Dragon was balanced, not quite elegantly, on a *chaise-longue*, taking great care not to cut the fabric. There were, Luther thought, enough *chaises-longue* around that they might have been a discount job lot. Actually they were: Sheraton had to be found something to do.

Luther stopped short, and carefully examined the reclined-upon and the recliner.

"No, won't do.", he said firmly.

"It won't?", came an unhappy response, "I've tried so hard to make it comfy for you."

"Of course, You have. But if You'll take the advice of a creature programmed for comfort, You'd be much happier in a gentleman's wing-chair, with lots of soft cushions to support Your back."

And after the immediate and necessary adjustment, He decidedly was.

"I didn't think you'd actually want tea, but if you do, you have only to say. But on the coffee table there's a dripping tap and mini-sink, a bowl of mineral water, one of milk, watered just the way I believe you like it, and one of gravy."

"Just the dripping tap will be fine. But, if I dare ask, might it just drip a little faster - you know, when it starts to gurgle, but not yet to trickle?"

And it was so. Whatever else, Dragon was assiduous to His guest's every wish.

"Now, there's a plate of smoked salmon, a bowl of custard, a beef casserole, and some fruit cake. That's what your master's mind seemed to suggest."

"The human I live with is hardly my master, thank You." "But I appreciate the gesture.", he added instantly seeing Dragon's face start to look hurt. "But if You really wanted to make a chap happy, then if the custard could be pink blancmange, and the casserole were to become a really vicious vindaloo, it would go a long way."

Dragon didn't mind this in the least. He loved feeling useful to people.

"The fruit cake is special. It was the fruitiest I could get an S&M kitchen to make."

"Looks it. You're still just an old sweetie at heart, aren't You?"

This being the unaffectedly nicest thing Dragon had heard in millennia, some thing, which, considering who He is, could not possibly be a tear, rolled down His face.

"Now is the coffee-table OK, or would you prefer the floor?"

"The floor, please. It makes eating so much more relaxed; no jumping down when you're full."

At which, all having been arranged to his contentment, Luther moved his head from left to right, and the contents of the dishes vanished so fast that those who didn't know him could easily assume he'd inhaled them.

"Seconds?"

"Do You need to ask? And is Your kitchen using portion-control, forgive my asking?"

Dragon took the heavy hint, and the contents of each dish were replaced by doubly generous portions. They lasted no longer.

Nor did the thirds, fourths and fifths. Normally he would have stopped after the fourths, since there were usually only that number of people to whom he could pretend to be starving. But today he was going to be satisfied he'd eaten enough.

The sense of contentment beginning its outward spread through Luther was interrupted when Someone uttered the foolishness of "I agree. It was peerless."

"Look, you.", said Luther, in tones not normally heard, at least not in that direction, in that room, "you can read the mind of anyone else you like, but not mine. Got that? Because if you haven't, we shall see just how strong your armour plate is when matched against my claws."

Since, like every other sentience ever to have become acquainted with Luther, Dragon knew exactly that this was not an outcome to bet on, He apologised. Well, actually he grovelled, lower-case and all, and put it down to stress, force of habit, and generally needing to keep one step ahead of the angels' schemings. Luther never bore a grudge towards anyone who fed him, and so his forgiveness was everything Dragon hoped for. Indeed, it may definitely be reported even in Gath, he purred. Just a little, but identifiably.

So Dragon thought he'd move things on a bit.

"I've made a few adjustments. Replaced a bit of the armour, and moved things around, and, well, I've got Ourself a lap. And the mind of that person who is not in any way your master seemed to indicate you quite like cashmere.

"So I don't suppose...."

Luther did suppose, of course. And as he curled himself up on Dragon's new made, but decidedly well-padded lap, the two forwent conversation as Luther's 80 decibel purring filled the chamber.

When they resumed, quite a while later, Luther finished describing his experiences in heaven - the ones I've already been a-telling you of, child. But Dragon looked more than a little puzzled.

"I'm not really quite sure where you managed to end up, - I'll get someone to check it all out - but it isn't supposed to be quite like that. And not being sure is worrying."

Luther thought he'd decided to avoid getting onto omniscience by asking what it should have been like, but out of his mouth came the inevitable words.

"But, and do excuse me for saying this, aren't You supposed to know anything and everything?"

"O absolutely. One does. One can know everything, and therefore in some sense One does know everything, given that One has to will it to be, but let's be honest, No-One in My right mind would ever let Themselves be aware of it all. And before you even think about trying to stop yourself thinking it, yes, it does explain a lot..

"Anyway. Heaven. It's meant to be that once you've got used to the light and realized that you have gone through death, and grown accustomed to your new body, then you don't need to go much further, not to begin with at least.

"You can stay there for a good long while, usually on the observation platform for your home world, looking down (or up, it all comes to the same thing), and thinking about how much easier it is to understand life now that you're dead, and you can look particularly on the people who matter to you, or you thought did until now, and watch them trying to live. You do get to intervene, if you want (before you've worked out there's not much point, obviously), mostly through prayer, but occasionally more directly if the emotional atmospherics are right and they've progressed far enough to be able to receive your input. But, of course, what you can achieve declines with time, as does your interest. Sooner or later you have to go on and pay attention to your own tasks.

"You see, heaven isn't where it's ended. You've got to start doing the real work of making yourself yourself. If you think you arrive in heaven having been transformed into something perfect, you're doing nothing but deluding yourself. Grace is abounding, but it's not that cheap. You're still the same tetchy, irritable, cantankerous mixture of gall and bile you always were. All you've done is show you've got the makings, got enough love in you to get going. What you have done on earth helps, don't mistake me, some are readier than others, got less work before them, but even they have got plenty left to do.

"Now then, the work is just yourself, to become more fully good, more fully loving, more fully compassionate and more fully penitent and forgiving. You see, Luther, the stuff about forgive us as we are forgiving others is essential; it's not an optional extra if you are going to be freed to be who you ought to be. It's basic to the whole business.

"You have to forgive. There is no choice at all: you have to. And that means commencing from exactly what they did to you. Every last little bit of it has to come to mind, and it has to hurt as much as it ever did, but without hiding.

"Get there, and then you can do, as you have to, the making of allowances, of every allowance, for all the things that formed them: their own pasts and pains, the pressures they were under, the ambiguity of doing anything. But give them all that, and I repeat it, you must, and voluntarily at that even though it's inescapable, there is still the residue that is their own simple evil, greater or lesser. The sins against you that mattered, they really were done with evil at the centre of them. Even nicest, nice people aren't nice.

"From somewhere, with a simple but absolutely clear knowledge of the depth of the evil directed at you, you have to find compassion, enough to stop holding on to the hurt, and accepting the consequences of the evil. Then, only then, you free them from you and you from them.

"And here's the nasty bit, the one you will recoil from. You have to accept that you, you alone, are totally responsible for what you are, what you have come to be as the result of that evil. But for you, there are no excuses and no allowances. Their upbringing evokes all your compassion, but yours is simply of no account. You made yourself. Even if you think you never did anything, you did it all. You are the self made man. You let evil hurt you. And that, my dear Luther, is sin.

"Even when you have all the best reasons and excuses in the whole world to justify your weakness, you have to throw them all away. Have to. But do it of your own free will. Accept the blame and responsibility for everything in your life.

"Done that? Then take all your talents, all your achievements, all your holiness, and throw them away too, for whatever they are, there is nothing there but inadequacy and waste.

"Indeed, whoever said salvation would seem just? But it is justice itself.

"Which brings with it another little task. If your talents must be thrown away, so must all your loves. Everything, everyone, no not them. But the feelings you bore, the bond with which you bound yourself to them, cast it all in the dust and tread it under your feet. You had children and would have killed for them? Excellent, but not any more. That's finished and done. It is over. I repeat, it is over.

"That is the real death you have to face. The earthly one is just a rehearsal.

"So you've got through that assault course of thistle paths, nettle fields and briar forests, and actually do know you have no excuses, no rights at all, no property, no goods, and that neither has anyone else in the end. You have taken all that off yourself, and reduced yourself to not very much except a bundle of need. Yes? If so, then you have something else to do.

"You have to love more passionately than the most infatuated love there has ever been. You have to make Romeo, Juliet, Abelard, Eloise, Antony, Cleopatra, the whole crew, look like amateurs, so passionate is your love. Or the greatest mystic you ever failed to understand but marvelled at, like Dame Julian or Brother Francis. You must surpass them. Yes, you. You have never loved until now.

"You have to love everything, that passionately, not because it deserves it, because it can't, but just because it is. No other cause but just being. As you are and I am.

"And then you have to accept the wonder of wonders, that you are loved that much yourself, and always have been, since before the world began, but it could never avail you anything until now that you love that much yourself.

"Got all that? So, my friend of friends, all that time you are leaving parts of yourself behind, letting them drop off, sometimes bit by bit, like a sliver of rust from a corrugated roof, and sometimes in a rush, like snow sliding off a fir tree, but ever losing them, and each bit gone makes you more purely you, going sure towards the you who is exactly you, your truest individuality. Who then, you find, is exactly identical to every other sentience in all creation.

"Which is the surety. There is nothing left of you, but everything is you. Then are you ready to enter the kingdom of heaven, because you have become like a grain of essential sand. Not one instant before. So don't talk to Me about faith. Faith is nothingness to Me, since I simply am. Forgiveness and love is the work. There is no alternative. But you have to choose it without any prompting.

"BTW, if on this way you have done the rejoicing you were promised, and the weeping, if you have eaten and drunk the food of life itself, received every grace imaginable, seen all glories - and you will have -, that all has to go too. You can not hold on to any of it. All your service, your hope, your faith, your charity, your praising, and all, has to be left behind. Because else they are possessions, and you will be glad that you have them, but you have to give away everything you possess. And the less that remains, the less you try to grasp anything at all, then the more you are yourself and possess all treasures and know that every glory was created for you.

"That is how you go from heaven to heaven until you reach heaven.

"As for those souls in hell? Well, they have killed their own souls. Committed suicide. Which is why it is so great a sin - but not the killing of the body. Suicide of the body needn't hinder you for a second. But suicide of the soul is total.

"And all hell is, all those things you saw? They are nothing but images and representations of one thing: the damned know what they have done, and still they would do it again. Don't ever think that hell is empty or thinly populated. You will have seen those who are choosing it every earthly day.

"Don't tell yourself you haven't seen it, you who observe like you observe. Just look round you at ordinary folk - it's not just the rich or powerful -, and see quite how many are intent on themselves alone until they have no soulful self left to have. There are crowds before hell's gates, eager to know it.

"A soul won't do for them; they have to be completely self-made. Gifts they never accept. Bribes - of course - that's just business, a legitimate purchase. Gifts never. No way. They're for jessies and pansies. So grace and souls are to be eliminated.

"So that, Luther, My protesting friend of friends, is what you should have seen. But I suppose you, Luther, could not, because your soul really is different, is inhuman. You have never done anything you cannot convict yourself of. So your fate was different. To become the observer incapable of action, capable of inaction, because you are nothing but nature."

Thank You for that comfort, thought Luther; talk about OTT.

CHAPTER 14

Come not between the dragon and his wrath.
Shakespeare
King Lear

Whenever, child, it happens that two people have to meet to discuss something that is at once difficult, embarrassing and important, then there are proprieties to be observed. Good will must be expressed, with ease and care and optimism. Yet, prepare they ever so carefully, there will be a moment when the task must be faced. At that point, it is certainly impolite not to be uncomfortably silent, but equally impolite and impolitic to let the silence extend into actual awkwardness. For which reason, since judging the exact quantity of silence demanded is an art too fine ever to be acquired, the obliquity, equal with circumlocution, is usual to be employed.

How long Luther's purrs had ceased cannot be said; when does a *moriendo* ever finish? But it had, and Luther decided to slide in the paper-knife.

"Dragon," he essayed, "may I ask You a personal question?"

This wording always constrains consent. So Luther slit the envelope of complicity further.

"Are You, well, You know, actually and really... Him... or... Them?"

A manoeuvre which seems risky, until it be recollected that Luther is nowise the suppliant. When was he ever?

"Mmm. It's a bit difficult to explain.", parried Dragon. Luther left him to continue.

"You see, I do have all power - that is, all that I need to have for what I need to do."

Not so much as a "mm" did Luther gift him in aid.

"And it's the same with omniscience. If there's anything I want to know I can know it. And so forth. So, yes, I am infinite, and there is, it is true, none beside Me. But... But... I am not uncountable."

Luther did not turn to see if Dragon was looking in any way as crestfallen as He sounded. It wasn't from mercy. This riposte needs be sharp.

"Ah! So although you're infinite, there is beyond and transcendent to you the realm of the uncountably infinite, against which you are, as it were, as zero."

If you can reduce infinity down to size, Luther had.

"You could say that.", confessed Dragon. "Than Me there can be no greater countable. And though countable, I am immeasurably and innumerably greater than any actual thing that can be defined."

Before D could regain his dignity, Luther nailed and prized him.

"Not uncountable, though." To this he added the pause momentary with the sigh piteous before completing the slice dolorous. "So, if You are not the utter transcendent, what in hell are You?"

To Luther's surprise, like the martial arts master who finds a novice using all the magisterial weight in leverage, Dragon was quite ready for this one.

"I am not I am who I am, but one does what one does."

To which gnomon he added, "I am sometimes like an eternally changing. Though not a process. People make of Me what they will. Do you know, I have even been spaghetti? But, dear friend of friends, the first one who notes that 'Dragon' contains 'Dagon' is getting smitten.

"Now we've got that all out of the way, we are going to get down to business, because it is I who do have to be dealt with, don't I, old chap?"

Luther resolved to give up Chess and take up Go. Or maybe Draughts. To the pub, and of beer, respectively.

About as ceremoniously as one might expect from One of His rank, Dragon shooed Luther on to the floor, and stood up. Luther jumped straight back in to the vacated hollow of the chair, and found that it was not even slightly warm. Dragons are very well-insulated.

"It all concerns the ministers and stewards of My heavenly truth.", began Dragon. "Now, it must be admitted that there are exceptions to what I have to say, and that as a bunch they've never been that brilliant at their allotted task, but it is the firm and collected opinion of all who have a say in these matters, that is to say Me, that those of your century are particularly lacking in the excellence department. They are, that is to say, spiritually challenged. And after due and careful consideration, and because We have immediate knowledge of these things, We are, of Our merest motion, to smite them."

"Smite them?", echoed Luther.

"Indeed.", resumed Dragon, "They are to be smitten.

"We have been long concerned concerning them and their ways, which are become loathsome in Our eyes.

"We have even visited and seen for ourselves how those who have QUESTIONS are received by Our ministers and priests. Believe

Us, you were not the first to be approached. But the only one to answer.

"So let Me ask a very simple question. Who is it that should be most familiar with the ways of heaven and the perpetual law of love, so that it is the air they breathe; that ought to be most excited by everything that is found out about the working of My universe, and seek to comprehend this new truth; that rightly should be the most plainly compassionate of all souls; that are given the task of raising people, ordinary and extraordinary, to share in the heights of heavenly prayer, meditation, contemplation and divine union; that are meant to ensure that all reach their highest potential; that have the duty to understand best all that the human mind can contain; that of all the people on the planet ought to know the most about the depths, divine and dark, of the human soul? Who? Mmm. Tell me, who?"

"Isn't that a rather extensive job description?", Luther parried.

"It's supposed to be, and it's supposed to require a lifetime of striving for centeredness and equanimity. We do make allowances. But they should show at-least-occasional signs of movement in that general direction."

"Are they really that much worse than before?", interposed Luther, even though he knew the task was pointless.

"There are, true, some perpetual issues they have to face. There is their official sin, for a start. They think they have been specially called to their office, that the idea has been specially planted in them by Benevolence. Maybe yes it has, maybe no it hasn't. But you see, it is just a little step from there to thinking that every thought in their head has been specially given to them by Providence. Ergo, if you disagree with them, you are disagreeing with Providence itself. Even if You are Providence Itself.

"One might expect that they'd work that one out for themselves. But it's not many, not all the way through. Then to this sin, add the cynicism of those for whom it's just a nice lifestyle; the ambitions of those who feel called to lead; the ruthless seeking of purple, red and white; the cowardice of those who don't believe and are afraid they'll be found out; and the eternal patronising of the eternally patronising.

"All that is usual and expected, and then we know too the ones who actually think they are succeeding in their job description. The mad, the evil and the evilly mad. Oh, We know them, and what awaits.

"All that is expected and usual. As is the hate. Of course, they justify it from the Word, despite all the Word says. Even the holiest have to hate someone. We know that.

"All those have always been there, and noted for weeding. But there was ever a goodly crop of faithful and diligent servants.

"But it's them that don't know what to say any more, how to rekindle in ordinary, unholy people the immortal longings that are always there to be followed. And they don't care that they don't know. They'd rather squabble than admit they've lost the plot. They'll offer an office the way they were taught, but don't see how it's one that holds neither mystery nor sacrifice nor call. They'll service, and that none too well, the few who find a way unaided to the way, but to those who've turned their backs then they have nothing to say that's useful.

"Success in the developing world they'll some of them claim, but not in the depravedly developed? But when the developing are developed, what then? I do not want the unthinking; I wait for the whole of the mind. They cannot deliver Me that.

"Be honest, My dear Luther; you know I'm right."

Luther couldn't say anything. Who could?

"I listened into one of their little conferences or councils or synods or whatever they call those wastes of the time I gave them. There was much division betwixt them as to whether a certain group, call them the X's because if it wasn't those it would be another group, should be welcomed as My children or expelled as My enemies. When a split is that sharp, anyone sensible looks for the real issue, the elephant, or, dare I say it, the Dragon, in the room. Not them. They were scared to face it.

"Then one day a particular, most fervent, prelate put it all in a single saying. In his country, said he, the X's are laughed at, which meant that he couldn't have X's around him, because he'd be laughed at too.

"And that was it really. I'm sure he'd willingly undergo martyrdom, if the cause suited him, but be laughed at? Never.

"Yet, how came his redemption but by One who took jeering and laughing and being pointed at and spat at, because that was His task? You see the point: whosoever shall be jeered at is greater than many preachers.

"If they can't and won't see that, I shall spit them and their words out of My mouth."

Dragon hadn't exactly been pacing around as he said this, but it was as well there were no valuable and fragile ornaments in reach of His tail. He stopped, and looked straight at Luther.

"Strange how one event so often sums it all up; reminds me of the Cities of the Plain. Would you like some more cake, by the way?"

Luther tried to change the tone a little.

"Isn't this where I'm supposed to ask You about what happens if there are even ten honourable ones left?"

He had more success than he expected. And less.

"Oh, there are oodles more than that. Oodles. But it won't do any good. Because they don't. They are to be smitten, and smote they shall be."

And He broke into a happy song:

> "A-smiting I shall go;
> A-smiting I shall go;
> A, O, Allelooh, Oh;
> A-smiting I shall go!"

There were a few more verses, but you get the general idea, child.

"I don't get to do nearly enough smiting. There wasn't that much in the original plans, in My hardly-humble certitude, so I'm not going to go all mimsy and merciful. No way. I'm not being done out of a good smite.

"Though, it is one of My more elegant smitings."

So Luther took the opportunity to answer one of life's great riddles.

"I must ask - everyone wants to know - what actually did they get up to in Gomorrah?"

If Dragon had had eye-lids, He would not have battered them for a second.

"The self-same as Sodom, the things made plain in the scriptures for those that care to read 32 books further on, or 13, or even 25, depending on version.

"It's ironic. The sodomitical clergy, the real ones, are those that get so righteously warm denouncing them that are anything but sodomites, at least if you take any notice of what the words actually say, like what the words themselves say you ought to.

"I like the irony. It's what makes this smiting so self-referentially elegant and post-modern and everything, not that the post-modernists are any of them going to join the finally-post-modern-and-everything jamboree."

Luther's head was not exactly not reeling, or realing.

"Since your head is giving you trouble, let Me spell it out: the Sodomites are those who abuse the messengers of the Hospitable One, and thereby deny that He offers grace and hospitality however He wants.

"Now have some more smoked salmon and I'll tell you how you are going to be the agent of My smiting."

Luther had a little light snack of a whole side of smoked salmon, two curries, and a pint of double cream. Unpasteurised, since you might just want to know.

"Feeling refreshed?", asked Dragon. "Then I'll continue.

"They are to be smitten. So I shall smite them. All.

"But ministers and stewards of the truth there must be. So that's your job. You are going to be My representatives on earth. All of them."

"What!", cried Luther, doing one of his more spectacular leaps, the ones that the worlds' greatest acrobatic teams talked about but never quite managed.

He recovered himself; there is nothing worth upsetting a side of smoked salmon for. "All of them?, and Why me?"

"Simply there's no-one better fitted for the job. Name me a wiser and better philosopher?"

Luther never could decide whether this qualified as a low blow or a simple statement of truth.

"As to the mechanics, We extract the soul of the next major cleric to be inaugurated, and substitute you. He gets brought here to meet Dame Jemima, and you get on with the job. Once you've got the hang of it, We repeat the process. Eventually, whenever anyone gets appointed, it's you that arrives."

It is not recorded how often that particular office had housed negotiations. And Luther, you will admit, is no push-over. But eventually a deal was done. He got to choose the order in which he took them over, he got to be as many real cats as he wanted, he could come back for a quiet chat as often as needed, and he got any extra powers he thought necessary. And he could exempt any clerics who *really* didn't need processing.

So it all began about two months later, after Luther had spent a fortnight in the Roman forum and a month in the Bahamas. Regular holidays and several numbered bank accounts (though only to contain reasonable sums {i.e. not scandalously unreasonable}) were also part of the deal.

he procession of prelates and clergy was centred on one figure, who was trying to look suitably overwhelmed; he thought that would come out better on television. As the figure reached his seat, momentarily his face went blank, but cleared at once. He sat down more elegantly than he had ever been known to, and somehow just inhabited his body to its fullest. There was a natural grace about him and a poise, which became more and more noted by the congregation, for the hours of the ceremony no longer trundled by but glided. The faithful felt unusually drawn to their new spiritual head, wanting to reach out and just

stroke his garments. When he picked up a child who'd brought him a posy, and sat her in his lap for a moment, everyone was more than a little wistful. His homily, too, had something quite unforced about it, and even the heads of state, for whom this had been a working inauguration, had an untried but strong sense that they wanted to do better. It was a good Sunday for many.

Elsewhere in the world, Archbishop Downelode's powers were beginning to fail. As Archbishops of Canterbury go, most of the C of E was mutedly wishing that he would.

Not so the Appointments' Committee; they needed his survival for a while yet. He had been the only feasible compromise candidate when the Committee had been even more than usually hopelessly divided. Neither unpleasantly orthodox nor worryingly unorthodox, having offended no-one in a long and slow career nor likely to, not politically incorrect nor yet particularly correct, he was sweet, biddable and amiable; and, above all else, he was aged seventy-one and very likely to see seventy-five. This provided four years for politicking and for a majority to emerge in favour of one of the three real candidates, all young enough to wait.

After his unexpected elevation, it had become obvious that the shock had made him a little more forgetful. Except on public view, this was a plus, since it meant that his Secretaries had a free hand. It was just unfortunate that he could not always be kept from the TV cameras. So they offered to write his sermons, and printed them in Large Type.

Now there was such a day. It was a state occasion, and it was his duty to show himself as Vicar to the nation and Padre to the Royals. When he paused for a moment in the midst of his sermon, losing the thread of a particularly homely simile, no-one was too worried. He would either find his place again, or if necessary his Chaplain would prompt him.

Ten seconds became fifteen, and while there was no actual concern, there was a sense that this was less than ideal. So his resuming his address should have brought reassurance.

But there was a most definite change. His stature became as vigorous as a fit forty-year old, losing the trembling stoop of the aged cleric. His face looked abruptly younger, and in a voice of such *basso profondo* that a visiting contingent from the Red Army Choir wondered as one whether he could be somehow recruited as an *Oktavist*, he firmly announced, "The Lord has, in this very moment, anointed me to announce anew the truths of the Christian message. And I shall now prove it."

Logicians of more pedantic cast might quibble as to whether it was actual proof, but that it was convincing, no-one could question. He leapt, in one perfectly balanced standing jump, to stand on the pulpit's reading desk, and then by another single bound transferred to the capital of a convenient stone column. From that he used hands and feet to run lightly upwards across walls, windows and galleries, and so found a footing in the clerestory passage, the very highest level of the Abbey.

And from that commanding position, he preached.

It was now an extempore sermon of plain common-sense, delivered with urgency and patent sincerity and straight-forward honesty, ducking no awkward issue. He installed into his hearers a sense that they themselves needed repentance and a conversion to new life. Not since the early Church, and rarely then, were words of such authority proclaimed. He might be more than eighty feet above the people, but they knew he was looking close and straight into every eye.

The Monarch was too well-trained to react. At all. The heir to the throne was of similar disposition, at least in public. A few more down-to-earth royals, however, so far forgot themselves as to join in the audible gasps at the Archbishop's ascent, and were actually seen to be listening to his words with unfeigned interest.

The sermon reached a rousing, possibly even rollicking, conclusion, and there was general - and for once genuine - applause for his stirring words.

And then utter, breath-held silence. For the Archbishop had begun his descent, slowly and smoothly retracing his path - but headfirst. If he fell, death would be certain and messy. Confidence returned when it began to be realised that despite his being upside-down, his flowing robes were nonetheless all immaculately in place and his pectoral cross still rested on his breast.

At the base of the triforium, he changed angle and direction, and, showing just how much he deserved to be styled "His Grace" took a leap onto the cresting of the quire-stalls, and used them to launch himself again. This time it was a layout Tsukahara leading into a two-and-a-half-twisting reverse double pike. That dismount saw him land perfectly and lightly on the balls of his feet precisely before the middle of the High Altar, where, not even slightly panting, he calmly intoned the opening line of "I believe in One God..." The Mayor of London wondered about a certain Opening Ceremony.

For the next twenty-four hours - at least - the many clips of this were watched on the Internet in such numbers that it seemed miraculous that the host sites never crashed. In such numbers too, did he attract users, that several pornographers abandoned their trade. A good business entrepreneur always knows when public demand has moved on to a new product.

From the Vatican, within the hour, there had come a fulsome statement, congratulating "our dearest Brother and Co-Worker of Canterbury" for his dramatic services to the universal Church by his restatements of ancient and timeless truth, and promising the little gift of a Pallium ere long.

That was Monday.

On the Tuesday, a sizeable delegation of senior Ministers and Pastors from the more traditional wing of the more traditionally extreme Southern Baptists called a Press Conference. They announced that nothing would ever again induce them to set so much as a toe into the water of their baptismal tanks. Caring about how, and how much, water was used in baptism was, they solemnly pronounced, nothing but pandering to vanity and meaningless externals.

On Wednesday morning, the Internet and media saw apparently confirmed reports that the Society of Friends and the Salvation Army had jointly announced that they sorely missed the true sacraments, and had been deeply moved towards the merits of the sacrifice of the Mass, benediction and perpetual exposition. In the afternoon came a lot more news releases; Pentecostalist Ministers and Apostles were said to have declared from a trampoline that henceforth they would count it an honour to preside at same-sex weddings. Some of the day's reports turned out, alas, to be the work of a hacker taking advantage of a widespread atmosphere of credulity. It was surely never very likely that the Pentagon was all going to be turned into a Trappist monastery, for example. When Archbishop Downelode declared that unless the wicked hacker repented, the flames of hell surely awaited, it was however entirely genuine. The hacker did public penance on the *Scala Sancta*.

Now, as to Thursday, there are still conflicting stories, but I tell you only what is known for certain.

The central architectural feature of Orthodox Churches is a great, richly decorated screen, the *Ikonostasis*. Through its doors, at various points in the holy liturgy, the clergy make solemn entries and exits, of which one of the more splendid and significant is for the reading of the Gospel by the Deacon.

The identity of the cathedral or basilica concerned is disputed. Personally, I think it not impossible that it happened in several, but I may be wrong. You've had cause to correct me before, haven't you child?

Yes, grandpapa? No, grandpapa? Does grandpapa care any more?

Anyway, what is certain is that during the entry, at the moment the Deacon was to place the sacred book on its stand, something caused the Deacon's arms to jerk with great force, and he threw the book high into the air. Sacrilege had been done!

Some eye witnesses say it was fifteen feet, others twenty, some thirty. It hardly matters. What does matter is that instantly the Patriarch jumped into the air, still holding his staff, and that as the volume was about to begin its descent, he caught it. With his teeth, his hands being otherwise occupied, and without there being the slightest mark to the book. He landed, so his followers say, far more nimbly than his Anglican exemplar, and certainly he was more encumbered. In his landing, by one fluid movement he returned the holy book to the Deacon's hands, as if it had never left them, and open, miraculously, at the right page. The action was caught on many a cell-phone, and Patriarch Bibliokatalambanos became more famed than Archbishop Downelode, which is only right. The Patriarch had averted tragedy and sacrilege; the Archbishop had not.

A few people say that an Ikon of the Theotokos Hodegetria was sign to smile afterwards; but since others say it was of the Theotokos Elousa, these reports are probably no more than understandable enthusiasm.

But, come the Friday of what was now known as the Week of the Leaping Archbishops, Luther got a text telling him to ease up a little and take his time. This suited him greatly, given his temperament, so he complied. Of course. And, being careful to think it only in qkqatt, he reflected on just how little smiting he had gotten away with.

When ancient schisms began to be healed, and bitchiness in the clerical world was in clear decline, it was plain something new was abroad. But unlike Jemima's ministry, this movement, which though of very different means had rather similar effects, was not to be brought to a sudden end.

CHAPTER 15

> Nothing, thou elder brother even to shade!
> Thou hadst a being ere the word was made,
> And, well fixed, art alone of ending not afraid.
> **John Wilmot, Earl of Rochester**
> **Upon Nothing**

From a windy path in a dark tight wood, find final a narrowest gate, and see beyond some house, not too grand, that has the amplest space, comfort, joy and rest. But to be entered, you must dislodge all luggage carried, and take only such books as you may write down yet yourself.

There was a well-known Oxford don of whom it was noted that if one of his pupils' essays merited criticism, his reproaches would be given in the veiled obscurity of an extinct and unknown language, to save that pupil from the sin of despair; whereas if one of their essays merited praise, to save their virtue from the sin of pride, his plaudits would be given in the veiled obscurity of an unknown and extinct language. But it shall not be so with us. Here is your report, child, written very plain.

It is time, then, you and I, child, to go down to the cellar. It's our little secret place, isn't it?, for our little private, cosy trysts we've been having for so long. It's where we do what we do and you are so good and loving to me, and I to you, that it has to be good. Good. Good for me. Good for you.

It's a strange fact, though, child, that I've never lived in a house with a cellar, not even for just a few days, he'll be no problem, we'll be glad to have him, not even for that. Not for a few hours. Garages, O yes, and in plenty. Cellars, never.

But there is a cellar. You know that. You do know that.

But there is a cellar and I must take you down there. The time is come. You must.

The mirrors are all framed in glory and ormolu, but silver thins in sulphurous air, and then ill reflects. It's like there's an images in the glass of them that can't come out.

And here, if I do not hurry, is the stone slab floor for sacrifices to God's unknown.

And here I will sit and take thought and listen for my spirits. But they don't speak now. I see them in the air, sometimes hanging still, sometimes dancing to a frantic beat, sometimes fluttering, sometimes with their lips muttering judgement, is it?

And in this cellar, here is not a false life. Here I sit surrounded by the forests of honour.

And look, see, my knives so sharp and fit and ready. Dissectings beneath them, behind them, and dishonouring.

I can not. Nor ever had design, nor was possessed of will or want, just but a dream to take away my hours.

It's true, is it not? You are no use now, not any more, child. I'm too old for you.

Imaginary friends end at eight, not that I ever have had any, and fantastic children at eighty, not that I'm eighty. You get me no heat; you do not warm me. But then, you don't come round any more to see if I'm alright. Your mother lets you cross three roads on your own, but you don't, not now. Mrs Doods said you'd been poorly, but what does she know? You're healthy; never had a day wrong in all your life. No, you have just let me be, and I forget what you used to look like, what you look like.

But I must still take you into the cellar. Down for the great ceremony. Shall I wear a pointed hat? I know you'll come.

And I'll wash my hands in your blood, and I shall rinse my soul in the sink, and it will do quite as well as ever.

Help me up, and then help me down. I cannot shift for that myself. Arthritis, you know. And the random flutterings of my heart, all chance.

I made mountains, you know, whole mountains. Gold and turquoise; just beautiful they were. And mine moved when you told them to. That's real skill, and now this is my final act.

Open the last door, would you, child? The dragon is waiting for an answer.

What will it read like? Maybe:

Prof ...., *peacefully after* .... *Cremation, 2.00p.m., 31st June. Family's and close friends' flowers only. Donations in lieu* ....

....

Flowers:	*nil*
Donations:	*nil*
Mourners:	*nil*

Or maybe something else. Either way, you've had it now, child.

No, no notice. There's no standing to suffice against it.

No notice of what takes mind or name or memory or record. Too strong, takes. It needs rest, but I can not. Let some sure thing steal me from me without me.

But what a world dies there and is never replaced! But every world, all them known of the children of man and woman, goes strait too for God's bonny kingdom.

Now, child, what did the dragon do next? Luther was safely on his task, and he at least had no more questions to ask. As for dragon, what His QUESTION was is *literally* inconceivable. Which was always the point.

Satisfied that everything He had decided to intervene in was taken care of for a good long while, and that He'd updated all the standing instructions accordingly, Dragon settled down to watch His plasma TV. From the Vatican was coming the first of its new celebrity series "Cat and List", in which a well-known, B-list, but decidedly mammalian, sometime superstar was asked what ten things they'd like to help change for the better in the world, were they to have the time and opportunity, the interview interspersed with footage of them playing with a fluffy kitten of their choice. Needless to say, this SublimerTV station was likely to put someone out of business.

Beside Him on the *pietre dure* coffee-table (He'd made it Himself and was really proud of it) was a six-pack of quadrillion-X lager and the remains of a pizza. Quattromilione formaggio, if you're interested.

Sat by His side was His ever-faithful Labrador. An intelligent, sapient and helpful friend is one thing, but you can't trust them to fetch the remote control whenever you need it.

And who this child was or is? I only know if there is life it can get itself but to chipped bone and occasion of puzzling ornament crazed.

Tired, I am tired.

Anyway, Nurse Child, it's time for you to get out the drugs trolley. There are patients to be seen. So we'd better stop for now.

My needle, child, my needling.

finis

AFTERWORDS and NOTES

¶ No cats, dragons, pterodactyls, butterflies, dogs, philosophers, children, harmless eccentrics, sinners, clergy, saints, humans not in any of the preceding categories, angels or other non-human sentiences were harmed in the writing of this book. It is probably the sad case that substantial numbers of human souls went to perdition, but, if so, it would have happened anyway and had nothing to do with this volume.

¶ This book uses only 100% organic thoughts. Unrecycled, it is hoped.

¶ It is a characteristic of these present, literally marvellous, times that anyone who writes humorously in terms that refer to religion will stand a very good (*anglice:* dreadful) chance of being accused of blasphemy, heresy or other like wickedness. The author therefore wishes to state plainly his wholehearted and unfeigned assent to the truths of the catholic and orthodox Church that have been and are received from the scriptures, creeds, councils and fathers. Nothing in this book lampoons or satires the substance of the faith. In each and every case, anything which is made fun of is one of the many distortions of doctrine found in our godless and god-ignorant society. Anyone who thinks otherwise has missed the point. So there.

¶ Luther was born on a farm near Ramsbury in Wiltshire, UK, in December 1979, and lived in various places in Hungerford, Leeds, Shadwell and Roundhay. Some incidentals in this book were suggested - albeit very elliptically - by events in his life and traits of his character. He was killed on 14th September 1996, apparently deliberately, by a hit-and-run driver.

¶ The sub-title "*una storia fiabesca delle chiave*" translates literally as "a fairy-tale-type history of the keys"; accordingly, let the reader understand, this can be as such neither a *roman à clef* nor a *roman à thèse*.

¶ The Greek word 'pharmakon' means poison, and the term 'pygous' refers to the region of the buttocks. A callipygous person, for example, has a beautiful backside.

¶ The person who became Muros would possibly use metric units.

¶ $e^{i\pi} + 1 = 0$ where $\pi \approx 3.1415$ and $e \approx 2.718$

¶ *Aula* is Latin, referring to the fore-court of a house, a hall, a palatial dwelling, or space for dwelling in.

¶ The distinction between different forms of infinity is a commonplace of modern mathematics; more properly it is the transfinite numbers discovered by Georg Cantor to which Luther refers.

¶ Some uninvented words used are to be found only in the full OED (eg 'aer'), and not always as headwords (eg 'Antartic'). Word inventions include eg the verb 'flet' from 'fletiferous', rather than from the noun forms 'flet'. Likewise, some apparent typos are actually proper usages, while some others are inventions. Or typos.